THE
CRIMSON
CANVAS

A Romantic Suspense Novel

By
JANA SAWYER

THE CRIMSON CANVAS: A Romantic Suspense Novel

SAWYER, JANA, Author
THE CRIMSON CANVAS
JANA SAWYER

Citrine Publishing Services, LLC
9810 FM 1960 West #295
Humble, TX 77338

In association with:
ELITE ONLINE PUBLISHING
63 East 11400 South
Suite #230
Sandy, UT 84070
EliteOnlinePublishing.com

ISBN: 978-1-961801-54-7 (Paperback)
ISBN: 978-1-961801-55-4 (eBook)

FIC027110
FIC027000

QUANTITY PURCHASES: Schools, companies, professional groups, clubs, and other organizations may qualify for special terms when ordering quantities of this title. For information, email info@eliteonlinepublishing.com.

PROLOGUE

Stepping onto the pool deck, the young woman with raven black hair greeted the man floating in the water with a cheerful "Good morning," savoring her delicious coffee as the morning sun cast long shadows over the pool. With a playful grin, she remarked, "Looks like you're running behind today. Don't let that secret slip!"

The man didn't respond; he just continued to float, so the woman moved closer to the pool.

"Good morning," she called out again, her voice louder this time. Then, she noticed it—and a surge of fear tightened her chest. The man's motions weren't deliberate; they were merely ripples in the water, spreading across the pool's surface. Beside his head, a dark hue tainted the water, spreading like ink, but it wasn't black—it was the stark red of blood.

The woman's world blurred into a surreal haze as the coffee cup slipped from her grasp, its fall towards the pool deck stretching into eternity before shattering into countless fragments upon impact. She flinched as sharp shards and warm liquid grazed her feet, but her gaze remained fixed on the man in the pool.

In the distance, a high-pitched woman's scream pierced the air, echoing through the neighborhood. It took the young woman a moment to realize that the scream was her own.

CHAPTER ONE

*D*espite the comfort of her surroundings, Sarah Kellerman yearned for something more. Her desire lingered in her mind as she ascended the grand staircase of the mansion. Each step, crafted from smooth marble, resonated with her every movement, while the elegant wood railing, imported from France, added a touch of old-world charm to the opulence surrounding her. Marble seemed to dominate the house, its chilliness striking Sarah, especially after returning from a long absence.

Pausing midway, she was captivated by a painting hanging on the wall. Smaller artworks surrounded it, but the central piece stole attention. It depicted her father, Anthony, seated at his office desk, with a towering bookcase behind him. His desk was bare, save for a closed laptop and a photo turned away from view. Sarah alone knew the hidden image, having painted it herself three years earlier, just before her mother's passing.

The most arresting detail was Anthony's expression – brooding and laden with a sadness that resonated deeply. Sarah had replicated it from memory, the same look her father wore long before cancer claimed her mother's life. She had expected him to question her choice, but he remained silent, perhaps unaware of his own melancholy or unwilling to confront it.

Shaking off the grip of the painting, Sarah resumed her climb to the second floor. Memories flooded her mind as she reached the top, the soft echo of her footsteps resonating through the empty halls. She recalled childhood laughter that once filled these rooms, now replaced by a haunting silence. The mansion seemed frozen in time, preserving moments of joy and sorrow alike.

As she wandered down the dimly lit hallway, Sarah's fingers trailed along the ornate wallpaper, feeling the intricate patterns beneath her touch. Each room held its own secrets, hidden behind closed doors and heavy drapes.

Soft light spilled from an open doorway at the far end of the hallway, beckoning her closer. With tentative steps, she approached the room. As she crossed the threshold, she found herself in the very office she had immortalized on canvas. The scene mirrored her painting with uncanny accuracy, every detail meticulously recreated.

Yet, there was a subtle divergence from her artistic interpretation. The laptop, once closed, now glowed with life, casting a blue hue across the room. And behind the office desk sat Anthony, not in the somber contemplation she had captured, but rather consumed by intense focus. His brow furrowed with such intensity that it seemed as though the lines etched upon it might split at any moment.

"Hey," she said softly, as if hesitating to distract him.

He glanced up at her, a wide smile filling his features. "Hey back, honey."

Sarah grinned at him. "You're working mighty hard for a man who's supposed to be retired."

He leaned back in his large, leather chair, the springs lodging a minor protest. "Only retired from being a state prosecutor, not from practicing law."

"I know; I'm just giving you trouble," she said with a light laugh.

Anthony chuckled, clearly enjoying the interruption. "And I'm glad I'm not going after criminals now." His smile wavered. "Too many years of that had a tendency to put me in a dark place. Corporate law is less stressful."

"I understand."

"You coming to the party tonight?"

She smirked . "I've already told you I am. You don't have to keep asking."

"Well, you don't have to, you know. It's a stakeholders' party and will be filled with a couple hundred lawyers talking legalese."

"It's fine. I won't be alone. Emily and Ashley promised to keep me company," Sarah assured Anthony, a faint smile playing at her lips. Emily and Ashley were not just friends; they were Sarah's steadfast companions since their days in grade school, their bond forged through years of shared laughter and tears.

"Will Lucas be joining us?" Anthony's inquiry, uttered while engrossed in his laptop, carried a weight that made Sarah tense involuntarily. Anthony sensed the question would have that impact, but he wasn't trying to be confrontational; he asked out of compassion and concern for his daughter.

"I… I don't think so, dad. I didn't invite him," Sarah confessed, feeling a pang of guilt for purposely overlooking Lucas in her preparations.

"His father's a member of the country club, you know. I extended the invitation to all the members," Anthony reminded her gently.

Sarah's response was a strained murmur, her discomfort palpable in the uneasy pause that followed.

Lucas held a significant place in Sarah's life, their history stretching back to their high school days. Though their relationship had experienced its ups and downs, Sarah couldn't deny her lingering feelings for him.

They had initially met in high school and dated casually, but Sarah had hoped for something more serious. However, Lucas was hesitant to commit, even though he clearly liked her. Despite this, their paths had crossed again after Sarah's return to St.

Louis from college in Massachusetts. Lucas had matured over the years, and their connection had deepened into something more meaningful.

Lucas Carter was the son of Leonard Carter, a successful business mogul from a long line of distinguished Carters, renowned in St. Louis as one of its leading families. Now a tennis instructor with a clientele bolstered by his father's connections, Lucas seemed to have found his footing in life.

Sarah took solace in Lucas's evident passion for his chosen profession, but, sadly, their relationship had cooled lately for reasons Sarah couldn't explain even though it was her decision to distance herself from him. Anthony knew this, but also knew that they still saw each other on occasion, which is why he inquired about his presence at the country club.

"Well, it's good that Emily and Ashley will be there" Anthony remarked, pushing past the awkwardness that mentioning Lucas had evoked. "Your friends will make for better company for you than my stuffy business associates. In fact, I wish I could hang with you guys, but I'm sure I'd just cramp your style." He gave her a wide grin filled with fatherly love.

"No, you wouldn't, dad. We'd love to hang out with you," she said, blushing a bit. It was not true, but it was a nice thing to say.

"Sure, you would," he responded sarcastically.

"Well, I guess I better get ready for tonight."

"You do that. I still have things to get done here," Anthony responded with a weary sigh, his demeanor shifting imperceptibly, as though concealing deeper thoughts. Sarah couldn't help but notice the subtle change in his manner.

"Is everything all right, dad?"

"Yes, honey. Just a tad fatigued," he replied, his expression softening with contemplation. "I think a swim might invigorate me," he mused, a gentle smile gracing his lips.

"That sounds good," she said with a nod, then turned and walked out.

At the opposite end of the hall, a grand bay window offered a sweeping view of the neighborhood from an elevated position. Sarah settled into the window seat, her gaze wandering over the lush greenery below, the quiet street lined with stately mansions, as she became lost in thought.

↗

Raised as an only child within the confines of a gated community, Sarah knew nothing but privilege from the moment she took her first breath. The many summers of her youth were often a blur of lazy afternoons spent lounging by backyard swimming pools, the laughter of her equally privileged friends echoing in the air. Yet, behind the façade of perfection, there lurked a sense of restlessness within Sarah.

Summers in St. Louis were merciless, a relentless onslaught of heat and unpredictability that kept its residents on their toes. Outside this sweltering urban sprawl lay Frontenac, a beacon of opulence nestled in St. Louis County, Missouri. Here, the affluent built their lives amidst a backdrop of manicured lawns and sprawling estates that would make any passerby pause in awe.

Sarah was no stranger to this world of luxury. The world outside her gated community beckoned with promises of adventure and independence, its siren call growing louder with each passing year. Even amidst the lavish vacations and clandestine forays into her parent's liquor cabinets, Sarah felt confined, suffocated by the weight of expectations that hung over her like a shroud.

It wasn't until her later teenage years that Sarah began to question the bubble of privilege in which she had been raised. The realization that not everyone lived in such opulence came as a shock, yet it failed to deter her spirit. Fueled by a thirst for life beyond the confines of her gated community, Sarah threw herself into the whirlwind of school activities, parties, and the fleeting romances of adolescence.

Her escape came in the form of a Bachelor of Fine Arts degree from Williams College in Massachusetts, a beacon of hope amidst the bleak northeastern winters she came to despise. Armed with her newfound freedom and a sense of purpose, Sarah returned to Frontenac, her childhood home, now feeling more like a gilded cage than ever before.

The 10,000- square- foot mansion that had once been a symbol of her family's success now felt suffocating, its walls closing in around her with each passing day. As Sarah stood on the precipice of adulthood, she knew the time had come to spread her wings and forge her own path, no matter the cost.

At the age of 23 , Sarah made the decision to bid farewell to her childhood home, venturing forth into a new chapter of her life. Her destination? A penthouse apartment nestled within the upscale enclave of Central West End. There, she found herself amidst a scene straight out of a postcard: picturesque sidewalk cafes exuding the irresistible scent of freshly brewed coffee, sophisticated Italian bistros, and avant-garde Asian fusion eateries tantalizing the palates of discerning diners.

As Sarah roamed the streets, she couldn't help but be swept away by the chic boutiques and antique shops that lined her new neighborhood. Each storefront seemed to pulsate with a vibrant energy, infusing the air with a palpable sense of style and sophistication that left her breathless.

A mere stone's throw away from her new abode lay the sprawling expanse of Forest Park, a verdant sanctuary amidst the urban jungle. There, shimmering lakes reflected the golden hues of sunlight filtering through the lush canopy of trees, offering a tranquil respite from the clamor of city life. Within this natural haven, a wealth of cultural treasures awaited discovery, from the renowned Saint Louis Zoo to the esteemed Saint Louis Art Museum, home to a breathtaking array of global masterpieces.

Her penthouse, an expansive sanctuary perched above the city, had a spacious room which Sarah transformed into her personal haven—an art studio bathed in the soft glow of natural light pouring through floor-to-ceiling windows. It was a space where creativity flowed freely, fueled by the generosity of her parents, Anthony and Monica, whose unwavering support made her dreams a tangible reality. From childhood, Sarah's keen eye for detail had set her apart, leading her down the path of Realism—a style that mirrored her uncanny ability to capture the essence of life in every paint stroke.

Her father, a distinguished state prosecutor and Harvard alum, often marveled at his daughter's remarkable recall and attention to detail. He joked that he wished he had witnesses with Sarah's acute perception, a testament to the profound impact her talent had on those around her.

As the years passed, Sarah's artistic journey took flight, igniting the local art scene with the brilliance of her vision. With each exhibition, her reputation grew, casting ripples that stretched far beyond the confines of her hometown. From regional galleries to the hallowed halls of New York City, her work captivated audiences and critics alike, earning her a place among the luminaries of the contemporary art world.

With the steady flow of sales came a newfound independence—a liberation from the financial tether of familial support. What had begun as a trickle soon swelled into a torrent, washing away any doubts and fears, leaving in its wake a sense of accomplishment and fulfillment that Sarah had long yearned for. In the glow of her success, she stood tall, a testament to the power of passion and perseverance in the pursuit of one's dreams.

And then Sarah's mother was diagnosed with pancreatic cancer. In a family where illness was a rarity, her sudden decline left everyone reeling. What began as a seemingly innocuous stomachache swiftly progressed into a battle for her life. Despite the doctor's prognosis of 12 months, Monica's brave fight came to an abrupt end within a mere four.

In the aftermath of her mother's passing, Anthony and Sarah found themselves adrift in a sea of grief, their world forever altered by loss. The days blurred into weeks as they grappled with the reality of their new existence, finding solace in the mundane tasks of funeral planning while navigating the numbness that enveloped them like a shroud.

Sarah, desperate to shield her father from the crushing weight of loneliness, moved back into the mansion. What began as a temporary arrangement soon became a permanent fixture of her life, her apartment standing as a silent testament to the life she once knew. Though she had initially clung to the idea of maintaining her independence, the pull of familial duty proved too strong to resist.

As time slipped by, the mansion became her sanctuary, a place of solace amidst the storm of grief that filled her heart. Believing that her art was a way out of this pain, Sarah bought additional art supplies to maintain a second studio at the mansion, not wanting to disturb the studio at her apartment. With each passing day, Sarah found herself drawn deeper into the familiarity of her childhood home, the memories of her mother etched into every corner. And so, two years slipped by within the embrace of those familiar halls, as she feverishly created paintings, each stroke of her paintbrush a silent prayer against the relentless tide of grief.

With a deep sigh, Sarah rose from the bay window and made her way to her bedroom to prepare for the evening's event. Her mind reflected on her last conversation with her father, the words echoing in her thoughts. As an attorney, Anthony always wore a perfect poker face, concealing his thoughts from the opposition while presenting arguments in court. Strategizing to keep his line of attack hidden was second nature to him. But Sarah wasn't fooled. She knew him too well. Something was gnawing at him, and the fact that he couldn't set it aside for the evening's social event struck Sarah deeply. This was unlike him; he was always cool under fire. Whatever was bothering him was big, and it concerned her deeply.

CHAPTER TWO

*A*nthony pressed the power button on his laptop, a ritual he performed with precision, and patiently waited for it to gracefully power down. Once the soft hum of the machine ceased, he meticulously arranged it at the precise center of his desk, mirroring the positioning depicted in the painting of his office. Sarah often teased her father for his attention to detail, playfully referring to him as "OCD." Anthony, however, took it all in stride, never refuting the claim, for he knew there was truth in her jests.

Afterwards, he indulged in a refreshing swim in the pristine waters of his backyard pool. Though its rectangular shape might have seemed mundane to Sarah and Monica, Anthony had chosen it for its practicality. Laps were his preferred exercise regimen, keeping him in commendable shape, especially as he approached his late sixties, despite easily passing for a decade younger.

With a swift change into his swimming trunks, he dove into the pool from its edge, gliding effortlessly through the water like a seasoned athlete. Swimming had been a lifelong passion; in his youth, he had even entertained dreams of pursuing it professionally, until his father's pragmatism redirected his ambitions towards a career in law. Despite the shift, Anthony excelled in his chosen field, carving out a life that had provided him with success and stability.

However, the loss of his wife had left an enduring void, one that would remain with him for the rest of his days, despite his efforts to cope.

In the tranquil confines of his backyard oasis, Anthony relished the solitude as he swam his laps. While the neighborhood Homeowners Association (HOA) regulations prevented him from erecting a privacy fence or stone wall, fencing around the pool was mandatory for safety reasons. Being a skilled lawyer, Anthony wasted no time in challenging the HOA's restrictions with characteristic aplomb. Drawing on his background as a state criminal prosecutor, he subtly reminded the HOA leaders of the potential risks involved in denying him this request, given the nature of his work. Reluctantly, the HOA relented, though not without considerable grumbling and pushback from some of the neighbors.

Yet, as tensions simmered, it became evident that Anthony's presence in the neighborhood brought with it a sense of respect and prestige, not to mention an added layer of security, courtesy of the increased police attention his status as a prosecutor garnered.

Anthony proceeded with the construction of a stone wall encircling his backyard. For building code compliance, including a gate was mandatory, something he would've done anyway. However, the gate was made of solid steel to deter prying eyes and required a key for entry. Mindful of fostering harmony with his neighbors, he opted to soften the starkness of the structure by planting tall hedges along both sides. This thoughtful addition imbued the area with a sense of natural beauty and tranquility. As the hedges flourished and intertwined, they gradually became a beloved feature of the neighborhood landscape, embraced by residents who found solace and joy in the lush greenery.

While Anthony enjoyed his evening swim, Sarah luxuriated in a hot bath. Though she typically opted for a quick shower before heading out, the allure of the oversized tub proved irresistible, coaxing her into a state of relaxation. Anticipation tinged her thoughts as she considered the stakeholders' event slated for the evening, set to unfold at the Westfield Country Club. While the prospect of reuniting with friends promised enjoyment, Sarah harbored reservations about the prospect of mingling with the staid business crowd. Their conversations invariably revolved around money, investments, and stock dividends – topics that held little meaning for her. As an artist, she found fulfillment in exploring the depths of the human spirit and the mysteries of life itself, pursuits she suspected held little interest for the attendees of such gatherings.

Yet, the presence of her friends Emily and Ashley softened her apprehensions. She felt guilty not inviting Lucas. She liked him. After all, they did have history together. But his preoccupation with material wealth sometimes clashed with Sarah's own values. Nonetheless, she couldn't deny the allure he held for her. He possessed intellect, charm, good looks, and a physique honed by years of coaching tennis. And the sex was good, for the most part. Though he harbored aspirations of turning professional, he gracefully accepted the reality when those dreams didn't materialize. Sarah admired his resilience, yet despite his admirable qualities, she remained uncertain whether he was the one meant for her.

Despite her reservations about their compatibility, she couldn't shake the expectations thrust upon her, particularly by her late mother, Monica. Sarah's promise to marry Lucas had been a white lie meant to bring comfort to her dying mother, a lie that now weighed heavily on her conscience.

The guilt lingered, exacerbated by her father's inquiries following Monica's passing. Sarah's evasive responses hinted at the uncertainty that clouded her future with Lucas, yet the topic remained a silent specter between her and Anthony, unspoken but ever present in their shared grief.

As the evening sun cast its golden glow upon the landscape, illuminating the sprawling lawns of the Westfield Country Club,

Anthony arrived in his fully loaded Porsche Taycan. The electric vehicle silently rolled up onto the club's circular driveway and stopped before the covered entrance. Trading places with a v alet, Anthony strode into the club in his pristine tuxedo. Possessing a charismatic and outgoing demeanor, he eagerly anticipated the evening's social dynamics. He relished the opportunity to mingle, exude charm, and network with finesse, all in service of fortifying the reputation of his esteemed law firm, the Kellerman Law Group.

Back at the mansion, miles away, Sarah stood before the ornate mirror in her bedroom, her slender frame adorned in a gown of midnight blue silk, its cascading folds hugging her curves with effortless elegance.

With meticulous care, she applied a hint of shimmering eyeshadow to her almond-shaped eyes, accentuating their depths, while a swipe of crimson lipstick added a touch of allure to her full lips. Her raven black hair cascaded in loose waves, framing her shoulders and delicate features in silken strands, a few loose tendrils dancing delicately around her face.

Surveying her reflection with a critical eye, Sarah adjusted the delicate pearls adorning her neck, their luminous glow complementing the rich hue of her gown. A pair of shimmering earrings adorned her ears, catching the light as she turned her head, adding a subtle sparkle to her ensemble.

With a final glance in the mirror, she smoothed down the fabric of her gown, the soft rustle of silk echoing in the room as she moved. Taking a deep breath to steady her nerves, she clasped a slender clutch in her hand, the weight of anticipation settling in her chest.

As she descended the grand staircase of the home, the click of her heels against the polished marble floor echoed in the silence, each step bringing her closer to the evening's festivities. With a sense of poise and determination, Sarah stepped out into the six-car garage, ready to face the night with her friends at the Westfield Country Club.

Sarah gazed at her reflection in the sleek window of her recently acquired BMW 328i. Despite her accomplishments in the art world at just 29 , where she had earned both financial success and the admiration of her peers, a lingering sense of inadequacy gnawed at her. Raised in a milieu of business-minded individuals, she couldn't shake the feeling of falling short of expectations. Despite her own achievements, she measured herself against the dynastic wealth of her friends, whose familial connections seemed to overshadow any personal accomplishments. While she had once tasted the allure of that world, Sarah had consciously chosen a different path, one rooted in her passion for art rather than the trappings of wealth and prestige.

Tonight's gathering at the country club served as a reminder of the divide between her choices and the expectations placed upon her. As Anthony's daughter, she often felt the weight of judgment from those who couldn't see beyond her deviation from the traditional path of success, marked by a law degree or a career in business. Hence, she often felt voiceless amongst the elite, and often thought they just humored her because she was Anthony's daughter. Despite the looming sense of unease, Sarah knew she would find solace in the company of her friends, who, she hoped, saw her for more than just her last name.

With a heavy sigh, Sarah settled into the driver's seat of the sleek Beemer, her hands finding familiar comfort on the wheel. As the engine roared to life, she activated the garage door, watching it ascend with a soft hum before guiding the car out into the twilight.

In the heart of Chesterfield, Missouri, nestled amidst the rolling green hills and whispering trees, stood the illustrious Westfield Country Club. A bastion of prestige and refinement, it stood as a symbol of exclusivity and old-world charm in the bustling modern world.

The estate sprawled gracefully over acres of manicured lawns, its grand Georgian-style clubhouse commanding attention with its regal presence. A sweeping driveway, lined with towering oak trees, welcomed guests into the embrace of luxury and tradition.

Within the clubhouse, the air was thick with the scent of polished wood and aged leather, mingling with the soft murmur of conversation and the clinking of crystal glasses. Mahogany-paneled walls held the secrets of generations' past, while plush velvet armchairs invited members to sink into comfort and camaraderie.

The heartbeat of Westfield lay beneath its verdant golf courses, where emerald fairways wove through lush valleys and around glittering ponds. Here, during bright sunny days, beneath the expansive Midwestern sky, gentlemen in crisp polo shirts and ladies in elegant attire strode purposefully across the greens, their laughter carrying on the breeze.

But Westfield was more than just a playground for the elite; it was a sanctuary of leisure and indulgence. Beyond the fairways, tennis courts echoed with the sound of swift volleys, and sparkling swimming pools beckoned under the warm Missouri sun.

There were no outdoor activities tonight, however . The evening had cast a serene hush over the familiar amenities of the country club: the tennis courts lay silent, the golf fairway deserted, and the pool shimmered under the moon's gentle gaze. All of the club's vibrant activity had been drawn indoors, congregating within the expansive embrace of the grand banquet hall.

Sarah guided her sleek BMW along the winding driveway, the soft purr of the engine contrasting with the stillness of the night. As she came to a graceful halt, a young man in a crisply tailored tuxedo emerged from the shadows, a practiced smile adorning his features. His greeting, though polite, carried an air of falseness. For him, the country club was a realm of transient roles and unattainable aspirations, yet he executed his duties with a professionalism that belied any personal discontent.

"Good evening, Ms. Kellerman," the valet offered, his voice carrying a note of deference as Sarah emerged from the car, the faint glow of the club's lights casting a soft halo around her. It was a scene replayed countless times, a fleeting encounter between worlds defined by privilege and service.

Returning the smile with a nod of acknowledgment, Sarah reciprocated the greeting. Despite the social chasm that separated them, there lingered a mutual acknowledgment of their respective roles in the intricate tapestry of club life. With practiced ease, the valet maneuvered the BMW away, disappearing down the driveway toward the secluded parking enclave reserved exclusively for the club's esteemed members.

With her clutch held firmly in hand, Sarah strode purposefully toward the club's entrance, the staccato rhythm of her heels echoing against the pavement.

"Hey there," a familiar voice called out from the shadows. Sarah turned, her gaze drawn to the soft illumination that bathed three figures in a warm glow. Standing beside a bench, beneath the gentle flicker of a nearby lamppost, were her friends Ashley and Emily, their graceful silhouettes adorned in elegant and sophisticated flowing dresses.

Ashley, statuesque and sleek with auburn locks cascading like a waterfall down her slender frame, carried herself with the picturesque beauty of a runway model. Emily, in contrast, exuded a sensual confidence, her shorter stature accentuated by curves that commanded attention from men and women alike. Ashley had adorned herself in a floor-length gown, its flowing fabric exuding timeless elegance and sophistication, while Emily opted for a daring ensemble, her dress teasing glimpses of skin in all the right places. Both women accessorized with a tasteful array of jewelry, striking the perfect balance between elegance and restraint, ensuring their adornments enhanced their beauty without overshadowing it. Sarah immediately felt self-conscience, as if she were underdressed for the occasion. Sarah's confidence faltered at the sight of her two friends as a wave of self-consciousness washed over her, a nagging doubt whispering that perhaps her attire wasn't quite fitting for the occasion.

Between Emily and Ashley stood Lucas, his athletic stature a testament to a dedicated workout regimen. His welcoming smile beckoned her closer.

Sarah forced a strained smile at Lucas, her hopes for a carefree evening with the girls quickly evaporating.

CHAPTER THREE

*A*s Sarah approached the small group, she was greeted by the sight of her girlfriends cradling glasses of sparkling Pinot Grigio, the liquid capturing the ambient light in a dance of refracted brilliance. Lucas, ever the embodiment of charm and easy demeanor, indulged in a mixed drink. Sarah assumed it was probably a rum and coke, which was one of Lucas's favorite drinks.

"We were wondering if you were going to show up," Ashley said, grinning.

"Yeah, Sarah, we're only here because you asked us to come," Emily added. "I love your dad, but this crowd isn't the usual one we'd hang out with."

Sarah laughed. "Me neither. I'm here to support my dad. He tried to talk me out of it, but he needs to know I'm here for him."

Ashley nodded. "That's nice."

Lucas swirled the ice in his glass and took a drink. "Sorry I didn't tell you I was coming. This is a good crowd for me to build my tennis business. I just have to listen to some boring stories and smile a lot and feign interest while I hand out my business cards."

"Boring stories? Feigned interest? Does that describe your relationship with most of your clients?" Sarah asked with good-natured ribbing.

"Pretty much so." Lucas took another drink.

They all shared a good laugh.

"Let's get inside; you need a glass of wine," Ashley said to Sarah, and then led them into the club.

The club hummed with energy, as conversation and laughter filled the air, predominantly from middle-aged lawyers mingling about. Behind the polished counters of the club's two bustling bars, several bartenders worked diligently, swiftly mixing drinks to ensure the guests remained content and refreshed. To alleviate the strain on these primary stations, two additional portable bars had been set up, offering further options for thirsty patrons.

Sarah made her way to one of the main bars, where the rich aroma of Pinot Noir beckoned her. As she watched the crimson liquid pour into her glass, Lucas stepped up beside her and exchanged his rum and coke for a Corona Sunrise, opting for the crisp bite of lager beer to accompany his tequila.

"Switching rum with tequila? You trying to knock yourself on your ass?" Sarah asked with a chuckle.

"Take a lot more than this, babe," he said as he sipped his drink. Looking around the room, he spotted some potential prospects among a gathering of younger male lawyers. It was almost like a clique in high school, the way they grouped together. "I think I see some new clients. They don't know it yet, but they'll be transferring funds to my bank account soon."

Lucas took another sip of his drink and walked toward the men, his demeanor exuding a charisma that would make any salesman envious. Sarah's gaze followed beside him, her admiration for his innate ability obvious. Lucas possessed a natural talent for sales, a trait he inherited from his father, who had harbored hopes of seeing him follow in his footsteps. However, despite his father's aspirations, Lucas harbored a disdain for sales jobs, viewing them as the least desirable roles within any industry. Though he never vocalized his sentiments, Lucas held firm to his belief that he deserved a career he found fulfilling. With a childhood spent on the tennis court, it seemed a natural path for him to pursue. His inherent Type A personality, typically suited for sales, found its place in his athletic pursuits. Despite any reservations, Lucas's father ultimately came to terms with his son's chosen path, accepting his decisions with a sense of understanding.

Sarah scanned the room, searching for Ashley and Emily. They had vanished while she and Lucas made their way to the bar, which struck her as unusual. At first, she thought they might have found some potential suitors, but then her eyes landed on them standing in the main hallway, gazing at a large painting. The artwork depicted the Westfield Country Club from a slightly elevated angle, showcasing its grand entrance and the sprawling golf course beyond, dotted with golfers and moving golf carts.

It had been Sarah herself who had been commissioned by the club to create that painting five years prior, before she gained wider recognition for her talent. She couldn't shake the feeling that her father's prominent membership status had played a role in her being chosen for the task, despite his assurances to the contrary. Regardless, she had taken an aerial photo from a helicopter and meticulously recreated it on canvas. Some might wonder why the country club hadn't simply enlarged and framed the photograph, but the club felt paintings possessed a timeless elegance that aligned with the club's aesthetic preferences. This was a sentiment that Sarah obviously agreed with, as evident by her artistic endeavors. Plus, duplicating the photograph in the form of a painting allowed Sarah to add personal touches, placing people and golf carts exactly where she envisioned them, rather than being confined to what the photo captured.

As Sarah looked at her painting from across the bar, she thought she could do much better now. It's the eternal struggle of an artist – always striving to improve. With each piece, comes more experience and sharper skills. Sometimes, artists can't help but cringe at their earlier work, even if it was once praised. But like all artists, Sarah had to face critics who didn't appreciate her creations. That's just part of the life of a creative person.

Sarah joined Emily and Ashley at the painting, greeted by their smiles.

"I've always loved this piece," Ashley said.

"Thank you," Sarah replied.

Emily took a sip of her wine. "Don't you have an exhibition soon?"

"Yes. September 12th at Clayton Art Gallery," Sarah said, her tone dry.

Ashley gave her a sympathetic look. "You don't sound too excited."

"Well... since my mom passed a few years ago..." Sarah let her words trail off, a gentle shake of her head accompanying her frown.

Ashley touched her arm. "I understand. I'm sorry."

"It's okay. I just haven't produced many new pieces. It'll mostly be older stuff."

"I'm sure it will be fine," Emily interjected. "In fact, it might be just what you need."

Sarah chuckled. "Yeah. I need more reasons to get out of the house."

Ashley focused on the part of the painting depicting the country club's entrance. "This is incredible, Sarah. You captured it perfectly."

Sarah laughed. "I painted this years ago. The groundskeepers deserve the credit for their precise trimming," she said modestly.

"Yes, but your attention to detail is unparalleled," Ashley insisted.

Emily finished her wine and turned to Sarah. "Maybe you can paint me." Then she quickly motioned to Ashley. "Or rather us."

Sarah laughed, then realized Emily was serious. "You're not joking, are you?"

"No, I'm not," Emily said firmly.

Sarah glanced at Ashley, who shrugged with embarrassment. It was true; they wanted Sarah to paint them. "Well, sure. I'm flattered. Let's talk about it soon."

Sarah glanced across the room and caught sight of Lucas, effortlessly engaging with a group of lawyers, exuding charm and confidence as he exchanged pleasantries and business cards. However, she couldn't help but notice his wandering gaze lingering on a few passing women. A twinge of jealousy flitted through Sarah, an unwelcome emotion she tried to push aside. Yet, she acknowledged its presence, knowing it was a natural human response. What troubled her more, however, was her own lack of intensity in feeling it towards Lucas. Perhaps her emotions had dulled since her mother's passing, or perhaps it was Lucas's habitual attention to other women that had desensitized her to it.

Nonetheless, Lucas's behavior was a stark reminder of the necessity to safeguard her own heart above all else. Yet, she was acutely aware that this self-preservation often meant erecting emotional barriers between herself and those who cared for her, potentially leading to feelings of isolation and loneliness.

Lucas caught Sarah's gaze and offered her a warm smile, signaling with a raised hand that he'd join her shortly before heading to the nearest bar for another drink. Sarah observed the bartender mix him another drink. It looked like it was probably another Corona Surprise and she realized she'd likely be driving him home later. Perhaps, she mused, it was his subtle strategy to steal some moments alone with her, something they'd been lacking lately. Sarah recognized her responsibility for this situation, finding solace in her alone time within the mansion's walls in recent times.

With his fresh drink in hand, Lucas navigated through the bustling crowd, making his way toward Sarah and her friends.

"Hey, ladies, enjoying yourselves this evening?"

"Of course," Emily offered as she sipped her wine. "And you?"

"I'm doing positively wonderful. I think I landed myself a few more clients," he announced with a buoyant tone, raising his glass to his lips. Sarah noticed a subtle unsteadiness in his movements as he sipped his drink.

Sarah now knew for certain she would be driving Lucas home tonight, her concern masked by a warm smile.

Lucas's gaze swept across the room, taking in the elegant decor and the elite crowd. "Your father has truly outdone himself with this event," he remarked, his admiration evident in his tone.

Sarah recognized Lucas's deep respect for her father, knowing it surpassed even Lucas's admiration for his own father. Anthony's influence stretched far beyond his role as an attorney; he held sway within the city's most exclusive circles, seemingly acquainted with every notable figure. Sarah and Lucas, along with their circle of friends, were born into this privileged world of opulence. While many of Sarah's peers reveled in their membership of the dynastic wealth crowd, Sarah couldn't shake the feeling of emptiness that pervaded their conversations. What once seemed glamorous and aspirational now felt hollow and superficial to her. As a child and teenager, she had been swept up in the allure of wealth and status, but as she matured, she found herself increasingly disillusioned by the endless discussions of materialism, social climbing, and name-dropping. The once-exciting tales of exotic travels and encounters with celebrities now left her feeling bored and disconnected. Despite her privileged upbringing, Sarah couldn't help but feel trapped by the expectations and conventions of her social milieu, longing for a deeper sense of purpose and fulfillment beyond the confines of her affluent lifestyle.

A cocktail waitress glided over, her poised demeanor exuding hospitality. "May I get any drinks for anyone?" she inquired with a warm smile.

"I would like another glass of white wine," Emily declared, her voice carrying a hint of eagerness.

"Me too," Ashley chimed in, her gaze already fixed on the array of bottles behind the bar.

Sarah returned the waitress's smile, her own request for a glass of wine conveyed with a gentle nod.

Lucas raised his already half-empty drink. "I'm good," he stated tersely, a hint of impatience tainting his tone, much to Sarah's chagrin. She couldn't help but notice his habitual disdain towards the club staff, his complaints about their performance and turnover ringing in her ears. It irked her that he failed to consider how his attitude might contribute to the very issues he lamented. She silently mused that perhaps a dose of empathy could bridge the gap between his expectations and the reality of the staff's challenges.

The three women put their empty glasses on the cocktail waitress's empty try, then she gave the group a pleasant nod and disappeared toward the bar.

"Can you believe how fast this year has flown by? It feels like just yesterday we were celebrating New Year's Eve!" Emily exclaimed.

Ashley interjected with a wistful sigh. "I know, right? Back in the day, it was all about having fun. Now, it's like I'm drowning in deadlines at work." As an interior designer, Ashley found immense joy in her craft, but the reality of being at the bottom of the totem pole in her company often meant she was buried under a mountain of projects, her passion tested by the relentless demands of her workload.

Emily nodded solemnly, her gaze distant. Like several of Sarah's friends, Emily found herself employed within the family business, her role situated in the realm of commercial real estate. It was a position easily secured, devoid of the usual hurdles such as experience or interviews; instead, it was simply a matter of stepping into an already awaiting role. However, the true test of her worthiness loomed in the future - the eventual passing of the torch, the moment when she would assume leadership of the company. Yet, despite her dedication and competence, Emily was keenly aware that this pivotal opportunity would likely be extended to her eldest brother. It was a stark reminder of the entrenched gender dynamics that persisted even in the modern era; a testament to the enduring tradition where the reins of power were still predominantly handed to the men of the family.

The waitress reappeared, gracefully balancing a tray laden with glasses of chilled white wine. With a sense of anticipation, each lady took a glass and enjoyed a sip of the sparkling liquid.

"Let's steer clear of work talk," Lucas interjected, his words belying the irony of his recent efforts to solicit clients for his own business. "Anyone been to any good concerts lately?"

All three women shook their heads in unison, indicating a collective absence of recent concert experiences. Emily, however, appeared momentarily lost in reflection before breaking the silence with a nostalgic query, "Remember when we used to hit the downtown clubs every weekend?"

Ashley's enthusiasm was palpable as she vigorously nodded in agreement. "Oh, absolutely," she chimed in. "And how we'd dance until dawn?"

Emily's grin widened, her eyes sparkling with memories of those exhilarating nights. "Those were the days," she exclaimed. "We definitely need to recreate that magic soon."

Ashley laughed. "Absolutely! But can we please make sure we have a good brunch spot lined up for the morning after? My head can't handle another round of mimosas without some solid eggs Benedict to balance it out."

Lucas took another drink. "Agreed. Brunch is non-negotiable after a night like that."

Sarah listened attentively, her thoughts drifting back to those wild nights of clubbing that once filled her weekends with excitement. Yet, amidst the memories of pulsing music and laughter, she couldn't help but recall the pounding headaches and queasy stomachs that often lingered long after the party had ended. It struck her how her friends conveniently omitted these less glamorous details, prompting her to ponder the tendency to romanticize the past, to selectively remember the joyous moments while conveniently glossing over the less pleasant ones.

Sarah joined the conversation. "I think next time we go to a club; we should make sure to pace ourselves, or at least try to."

The other three fell silent and locked their eyes on Sarah with an intensity that made her uneasy.

"Kill joy!" Emily humorously exclaimed in an attempt to lighten the mood.

"I'm just sayin'," Sarah laughed.

Lucas grinned. "No promises. But hey, who needs sleep when you've got good company and great memories to make, right?"

"Yep, memories," Ashley remarked, her voice tinged with a hint of nostalgia, punctuated by a sip of her wine. "In the end, they're all we're left with."

Lucas raised his glass high. "Amen!"

Emily joined in and held her wine glass up. "Cheers to that! To friendship, adventures, and never-ending brunches!"

Laughter erupted, and they all joined in the toast, clinking their glasses together before taking a celebratory sip.

While Emily, Ashley, and Lucas animatedly discussed their careers, travel plans, and trendy restaurants they were eager to try, Sarah found herself disengaging from the conversation. Her gaze settled on her father, Anthony, who commanded the room effortlessly, blending social charm with business acumen. He thrived in this environment, seamlessly transitioning between the roles of gracious host and savvy businessman. Sarah couldn't help but feel a pang of reverence for her father's ability to navigate the intricacies of their upscale world.

As she watched him work the room with practiced ease, she couldn't shake the feeling that this wasn't the life she envisioned for herself. While genuinely happy for her father's success, a growing sense of unease stirred within her, a yearning for something more meaningful and authentic beyond the glittering facade of their privileged existence.

Sarah longed to break free from the suffocating safety net that had always surrounded her, to dive into a world of true freedom and face genuine risks—risks that made her feel alive. She knew no one could grant her this liberation; it was a journey she had to undertake on her own, a daring leap into the unknown to discover her own strength. Sadly, she doubted any of her friends would ever emerge from their cocoon of wealth long enough to truly understand her.

CHAPTER FOUR

*I*n the sprawling expanse of the country club's grand hall, Anthony was entrenched in a conversation of distinct purpose. Every word spoken remained dedicated to the primary objective of the social gathering, ensuring its essence remained undiluted amidst the surrounding festivities. The clink of glasses and murmur of conversations enveloped him in the familiar atmosphere he had become accustomed to when mixing business with socializing.

As Anthony moved through the crowd, his gaze found two familiar faces amidst the sea of suits and cocktail dresses: Stephen Millstadt and James Harris, two junior partners from his law firm.

The two men, both seasoned lawyers in their forties, shared a bond that stretched back to their law school days at St. Louis University. Their careers had been forged in the crucible of smaller law firms specializing in family law.

Anthony first encountered Stephen on the pristine greens of the Westfield golf course, introduced by a fellow member who spoke highly of Stephen's talents. Despite Stephen's limited experience in corporate law, his hunger for success and genuine dedication to client welfare left a lasting impression on Anthony.

So much so that Anthony wasted no time in offering him a position at his firm. Stephen, in turn, recommended James for another role within the company. Anthony found amusement in the dichotomy between the two men; Stephen, with his athletic prowess and love for the fairway, stood in stark contrast to James, whose penchant for board games and leisurely pursuits, such as reading, belied his dedication to his craft.

Though Stephen once jested about James's gaming companions, their shared passion for the law served as the foundation of their friendship, transcending superficial differences.

Stephen and James were dedicated to their work at Kellerman Law Group, often putting in extra hours. Stephen had the time to spare since he was divorced and didn't have children, while James seemed to be a lifelong bachelor with few commitments.

It wasn't long before Anthony took notice of their hard work and long hours and extended invitations for them to join the ranks of junior partners at Kellerman Law Group.

"Hi, Anthony," Stephen greeted with a grin, raising his glass in salute as Anthony approached.

"Hey, boss," James chimed in, taking a sip of his diet cola with a hint of childlike innocence.

"Stephen, James, always a pleasure," Anthony replied. "You guys enjoying the party?"

"That would be a resounding 'yes'," James replied, excitement evident in his voice. Mingling with the city's elite was a thrill, even though he secretly doubted its impact on his career. Socially shy, he still relished the opportunity to feature in photos, hoping they might find their way into influential magazines. Plus, he couldn't wait to share the snapshots with his gaming buddies, fellow law student graduates, and childhood pals for some bragging rights.

Stephen took a more practical approach. "I'm doing my bit to promote the law firm," he explained, raising his drink with a grin. "And hey, free drinks are always a plus."

Anthony smirked. "Free for you and everyone else, but it's costing me a pretty penny."

"And it's all tax deductible," Stephen quipped with a grin. "The best part? No need for an accountant; I've got tax law down pat, if I do say so myself."

Anthony cocked his head and playfully jabbed at Stephen. "You sound like you're aiming for a promotion, Steve."

"Well… duh. That house in the Hamptons isn't going to pay for itself."

"Do you have a house in the Hamptons?" Anthony asked.

"Not yet; I'm talking about the future."

Laughter danced through their conversation for a fleeting moment before they were interrupted by the arrival of Nick Pernod, a well-known figure in the business world, who achieved success at an early age. In his mid-thirties, Nick was younger than most of the crowd present this evening at the country club, with the exception of Sarah and her friends.

"Gentlemen, what a pleasure to see you all," Nick greeted, his voice smooth as silk as he joined their circle. He was a handsome, towering figure, broad-shouldered and formidable, exuding confidence effortlessly. Clad in a sharp Armani suit, he epitomized cool and collected, a man who remained unfazed in every situation. With stakes in over a dozen technology firms, known and unknown, Nick held an enigmatic aura, leaving his other ventures to the imagination.

"Ah, Nick, always a pleasure," Anthony greeted, his attempt to conceal his surprise evident as he offered a handshake.

Nick flashed a charming smile, his eyes sparkling with a hint of mischief. "Oh, just thought I'd grace this event with my presence," he replied with a wink. "I know it's a private event, but one of your guests, who is a member of the club, used their guest privileges to invite me along. Hope you don't mind."

"Of course not."

"Good, because truth be told, I've been itching to chat with you, Anthony."

Anthony arched an eyebrow, intrigued. "Oh? What about?"

Nick leaned in closer, his tone conspiratorial. "I've been eyeing your firm for a while now, Anthony. I see great potential there, and I want in."

A ripple of surprise passed through the group as they exchanged glances, the implications of Nick's words sinking in.

"You want to invest in the firm?" Stephen asked, eyebrows raised in disbelief.

Nick nodded, a confident gleam in his eyes. "Absolutely. I believe in what you're doing, Anthony. But here's the kicker," he added, leaning back with a grin. "I can't. Seems I missed the memo that only attorneys can be stakeholders in a law firm."

The group chuckled at the irony of the situation.

"Well, Nick, I appreciate the vote of confidence," Anthony said, a smile tugging at his lips. "Who knows, maybe one day we'll find a way to make it work. But don't view your visit as a waste of time. Enjoy the drinks and the mingling."

"Dad," Sarah's voice came from behind Anthony, drawing everyone's attention to his attractive daughter. As Sarah glanced at Nick, he flashed her a disarming smile, briefly diverting her attention.

"Yes, honey?" Anthony inquired, gently guiding her attention back to him.

"I just wanted to tell you we were leaving. Thanks so much for inviting me and the others."

"Sure thing. Thanks for coming." He gave her a warm hug.

As they separated, Nick stepped forward, his hand outstretched. "Hi, I'm Nick."

"I'm Sarah," she responded as they shook hands.

"A delight to make your acquaintance," he said, his tone carrying a hint of flirtation.

Sarah blushed slightly. "Likewise," she replied. Then, breaking away from Nick's gaze, she nodded farewell to Stephen and James before turning to walk away. Nick's lingering stare unsettled Anthony, though he concealed his emotions behind a stoic facade.

Nick turned his attention back to the men and made small talk, mostly about his businesses, new acquisitions, stocks, and golf game. Anthony listened with a polite smile, but his interest was minimal. He shared his daughter's disdain for those who could only discuss business and sports. Yet, Anthony was deeply entrenched in this lifestyle with no real escape, and at this point in his life, he had no desire for one. That door had closed decades ago. After dominating the conversation, Nick bid adieu and moved on to another group.

Anthony turned to Stephen and James with a forced smile, but his demeanor had clearly shifted, his expression growing solemn. His junior partners noticed the change immediately.

"What's up, Anthony?" Stephen asked.

"I need to talk to you both about something," Anthony replied somberly.

He leaned closer to the two men and spoke to them in hushed tones.

Lucas sat silently, his eyes shut, in the passenger seat of Sarah's Beemer as she drove them through the serene streets of Shaw, a neighborhood nestled in the heart of St. Louis. The area boasted a peaceful ambiance with its canopy of trees and lofty Victorian residences shaded within lush greenery. Tower Grove Park, a hallmark of the community, boasted a 19th-century palm house, charming pavilions, and a serene water-lily pond where nature balanced with the urban landscape. Nearby, the Missouri Botanical Garden contained diverse conservatories international gardens, while the historic Compton Hill Reservoir Park boasted a majestic Romanesque-style water tower, adding a touch of grandeur to the skyline.

Lucas, despite his proficiency as a tennis instructor, found himself humbled by the opulent Victorian home he called his own, a legacy bestowed upon him by his father's wealth. While his career afforded him a comfortable living, it paled in comparison to the affluence required to maintain such a residence. Yet, he had chosen this prestigious neighborhood not solely for its cultural allure but also for the status and prestige it granted him.

"I noticed you talking to Nick Pernod," Lucas remarked, his eyes still closed as the wash of streetlight flowed through the car's windows, as though even that subdued glow felt too intense.

"Yeah, he introduced himself when I talked to my dad. I guess they're friends. You know him?"

"Only by reputation. He owns a computer software firm that my dad did business with." Lucas paused for a thoughtful moment. "My father was really impressed with him," he added with a mix of sadness and pain.

Sarah understood the weight of Lucas's perceived disappointment to his family by opting for a potentially unstable career that had a lifespan limited by his own physical abilities. It was a shared trait between them, both pursuing unconventional paths. While her own journey as an artist garnered support from her parents, she couldn't shake the notion that her gender played a role.

Observing her friends' mothers predominantly as stay-at-home women, Sarah recognized it as more than just a generational norm; it reflected the privileged portion of society. It seemed a throwback to the 1950s, where women tended the home while men moved into the workforce.

Yet, in today's reality of soaring expenses, dual-income households were a necessity more often than not, a fact lost on the elite. They looked down on those struggling to make ends meet, oblivious to their own advantage of inherited wealth and generational businesses. Merit had little to do with their lofty positions; it was the cushion of trust funds and handed-down prosperity. Sarah's peers, many basking in self-congratulatory achievements, were often blinded by their own illusions of success.

Sarah found herself ensnared in the very cycle she critiqued. Despite her awareness of the privileged existence she inherited, she defiantly pursued the bohemian path of an artist, a stark contrast to the corporate circles she traversed. Yet, she grappled with the contradiction of her choices. On one hand, she resisted the label of hypocrisy, acknowledging her human craving for creature comforts—a sentiment amplified by the allure of her opulent upbringing. The appeal of her gas-guzzling status car and the luxurious swimming pool, complete with underwater lights, sliding board, and diving board, nestled behind the mansion walls of her gated community, proved difficult to resist. Caught between her ideals and her desires, Sarah wrestled with the tension of authenticity versus indulgence.

Nick Pernod, the guy who sparked jealousy in Lucas, fully embraced his privileged upbringing. He dove headfirst into the opportunities handed to him by his family, turning them into even more wealth. Lucas could've followed suit, but he went his own way, much like Sarah. At first, she admired Lucas for his independence, but lately, she started to question if his choices were driven by rebellion against his father or just plain laziness. After all, he had the freedom to set his own hours while still benefiting from the family's financial support.

Sarah had a hunch that Lucas's father continued to fund him out of a sense of pride. Cutting off the financial support to Lucas, which would force him to live a life of the lower classes, would certainly tarnish the esteemed Carter family name, a pillar of respect in St. Louis society. Lucas likely understood this dynamic and capitalized on it, knowing his father couldn't bear the shame of his son living anything less than a comfortable life.

Sarah pulled her BMW to a halt in front of Lucas's home, situated amidst the quaint streets of Shaw's historic district. The house boasted several thousand square feet, complete with a charming wraparound porch and a striking circular turret adorning the front right corner. It was undeniably spacious for just one person, but typical for the social circles Sarah and her friends frequented.

Lucas slowly turned his head and blinked at his house through the alcohol haze. "Thanks for the ride."

"No problem, and I'm sure the country club will watch over your Tesla until you pick it up tomorrow," she said with a wide grin.

He casually glanced over at her, then drew nearer, their lips meeting in a kiss that gradually grew intense. They held each other close, losing themselves in a passionate kiss. When they finally separated, they gazed deeply into each other's eyes. Under the soft glow of the moonlight, Lucas tenderly traced the outline of Sarah's jaw with his fingertips. She nestled closer, her breath hitching in anticipation as his hand trailed down the curve of her neck, sending shivers down her spine.

"You want to spend the night?" Lucas asked so softly it was barely audible.

Sarah subtly shook her head. "No... I... shouldn't."

"How about coming in for a while then?"

"If I do, I'll end up staying, you know that."

Lucas leaned back in his seat, letting out a heavy sigh as he watched the trees, which lined the street, sway gently in the breeze through the windshield, their leaves shimmering beneath the streetlights.

"I just don't know what's going on between us," he murmured with a tinge of frustration lacing his words. There was no anger in his tone, only a blend of confusion and anguish.

"You know what it is," Sarah said with some guilt as she glanced out the driver's side window.

"Your dad?"

She nodded. "He just hasn't been the same since my mom died."

Lucas turned to her, but she was still looking away. "He seems to be doing fine to me. I mean we both saw him tonight. Everybody saw him. He was having a blast."

"He's good at masking his troubles, bottling things up until they boiled over. I've watched him do it his whole life. So did my mother, but she was always there to talk him down from the ledge so to speak when the pressure got too great. But now she's gone and it's up to me to fill that space."

"It is <u>not</u> up to you. Anthony is a fantastic guy and you love him and support him, but it is not your responsibility to give up your own life… your happiness… to watch over him like he's a child."

Sarah's glare bore into him, tears glistening in her eyes, and in that moment, he felt an immediate pang of regret for his words. "Don't tell me what I'm responsible for. My dad needs me right now and I plan to be there for him."

"Okay, okay," he said softly as he wondered what damage he may have just inflicted on their relationship.

"I need to go," Sarah said curtly without looking at him.

"All right, I'm sorry," he uttered, his words hanging in the air, awaiting any response from her, but she only answered him with silence. Feeling awful about the situation, he stepped out of the car, and watched her BMW disappear into the distance, his gaze fixed on its retreating form in the street.

Sarah had hoped to sleep in, but, as usual, it didn't happen. Without even glancing at her phone, casually charging on the bedside table, she knew it was just past 7 a.m. It seemed she was fated to rise at that hour without fail.

In college, she used to be a night owl, dragging herself to morning classes. Back then, she could manage on very little sleep, being in her late teens and early twenties. She never valued it then, took it all for granted, like her friends did. They could stay up late, partying, and drinking, living life freely without parents around, then breeze into class the next day. Their clothes might be messy and their hair untidy, especially the boys', but who minded? Not their professors, nor their classmates who often partied with them. But those days were now distant memories. Regardless of how late she stayed up, Sarah inevitably found herself rising early to start her day.

Sarah's thoughts returned to last night and the surge of irritation she felt as she left Lucas standing on the street. They had shared a tender, intimate moment, yet he had managed to ruin it. She resented his tendency to question her decisions; after all, she never questioned his—at least not to his face. She had always afforded him the space to navigate his own choices, and she expected the same consideration in return.

Sarah perched on the bed's edge, stretching as she released a contented yawn. The faint sound of footsteps echoing down the hallway made her smile. Her father, like her, always rose early. He was a morning person for as long as she could recall. The muffled steps suggested he was making an effort to be considerate to avoid disrupting her slumber. From the sound of it, he seemed to have entered his office, engrossed in his early morning routine.

Sarah put on her slippers and robe before quietly making her way out of her room. She silently moved down the hallway and descended the stairs toward the first floor. She pondered stopping by her father's office to say hello, but decided against it. She thought he'd probably be processing last night's events and planning his next moves.

She chose to give him some space, at least until she'd had her first cup of coffee. That thought brought a grin to her face.

As she descended the stairs, Sarah paused beside the painting of Anthony in his office. The thought of replacing it with something fresh crossed her mind. She knew her father wouldn't object; he trusted her judgment on such matters, as did her mother before she passed. Yet, Sarah couldn't decide on the spot. She'd have to wait for inspiration to strike. When it did, she vowed to pour her heart into crafting the perfect replacement. With a mental note made, she added it to her to-do list and tucked it away for later.

Sarah entered the spacious kitchen which was situated at the back of the mansion. It was a haven of both function and comfort. High ceilings were illuminated by recessed lights, casting a soft, even glow over the room. Gleaming marble floors stretched beneath, reflecting the warmth of the ambient lighting. Generous countertops offered ample space, while sleek cabinetry lined several walls. Floor to ceiling windows spanned the entire length of the back wall, flooding the space with natural light. Their sheer size offered panoramic views of the surrounding landscape. Adjacent to the kitchen, down a nearby hallway were double doors that opened onto the backyard pool.

Sarah brewed herself a cup of coffee with a simple coffee pod, listening as the aromatic liquid filled her cup. Amidst the gentle drip, she caught the faint sounds of her someone—her father—descending the stairs and slipping out through one of the numerous side or back doors. She concluded it was the latter, leading to the pool area where he traditionally kickstarted his day with a brisk swim. Glancing at the analog wall clock, a relic of charming antiquity chosen by her mother, she noted it was 7:09. Anthony's punctuality was legendary; his morning swim always commenced at the stroke of 7 a.m. Sarah chuckled at the notion of her father potentially breaking his routine, contemplating a Guinness World Record entry for tardiness. Perhaps the previous night's festivities had left a deeper impact than she realized. Nonetheless, if a slight delay meant furthering his business goals, sacrificing nine minutes of the morning was a trivial price to pay.

With her coffee brewed, Sarah added a splash of half- and- half and a spoonful of sugar before opting to join her father by the poolside. Making her way through the short hallway, she reached for the double doors. Despite the morning sun casting a shimmering reflection upon the water's surface, she could still make out her father's silhouette submerged beneath the pool's surface as she glanced through the door's windows. His arms and legs gracefully swayed back and forth. She noticed he seemed to be swimming slower than usual, attributing it to the tiring social event from the night before.

Stepping onto the pool deck, Sarah greeted her father with a cheerful "g ood morning" as she savored her delicious coffee. With a playful grin, she remarked, "Looks like you're running behind today. Don't let that secret slip!"

Anthony didn't respond; he just continued to float, so Sarah moved closer to the pool.

"Good morning, Dad," she called out again, her voice louder this time. Then, she noticed it—and a surge of fear tightened her chest. Anthony's motions weren't deliberate; they were merely ripples in the water, spreading across the pool's surface. Beside his head, a dark hue tainted the water, spreading like ink, but it wasn't black—it was the stark red of blood.

Sarah's world blurred into a surreal haze as the coffee cup slipped from her grasp, its fall towards the pool deck stretching into eternity before shattering into countless fragments upon impact. She flinched as sharp shards and warm liquid grazed her feet, but her gaze remained fixed on her father in the pool.

In the distance, a high-pitched woman's scream pierced the air, echoing through the neighborhood. It took Sarah a moment to realize that the scream was her own.

CHAPTER FIVE

*I*n the heart of Frontenac, Missouri, lay Greenwood Estates, a picture-perfect enclave nestled along a single, meandering road. Guarded by an elegant, automated gate at one end and cradled by a cozy cul-de-sac at the other, it stood as a sanctuary of luxury and tranquility. Stretching proudly along this prestigious avenue were grand mansions, each a testament to opulence and refinement.

From its bustling entrance off Clayton Road to its serene cul-de-sac, Greenwood Estates hummed with life, particularly in the warm embrace of summer. The diligent hum of lawnmowers filled the air as meticulous landscaping adorned the surroundings. Amidst this symphony of activity, special projects sprang to life—a new pool taking shape here, a stylish renovation unfolding there, each a testament to the ever-evolving dreams of its residents.

Yet amidst the grandeur, there was an understated elegance—a respectful distance between driveways that allowed for a sense of seclusion if desired, yet fostering a sense of community when neighbors came together, drawn by the shared bond of their exclusive haven. Greenwood Estates wasn't just a neighborhood; it was a tapestry of stories, a mosaic of dreams, where privacy and camaraderie danced in perfect harmony beneath the shade of ancient oaks and the glow of evening sunsets.

This morning, the air was heavy with a sense of foreboding as those cherished stories took a very sudden dark turn, leaving shattered dreams in their wake. The neighborhood stood cloaked in an eerie silence, a stark contrast to the usual lively atmosphere that graced its luxurious streets. Police cars littered the circular driveway, their flashing lights casting ominous shadows against the imposing facade. News vans lined the streets, their satellite dishes pointing towards the sky as they broadcasted the shocking events that had unfolded on the mansion grounds.

Neighbors peeked from behind their curtains or stepped quietly onto their porches, casting furtive glances at the unfolding scene. The street lay in hushed stillness, save for the approach of an ambulance, its flashing lights illuminating the path as it rolled toward the mansion. Though the siren remained silent, the urgency hung thick in the air, palpable to all who watched on.

Amidst the solemn atmosphere of the mansion's interior, Sarah found herself caught in a storm of conflicting emotions. The spaciousness of the mansion allowed her to settle in the formal living room, far removed from the hallway that stretched towards the pool. This room, adorned with elegant furnishings and polished surfaces, was a seldom-visited sanctuary, reserved for special occasions and festive gatherings. But there was nothing special or festive about today.

Surrounded by the quiet murmurs and downcast expressions of emergency personnel that moved about the house, Sarah was embraced by the comforting presence of friends, primarily Emily and Ashley, as well as Lucas. If there ever was a time she needed her boyfriend, ex or otherwise, that time was now. Their words of solace and gentle gestures served as a lifeline in the midst of her overwhelming grief, offering a semblance of comfort in the wake of her father's shocking and unexpected passing.

Yet, despite the warmth of their support, Sarah couldn't shake the lingering sense of unease that clung to her like a heavy fog by just being in the home. The once-familiar halls of the mansion now seemed to loom ominously, each shadowy corner whispering reminders of her father's absence. What was once a sanctuary of laughter and love now felt eerily silent, the weight of her loss casting a pall over every cherished memory of her father and mother. In the midst of this emotional tempest, Sarah found herself grappling with a profound sense of isolation, her heart aching for the comfort of her father's presence amidst the unfamiliar chill of the mansion's walls.

Sarah's keen eye for detail didn't fail her as she observed the presence of an unfamiliar figure amidst the uniformed police officers and EMTs. Unlike the crisply attired officers, this man, likely in his fifties, stood out in a slightly rumpled suit that seemed out of place in the elegant surroundings. With a gruff demeanor, he walked alone through the mansion's halls, his sharp gaze taking in every detail of the layout and décor, occasionally speaking quietly to the uniformed police officers, as if giving them instructions. Curiosity piqued, Sarah pondered the purpose of his presence. It dawned on her that he must be a police detective, but she couldn't fathom why one would be necessary for what appeared to be a straightforward accident.

As Sarah caught sight of the man peering out of a back window, a surge of determination overcame her, and she abruptly came to her feet.

"Sarah?" Ashley's voice rang out, tinged with concern as she noticed Sarah's sudden movement and focused gaze on the stranger.

"I'm going to go have a chat with that man," Sarah declared, her tone as nonchalant as if she were merely joining a casual conversation. Ignoring Ashley's apprehension, Sarah began to make her way across the room.

Lucas watched her with growing concern. "Sarah, sweetheart, maybe it's not the best time for that," he interjected, his worry evident in his voice.

Lucas's use of the term 'sweetheart' grated on Sarah's nerves. While she appreciated his caring nature, she couldn't help but feel irritated by the implication that he saw her as fragile and delicate.

True, she was feeling vulnerable at the moment, but she was also curious about the presence of this man—possibly a detective—in her own home. She didn't want to be treated with kid gloves; she wanted answers.

As Sarah neared, the man pivoted, sensing her presence. Before she could speak, a scene outside grabbed her attention. Her father lay motionless in the pool, police documenting the grim discovery. The water danced serenely, oblivious to the tragedy unfolding. A camera captured the broken coffee cup on the deck, a poignant reminder of Sarah's shock.

Sarah recoiled, horror washing over her anew at the sight of her father's lifeless form. The memory flooded back: the coffee cup slipping from her grasp, her frantic attempts to rouse him, the futile struggle to pull him from the water. Every detail burned into her mind with painful clarity—stumbling back into the house, her frantic search for her phone, calling 911—a chaotic whirlwind of emotion and action.

"Hi," Sarah said with an edge in her voice, like one might use with a customer service representative just before lodging a complaint.

"Hello," the man said in return, without emotion.

"I'm Sarah Kellerman," she began, her voice catching. "I'm the one who called 911 when I found..." She stopped, swallowing hard against the rising emotions. "When I found my dad in the pool," she managed finally, unable to utter the words " father's body" —it was still too painful.

"I'm Detective Nelson," the man introduced himself, offering his hand. Sarah shook it mechanically, her mind elsewhere. "I'm really sorry about your loss," he added sincerely, his words carrying genuine empathy, a gesture that Sarah found comforting.

"You're a detective?" Sarah asked, though she already knew the answer. She had known even before she approached him, before he introduced himself. She realized it was a habit she'd picked up from her father, a subtle influence guiding her actions. Asking questions she already knew the answers to was a skill she understood well—an essential tactic for an attorney as her father often reminded her.

"Yes," he said with a nod.

"What kind of detective?"

"Homicide," he stated, casting a curious glance her way, as if searching for her reaction.

And he got one. "Why?" she gasped, disbelief etched across her face. "It was just an accident, right?"

"Probably," he said, pausing a moment before continuing. "Did he go swimming in the morning often?"

"Yes. Every morning at 7 a.m. . Like clockwork. Never missed as far as I remember." She eyed the detective, trying to read him. "Are you suggesting my dad was…?" Her voice trailed off, the question lingering in the air, heavy with uncertainty.

Nelson spoke in an easy, calming manner, in an attempt to settle her worries. "I'm sure it was an accident, Sarah. May I call you Sarah?" She nodded without saying a word. "Your father was a public figure. A high-profile public figure. And as a state criminal prosecutor—"

"Former prosecutor."

"Yes, former prosecutor. Nonetheless, during his time with the state, he put behind bars some people who might hold a serious grudge."

Realization sinks into Sarah and her eyes widen with fear. "So, you're saying he was murdered?"

"I'm not saying any such thing. I'm just stating the facts of his profession. Former profession. Besides that, when someone— anyone—dies under potentially mysterious circumstances, we are required to investigate. It's just standard procedure."

Nelson reaches out as if to give her comforting touch on her arm, but he stops short of making contact. "I'm sure this will turn out to be a tragic accident. Again, I'm very, very sorry for your loss."

Sarah nodded, ready to leave, but Nelson's voice grabbed her attention. "Sarah," he called, halting her retreat. She turned back to face him.

"I noticed a surveillance camera near the pool area. May I have the footage?"

Surprise flickered across Sarah's features. The detective had assured her of her father's accidental death, yet his request for surveillance footage contradicted that assurance. Her mind raced, but she reminded herself of his claim about standard procedure. Maybe she was just being paranoid.

Though she had no reason to refuse, Sarah knew denying the request would only lead to more trouble. If she did, the detective would simply obtain a court order. It seemed pointless to resist, especially when the footage held the truth she sought.

"Sure," Sarah said.

"Thanks, I'll get the department tech guys out here to retrieve it."

"Will they be here today?" Sarah inquired; her concern evident.

"Maybe, but most likely tomorrow," Nelson confirmed, noting her subtle grimace. "Is there a problem?"

"I don't feel comfortable staying here," Sarah confessed, her unease palpable.

Sympathy washed over Nelson. "You should probably stay with a friend or in a hotel," he suggested, his tone gentle yet authoritative.

Sarah nodded in agreement, grateful for his understanding.

"If you're not here, may I have access to the house?"

"Yes. I'll give you a key."

"Thank you," Nelson said, extending a card from his wallet. "Here's my number. Call me anytime for any reason."

"Okay, Detective," Sarah replied, tucking the card away before rejoining her friends, her mind still swirling with unanswered questions.

Sarah walked across the spacious living room of the mansion, her gaze wandering aimlessly across the elegant furnishings that had once been a source of comfort. Now, they seemed to mock her with their opulence, a stark reminder of the life she had lost. The memory of her father, Anthony, floating lifeless in the pool haunted her every thought. The once-grand estate now felt suffocating, each room echoing with the absence of her parents' presence. She longed to escape its confines, to find solace in the embrace of familiar faces.

Ashley approached her with eyes brimming with concern as she gently placed a hand on Sarah's shoulder.

"Sarah," she said softly, her voice a gentle melody amidst the oppressive emptiness of the room. "You shouldn't be alone right now. Come stay with me for a while. You know you're welcome for as long as you need."

Sarah's heart swelled with gratitude for Ashley's offer, a lifeline in the midst of her despair. Just as she opened her mouth to respond, Emily appeared.

"I, um, I could also offer my place," she said, her cheeks flushing with embarrassment for not thinking of asking first, as she shifted nervously on her feet. Sarah offered her a small, reassuring smile, touched by her friend's gesture of kindness.

"Thank you, Emily," she said softly, her voice carrying a note of appreciation. "But I think I'll take Ashley up on her offer."

"Sarah, may I speak with you for a moment?" Lucas's voice cut through the air, drawing Sarah's attention. He approached with a respectful distance, mindful not to disrupt the intimate exchange she shared with her two closest friends. He understood his role in her life at that moment and respected the boundaries she needed.

With a nod, Sarah acknowledged the flood of emotions swirling within her. Despite feeling overwhelmed, she found comfort in the presence of her friends, knowing they were there to support her in any way they could. Stepping away from Ashley and Emily, leaving them to quietly conversed amongst themselves, she made her way over to Lucas.

"Sarah," he said, his voice low and patient. "My door has always been open for you. You know that. You've spent the night plenty of times in the past. I would really like for you to consider staying at my place."

"I don't know," Sarah said, her voice tinged with uncertainty. The inner conflict was palpable. She was really considering it but was torn and not sure it was a good idea.

"Please, at least one night. Decide tomorrow if you want to stay." There was no desperation in Lucas's tone. He wasn't begging; he was negotiating. Sarah wasn't sure how she felt about that.

Sarah hesitated, her heart struggling between the comfort of familiarity – staying with Lucas – and the uncertainty of the unknown – staying with Ashley. She'd been friends with Ashley for many years, but they'd never lived together. Arrangements like that have been known to destroy friendships. The idea of living with Ashley was tempting, but she couldn't shake the fear of how such arrangements have been known to destroy a friendship.

Yet, she knew she wasn't ready to reopen old wounds with Lucas, to dive headfirst into a relationship still marred by past hurts. But in that moment, with the weight of her grief pressing down upon her, she found herself relenting.

"Okay," she whispered, her voice barely above a whisper. "Just one night."

Ashley didn't take offense when Sarah mentioned she'd be staying with Lucas for the night. She completely understood the decision. After all, Lucas was more than just a friend to Sarah, albeit in a somewhat undefined way. Ashley knew that Sarah and Lucas's relationship had shifted into uncertain territory, and the complexities of the situation undoubtedly stirred up Sarah's emotions, leaving her feeling even more conflicted about where things stood.

Ashley, Emily, and Lucas shared one unanimous belief: it was imperative for Sarah to leave the mansion as swiftly as possible. Each moment spent within its confines seemed to burden her with an unbearable weight, draining the life from her. They recognized the urgency of changing her surroundings before she succumbed entirely to the suffocating atmosphere of the mansion.

As Ashley and Emily accompanied Sarah upstairs to her bedroom to assist her with packing, Lucas remained in the living room, giving them space. Halfway up the staircase, Sarah's gaze drifted towards the majestic painting she had crafted of Anthony in his office, a painful reminder of her loss. Despite its soft, earthy tones, a subtle hint of red seemed to seep through, overwhelming her senses. She remembered mixing the red in to make some of the details pop, but now it felt as though the red had intensified as if the painting itself was bleeding, a sight too agonizing to bear. Hastily tearing her gaze away, Sarah hurried upstairs, hoping her friends hadn't noticed the discomfort the painting now evoked within her.

Lucas's request for a light pack was met with earnest attempts from Ashley and Emily, yet the task quickly revealed itself to be a futile endeavor. The prospect of an indefinite stay demanded more than a minimal assortment of essentials. Each item reflected Sarah's uncertainty about when she would feel ready to return to the mansion. Clothes were carefully folded, toiletries meticulously arranged, and personal care items gathered with thoughtful consideration.

Before leaving the mansion, Sarah gave Detective Nelson a spare front door key and the alarm code. He assured her that he'd personally make sure the house was locked up and the alarm set before leaving. He speculated that neither he, nor any other police officer, would need to return to the premises after tomorrow.

In a gesture of kindness, Detective Nelson arranged for police officers to clear a path from the garage, where Sarah's BMW was parked, to the street. The driveway and the street in front of the house were jammed with news vans from both local and national networks, making it challenging for anyone to navigate to their cars, but Sarah made it out of the neighborhood easily.

Unfortunately, Emily, Ashley, and Lucas weren't granted a police escort to their cars, which were parked on the street in front of the mansion, leaving them to face a barrage of questions from journalists. They chose to keep their heads down and remain silent as the reporters bombarded them with inquiries. Though Lucas simmered with anger and shot menacing glares at some journalists, it did little to deter the onslaught of questions directed at him.

As they departed the neighborhood, several networks managed to capture good footage of them driving away. Each of them drove luxurious cars—Lucas in a Mercedes, Emily in a Lexus, and Ashley in a Porsche. The networks aimed to spin Anthony's tragic death into a commentary on class disparities. Death within affluent circles made national headlines, yet shootings in impoverished neighborhoods barely registered on the news radar.

By that evening, the passing of Anthony Kellerman had stirred waves across the nation, seizing the spotlight on every news platform. It marked a sorrowful follow-up to the loss of Monica, the family's beloved matriarch, just two years prior. Anthony's renown stemmed from his role as a state prosecutor, a career that often remained in the shadows for many. Yet, Anthony's courtroom theatrics had propelled him into the national spotlight, his cases splashed across the screens of CNN, MSNBC, and FOX News. Though fleeting, his moments of fame surpassed the typical 15 minutes, his courtroom performances becoming the stuff of legend in Missouri and beyond. It wasn't a deliberate pursuit of celebrity; it was simply Anthony being Anthony—wholeheartedly devoted to every endeavor he undertook. Monica would jest about their family's dual artistic streaks, with Sarah's success as a painter complementing Anthony's legal flair. He took it all in his stride, believing in giving his all to present a compelling case. And now, in the wake of his passing, the echoes of his legacy reverberated from coast to coast, a testament to the impact he had made on the legal landscape and beyond.

But the news coverage had a dark side. It spilled over into social media, making Sarah, the last living member of the Kellerman family, a prime target. Her image was everywhere, and she became the focus of vicious posts from anonymous users pounding away at their keyboards. Comments like "a lawyer's death is welcome, and a rich lawyer even better," and "boohoo, poor little rich girl can now drown her sorrow in her millions" bombarded her feed. Cruel taunts such as "your turn to go swimming, Sarah" and "hopefully you'll be next, girl" cut deep. Overwhelmed, Sarah slammed her laptop shut, and, sobbing uncontrollably, later buried herself in her bed for days.

CHAPTER SIX

*S*arah sat quietly in Lucas's living room, a glass of red wine in hand, but her thoughts were far away. Despite the warmth of the room, she felt a heavy sadness weighing on her heart. The rich mahogany woodwork seemed to blur before her eyes, the ornate patterns now nothing but a distant backdrop to her melancholy. The polished hardwood floors, usually gleaming with light, now seemed dim and lifeless.

Lucas moved closer in hopes of being a comforting presence beside her. The soft glow of the setting sun through the large windows cast gentle shadows across the room, but it offered little solace to Sarah's troubled mind. They sank, side by side, into the plush velvet sofa together, its deep hues of burgundy and emerald offering a small measure of comfort in their shared sorrow.

Before them, the grand fireplace stood as a silent sentinel, its marble facade a stoic reminder of the passage of time. Lucas reached out, his hand finding hers, a silent gesture of support in her time of need. Above the mantel, the gilt mirror reflected their subdued figures, a stark contrast to the room's usual vibrancy.

On the mantel, the delicate porcelain figurines stood as silent witnesses to their shared history, their presence a reminder of the fragility of life.

"You can stay as long as you need to," Lucas offered softly as he sipped his wine.

"Thank you," Sarah murmured softly, her voice barely above a whisper. She was well aware of Lucas's perpetual offer of an open door, yet uncertainty lingered in her mind. While she harbored a deep-seated love for him, she couldn't shake the nagging doubt that their relationship had reached its natural conclusion. Despite this, she found solace in his presence, a familiar comfort during her time of distress.

"Lucas," Sarah's voice in a hushed tone, her eyes glistening with unshed tears. "I just...I don't know how to deal with this."

"I know, Sarah," he murmured softly. "Losing your dad...it's unimaginable."

Sarah nodded, a lump forming in her throat as memories of her father flooded her mind. "He was everything to me," she admitted, her voice trembling with emotion. "The person who was always there after my mom died. And now he's gone."

As Sarah spoke those words, a realization washed over her like a wave crashing against the shore. It struck her that she thought she'd moved in with her dad after her mom passed away because she believed he needed her, but she now understood it was she who needed him. Being an only child, her parents had been her steadfast companions throughout her upbringing. Even as an adult, Sarah had clung to the closeness they shared, cherishing the bond they had nurtured over the years. Now, with both of them gone, she felt adrift, as if a vital anchor had been suddenly wrenched from her grasp, leaving her to navigate the turbulent waters of life alone.

Gently, Lucas squeezed her hand, his touch offering a silent promise of support. "You don't have to face this alone," he reassured her, his gaze unwavering. "I'm here for you, Sarah. Whatever you need, I'll be right here by your side."

Tears spilled from Sarah's eyes as she leaned into his embrace, seeking solace in the warmth of his presence. "Lucas," she whispered, her voice choked with emotion, "You're my rock in all of this."

As they sat together in the quiet embrace of shared sorrow, the weight of grief seemed momentarily lighter, replaced by the gentle comfort of companionship. And in that fleeting moment, Sarah found herself grateful for the unexpected kindness of her ex-boyfriend, whose unwavering support served as a beacon of light in the darkness of her grief.

Lucas fought the urge to talk about it with her. To discuss what she thought she should do going forward. Besides being inappropriate, it would have simply been wrong. This was not the time for talk, not unless she wanted to talk, and clearly she didn't. This was the time to let her just be. To do whatever she wanted to do. And for now he could see that she wanted to drink wine and let the night envelope her, and leave whatever decisions she needed to make until tomorrow, or next week, or whatever.

Lucas's thoughts raced as he considered the myriad decisions looming on Sarah's horizon. He couldn't help but wonder about her intentions regarding the mansion. Would she choose to make it her permanent residence once more, or perhaps opt to sell it? And then there was the matter of her father's law firm. With her impending inheritance, she would soon become its principal stakeholder. The weight of these questions hung heavy in the air.

But he resisted the temptation to broach the subject with her, knowing it wasn't the right moment. It wouldn't have been appropriate, and it certainly wouldn't have been helpful. Now wasn't the time for discussion, not unless she initiated it herself, which she clearly didn't. This was a time for allowing her to simply exist, to be in the moment without the weight of decisions pressing down on her. It was evident that she sought solace in the simple act of sipping wine and letting the night wrap around her like a comforting blanket, postponing any difficult choices for another day, another week, or whenever she felt ready.

As the evening's shadows crept into the room, Lucas drew nearer to Sarah, his heart thrumming with anticipation. He pressed his lips to hers, a tender gesture laden with uncertainty. To his delight, Sarah responded, her own lips yielding to his with a sweet surrender that sent a jolt of electricity through him.

Setting aside their glasses of wine on the coffee table, Lucas enveloped Sarah in his arms, drawing her closer until there was no space left between them. Their kiss deepened, ignited by a newfound fervor as their tongues entwined in a surge of passion. In that moment, the world outside faded away, leaving only the intoxicating warmth of their embrace.

After a while, Lucas gently took Sarah's hand, leading her upstairs to his bedroom. There, they found solace in the spacious four-poster bed, its sturdy columns standing like guardians, enveloping them in the comfortable embrace of its canopy.

Sarah lay upon the soft expanse of the bed, her anticipation palpable in the air as Lucas's hands moved with a tender reverence, slowly undressing her, each garment shed like a layer of inhibition falling away. His caress was a crescendo of desire, igniting flames that danced across her skin.

With each piece of clothing relinquished, Lucas mirrored her vulnerability, shedding his own layers until they were both laid bare, skin to skin, heart to heart. The room was a sanctuary of whispered promises and unspoken desires as they surrendered to the intimacy of the moment.

As they finally came together, their lips met in a tender kiss, and Sarah and Lucas became lost in each other. She lay tangled in the sheets, her heart racing with anticipation as Lucas's warm breath danced against her skin and she felt a wave of desire wash over her. His touch was electric, sending shivers down her spine as he explored every inch of her body with a reverence that took her breath away. Their hands roamed freely, tracing the curves of each other's bodies with a hunger that bordered on desperation.

His lips trailed down her neck, each one sparking excitement within her. His hands moved over her skin with a blend of tenderness and passion, mapping out every contour, every inch of her skin. Each touch, each kiss, was deliberate, as if he were committing her body to memory. As he moved lower, his lips followed, exploring her breasts, leaving a trail of heat in their wake. His tongue flicked over her nipples, drawing soft moans from her lips, her back arching to press closer to him. Sarah's fingers tangled in his hair, her breath hitching with every touch. The world outside ceased to exist; there was only Lucas and the intoxicating sensations he elicited.

Lucas's hands continued their journey, tracing the curves of her waist, the gentle swell of her hips, before finally settling on her thighs. He took his time, savoring the feel of her, the way her skin responded to his touch. His kisses followed the path of his hands, leaving no inch of her untouched. When he reached the apex of her thighs, he paused, his breath hot against her most sensitive spot.

Sarah gasped, her hips lifting off the bed as a wave of pleasure washed over her. He took his time, exploring her with a reverence that made her feel revered. His tongue moved in slow, languid strokes, teasing her, driving her closer to the edge with each passing moment. Her moans filled the room, mingling with the sound of their heavy breathing. Sarah's hands clutched at the sheets, her body a taut bowstring, ready to snap.

Just when she thought she couldn't take it anymore, Lucas pulled back, his eyes dark with desire as he moved up her body. He kissed her deeply. The kiss was a promise, a silent vow of the pleasure yet to come. Sarah's body quivered with anticipation, her breath coming in short, ragged gasps. Lucas's fingers roamed over her body, his touch a tantalizing mix of tenderness and urgency.

When the time was right, he positioned himself to enter her, his eyes locked onto hers. Slowly, he entered her, their bodies becoming one. The sensation was exquisite, a perfect blend of pleasure and intimacy. They stilled for a moment, savoring the feeling of being joined, hearts beating in unison. The connection between them deepened, an unspoken bond that transcended words.

Their bodies began to move together in a slow, sensual rhythm, a dance as old as time. Each thrust, each movement, was a testament to the depth of their connection, a physical manifestation of the emotions that had been building between them all night. Lucas's hands gripped her hips, and the pleasure built between them, a crescendo that grew and grew, driving them higher and higher.

Sarah's hands roamed over Lucas's back, her nails digging into his skin as she urged him on. Her breath came in short, ragged gasps, each one a testament to the intensity of their passion. Their kisses were a desperate melding of mouths and tongues, a primal expression of their need. The world outside ceased to exist; there was only the two of them, their bodies moving together in a dance of love and desire.

The rhythm between them quickened, their movements becoming more frantic, more urgent. The pleasure built to an almost unbearable intensity, a pressure that grew and grew, threatening to overwhelm them both. Sarah's body trembled beneath him, her moans becoming cries of ecstasy as she teetered on the edge. Lucas's thrusts became more forceful, each one driving them closer to the precipice.

Finally, the wave of pleasure crashed over them, a tidal wave of ecstasy that left them both trembling and breathless. Sarah cried out, her body arching off the bed as her release washed over her. Lucas followed moments later, a low groan escaping his lips as he spilled into her, their bodies trembling with the force of their shared climax.

They collapsed together in a tangled heap, their bodies still shuddering from the intensity of their lovemaking. The room was filled with the sound of their heavy breathing, the steady beat of their hearts slowing as they came down from their high. They lay wrapped in each other's arms, their bodies still entwined, finding solace and connection in the aftermath of their passion. They slipped off to sleep, the world outside forgotten, at least for a while.

In the days that followed, Sarah and Lucas strolled through Missouri Botanical Garden, known as Shaw's Garden, a short walk from

Lucas's home. Amidst the vibrant hues of the Garden's blossoming flowers, their conversations flowed between shared moments and silent reflections. Occasionally, they walked hand in hand, though often they simply walked alongside each other. Sarah cherished Lucas's presence during her time of need, yet she understood it wasn't a promise of forever. This realization brought moments of guilt, yet she appreciated Lucas's understanding of their situation and his reluctance to push for more commitment.

Sarah chose to let her phone calls go to voicemail, immersing herself in the present, while Ashley and Emily's concerned check-ins served as gentle reminders of support. Detective Nelson left a single message, marking the conclusion of the investigation and the securing of her father's mansion, which added a layer of closure to the whirlwind of emotions. Amidst the beauty of the garden, Sarah found herself yearning for time to stand still, to hold onto these fleeting moments indefinitely, yet the reality of her father's passing loomed heavy. With the weight of funeral arrangements pressing down, particularly since there was no surviving immediate family on Anthony's side to help out, she reluctantly surrendered the task to the capable hands of the funeral director, knowing that she wasn't emotionally prepared to face it alone.

The day of the funeral dawned, casting its shadow over Sarah's heart with a mix of relief and dread. The sun hung low in the St. Louis sky, casting a golden hue over the sprawling grounds of Rolling Hills Memorial Park on the outskirts of Frontenac. It was a solemn day, one where the air seemed heavy with grief as hundreds of mourners gathered to bid farewell to Anthony Kellerman.

The gathering was a blend of professionals, including attorneys and staff from the Missouri State Prosecutor's Office, as well as lawyers in private practice. Among them mingled businesspeople and lifelong friends of Anthony, tracing their connections back to his youth.

The gravesite was adorned with wreaths of white lilies and roses, their fragrance mingling with the scent of freshly turned earth.

One by one, speakers approached the podium beside the gravesite, weaving a tapestry of memories — some laced with humor, others steeped in sorrow — all bound by the weight of loss. Amidst the sea of faces, Sarah stood at the forefront, nearest to the gravesite. She had quietly informed the funeral director beforehand that she wouldn't be speaking; public addresses were never her forte, and she held her thoughts about her father as sacred, reserved for intimate circles. Thus, she deferred to the professionals, allowing them to share their poignant anecdotes of her father. As the last speaker concluded, the minister, a non-denominational Christian, offered a few solemn words before Anthony was laid to rest. Though Sarah was raised in a Christian environment, her faith was more of a cultural echo than a fervent belief. Their family held loosely to the notion of a higher power, finding solace in their own quiet reflections rather than formal religious practices.

Sarah stood at the edge of the gathering, her heart heavy with loss. She watched as the casket was lowered into the ground, her father's final resting place. Beside her stood Ashley and Emily, their presence a comfort amidst the sea of mourners. Sarah's eyes swept over the crowd, recognizing familiar faces, some offering condolences, others silently paying their respects.

Ashley embraced Sarah in a comforting hug.

Sarah's voice trembled with emotion as she spoke. "He was so full of life and ambition. A true force of nature. And now..."

Emily reached out, squeezing Sarah's hand gently. "Yes, he had a very vibrant spirit."

Sarah managed an appreciative smile.

As the ceremony drew to a close, Sarah felt a familiar presence at her side. She turned to see Lucas, his eyes filled with a mixture of sadness and regret. He had given Ashley and Emily space to be near Sarah since she had gone days without seeing them.

His eyes spoke volumes of sorrow and condolences, bridging the silence between them. After spending the last several days together, words felt unnecessary in their shared understanding. Though they had grown apart in recent years, this moment of shared grief strengthened the bond between them.

Sarah, Lucas, Ashley, and Emily stood in silence as the last of the mourners paid their respects, each lost in their own thoughts and memories of Anthony. And as the sun dipped below the horizon, casting long shadows across the cemetery, Sarah knew that although her father may be gone, his legacy would live on in the hearts of those who loved him.

As they made their way across the cemetery grounds towards their parked cars, Sarah's gaze fell upon James and Stephen, the two junior partners at Anthony's law firm, engaged in what seemed to be a subdued yet intense discussion. Upon catching sight of Sarah's curious glance, their demeanor swiftly changed. With understanding smiles and nods, they conveyed their recognition of her profound loss. Shifting into a more composed exchange, they briefly resumed their conversation before casually turning and strolling away in opposite directions.

Then she noticed the young and successful businessman, Nick Pernod, approaching his sleek, electric Mercedes Benz. Considering the path he had walked, it seemed plausible that he had been conversing with James and Stephen. If not, then he had certainly walked by them. He didn't seem to notice her as he settled into his car and drove off. Sarah couldn't shake the realization that he hadn't approached her during the service to offer his condolences. It struck her as peculiar, especially considering the flirtatious encounter they had shared at the country club. Despite herself, she couldn't deny the faint stirrings of attraction she felt toward him.

As Ashley and Emily bid their farewells and headed towards their cars, Sarah and Lucas made their way to Lucas's car, only to find a figure lingering nearby. It was Detective Nelson.

Lucas's frustration was palpable as he let out a resigned sigh. "How thoughtless of him to be here," he muttered. "You don't have to talk to him right now."

Sarah offered a reassuring smile. "It's fine. I don't mind. Why don't you wait here?"

Lucas looked surprised by her response. "Are you sure?" he asked, hesitating.

Sarah nodded, determination in her gaze. "Absolutely. He might have some valuable information."

Lucas relented, slowing his pace as Sarah approached Detective Nelson. "Hello, Detective," she greeted him, her voice steady despite the nerves fluttering within her.

"Hi Sarah. You can call me Brock. I want to give you my condolences on the loss of your father," Detective Nelson said, his tone gentle.

She faintly remembered seeing his full name on the card he gave her. "Thank you, detec—Brock. I believe you already offered your condolences at my house on the day of."

Nelson shrugged, a tinge of embarrassment crossing his features. "It's not uncommon for police officers to attend the funerals of victims."

"Was that what my dad was? A victim?" Sarah inquired, concerned.

"Of an accident, yes. Not a crime."

Sarah breathed a sigh of relief. "The surveillance footage showed that?"

"Umm… not exactly, but we have no reason to believe there was foul play."

"I'm confused."

"The camera by the pool area wasn't working."

Sarah was stunned. "Really?"

"Yes, but don't be alarmed. I encounter this situation frequently. In fact, the mansion has seven cameras, and three of them weren't operational."

"The cameras were broken?" Sarah echoed, disbelief coloring her words.

"No. The 'video loss' on CCTV security cameras can stem from various factors—poor power supply, unstable network, camera software glitches, to name a few. My guess is Anthony hadn't had them serviced in a while. Unfortunately, it's a common issue," Detective Nelson explained, his tone matter-of-fact.

Sarah blinked, processing his words. "So...how can you conclude it was an accident then?"

"We lack any evidence to the contrary. The four functioning cameras captured nothing. There's no suspicious evidence in the home. Moreover, you were present that morning and noticed nothing unusual. Your statement even mentioned hearing him moving around the house before you... found him. So, the case is closed," Nelson replied, his tone steady.

"That's reassuring. But still...the pool camera not working?" Sarah pressed, a hint of skepticism in her voice.

Detective Nelson sighed with a tinge of frustration. "I can't tell you how often we encounter this situation. So much vital information is lost due to faulty cameras. We stress the importance of regular servicing, but..." He trailed off, shaking his head in dismay. "Sorry, I have nothing more to tell you."

"That's understandable. Thank you," Sarah replied, her tone accepting.

"Again, my condolences for your loss." With that, he turned and walked away.

Lucas returned to Sarah's side. "What did he want?" he inquired softly.

"He came to tell me that the case is closed. My dad's death was ruled an accident."

Lucas chose his words carefully. "As awful as it is, at least he wasn't the victim of a crime. That's somewhat of a relief, isn't it?"

Sarah responded dryly, "Yeah, definitely."

"Are you okay?"

"Yes. Let's just leave," Sarah said as exhaustion from a very long day was settling in.

They climbed into Lucas's car and drove toward the cemetery's exit. Sarah's eyes roamed over the rolling green hills and the solemn gravestones that dotted the landscape. She tried to convince herself that it was a positive outcome, that her father hadn't been the victim of foul play. After all, it was what she had insisted on from the start. Yet, an uneasy feeling lingered within her, whispering that there was more to the story than met the eye. Much more.

CHAPTER SEVEN

*S*arah found herself gravitating towards Lucas more and more in the following weeks.

A heavy, gloomy cloud hung over her, stubbornly refusing to dissipate. She attempted to conceal her mood from Lucas, though he saw right through her facade. He did his best to comfort her, while allowing her the space she needed. Detective Brock Nelson's words echoed relentlessly in her mind, especially the bombshell about the key surveillance camera going haywire. Sure, he mentioned two others on the fritz, but it was the one she depended on that stabbed at her consciousness like a persistent thorn. That footage held the key to unlocking all the mysteries of that tragic morning, but alas, it was lost to eternity.

Sarah found herself fixated on the image of her father diving into the pool, only to misjudge the distance and collide with the edge, rendering himself unconscious. No matter how she replayed the scenario in her mind, it refused to align with reality. He had plunged into that pool countless times—not just hundreds, but thousands of times. She grasped the common wisdom that familiarity could breed carelessness, as evidenced by the prevalence of car accidents near one's own home. However, her father's meticulous nature, shaped by his OCD tendencies, made it difficult for her to believe he could be careless, even in familiar surroundings. In her eyes, his attention to detail transcended every situation, leaving her with lingering doubts about the circumstances surrounding the pool incident.

While Lucas was away attending to his tennis clients, Sarah retreated to her apartment studio, hoping to find solace in painting. Yet, despite her best efforts, motivation eluded her like a fleeting shadow. Initially optimistic that she could paint her way out of this funk, she found herself repeatedly confronting the haunting specter of her father's demise. No amount of paint splattered on the canvas could banish the relentless echo of images of what she imagined happening that morning at the mansion.

One afternoon, Sarah found herself lost in her art, half a bottle of Opus One Napa Valley Red Wine fueling her creativity. Initially aiming to capture the tranquil beauty of the mansion from the street, her brush soon took on a life of its own, morphing the scene into a haunting tableau straight from her darkest imaginings. With each stroke, emergency vehicles—police cars, ambulances, fire trucks—emerged, casting an ominous shadow over the canvas. Startled by the disturbing turn her painting had taken, she set her brush aside and stepped back, only to be met with a jarring realization: the predominant color of her creation was a deep, unsettling red. Despite the unsettling nature of her subconscious expression, she couldn't deny the cathartic release it provided, even as she grappled with the unnerving, morbid scene before her.

Raising her half-empty glass of wine, she cast a contemplative gaze between the ruby hues swirling within and the strokes adorning her canvas.

"I guess I'm in a crimson mood," she remarked, a sardonic edge lacing her words, before draining the glass in a single gulp.

Sarah's phone buzzed, displaying a local number she didn't recognize. Typically, she'd let such calls slide to voicemail, but today was different. With a wry acknowledgment of her inebriation, she answered, "Hello?"

"Sarah?" The caller hesitated, his uncertainty palpable through the line.

"Yes."

"It's Stephen Millstadt. I'm with..." His words faltered.

"I know who you are, Stephen," Sarah acknowledged, grateful for his discretion in hesitating to mention her father's firm by name. It was too soon, too raw for her. She also noted his call must be from his personal mobile phone, sparing her the jolt of recognition that would come with dialing from the office line. It was a small consideration, but one she appreciated, nonetheless. "What's on your mind?"

"I know this is sudden, but could James and I meet with you today? There's something important we need to discuss."

"Today?" Sarah's reluctance was evident in her voice. "Is it urgent?"

"Well...not necessarily today, but soon," Stephen admitted cautiously.

"Would it be possible for us to meet elsewhere?" Sarah's request hung in the air, laden with unspoken apprehension. The prospect of revisiting her father's office, his domain, felt like tiptoeing on the edge of an emotional precipice. She wasn't sure she could handle it, not yet. Not now. The mansion, too, held memories too raw to confront. Losing her mother had been a slow, expected ache. Her father's sudden departure felt like a violent rupture, an ambush by Death itself.

Stephen's response was a lifeline in the darkness. "We'll come to you," he assured her gently. "Wherever you feel comfortable meeting."

She hesitated in her response for a long moment. So long that Stephen had thought he lost her. "Hello?"

"I'm still here," she said. "Would you and James want to come by my studio? I'm in the Central West End."

"Sure," he said cheerfully, clearly relieved that they were going to meet with her today. She admitted to herself that the urgent phone call certainly piqued her interest. "Can we come by in an hour?"

"That's fine," she said. "I'll see you guys then."

With Stephen and James due to arrive shortly, Sarah scrambled to ready herself. A brisk shower refreshed her, followed by her tried-and-true skincare routine. As she applied moisturizer and makeup, she aimed for a polished yet natural appearance, using the familiar ritual to ground herself as she sobered up.

A touch of foundation evened out her complexion, masking any traces of fatigue, while a subtle blush added a healthy glow to her cheeks. Her freshly washed hair fell in soft waves around her shoulders, framing her features effortlessly. Opting for simplicity, she adorned her ears with simple hoop earrings, then swiftly selected an outfit: a sleek black blouse paired with tailored trousers, a timeless combination exuding professionalism and sophistication.

Surveying herself in the mirror, Sarah's nerves flared as she contemplated the purpose of the impending meeting. With a calming breath, she made her way to the living room, her anticipation mounting with each passing moment.

As the appointed hour drew near, the buzz of the doorbell jolted her from her thoughts, signaling the arrival of Stephen and James. Gathering her composure, Sarah took one final moment to check her appearance in a full-length mirror, and steeled herself for the task ahead before buzzing them in.

Sarah walked the expanse of her living room, her steps echoing softly against the polished floors as she waited for Stephen and James to take the long elevator ride to the top floor of the building. Through the floor-to-ceiling windows that framed her urban sanctuary, she glimpsed the world beyond, a sprawling tapestry of concrete and steel stretching to the horizon. Her gaze fell on a solitary hawk, its wings slicing through the air with effortless grace. Sarah found herself mesmerized by the bird's aerial ballet, a silent observer to its hunt. The hawk suddenly plummeted out of sight in pursuit of whatever prey captured its attention.

A sharp rap at the door jolted Sarah from her trance. She crossed the room, her hand hovering over the doorknob. With a deep breath, she opened the door to Stephen and James, offering a smile that they returned.

"Come on in, guys," Sarah beckoned, gesturing with a sweep of her hand. They entered, casting curious glances around the open, roomy penthouse apartment. It was evident they hadn't visited before, their expressions a mix of surprise and admiration. Sarah couldn't help but feel a twinge of self-consciousness; she knew they toiled long hours for her father, and likely lived in much more modest abodes.

Stephen turned and handed her a fat manila envelope.

"What's this?" Sarah inquired; her curiosity piqued.

"Your father had Lyle prepare this," Stephen explained gently. "I told him you weren't up for coming to the office at this time, so he asked me to give you this copy."

Sarah nodded solemnly, her heart heavy with the weight of understanding. She knew exactly what this was. Lyle Parmentier, one of her father's senior partners, had been tasked with drafting her father's last will and testament.

"I can go over with you if you'd like," Stephen said.

"No, that's all right," Sarah said dismissively, tossing the envelope onto a stand near the door. "I already know what's in it." It was a statement of fact rather than a boast. With no siblings to share the inheritance, Sarah was well aware that everything belonged to her by default.

James broke his silence with a sudden question. "Did you know he gave you control of the firm?" His tone revealed that he himself was surprised by this information.

Sarah's jaw dropped, a mixture of shock and bewilderment crossing her features. "Ummm...no...I didn't know that," she stammered, her mind reeling at the revelation. The weight of owning her father's vast estate was one thing, but the responsibility of controlling a prestigious law firm was an entirely different matter altogether.

Stephen interjected, his voice calm and reassuring. "You can discuss all the details with Lyle and figure out how to move forward."

"Okay," Sarah murmured, her voice faint as she absorbed the weight of this sudden development, feeling as though she'd been struck by a blunt object.

The three of them stood in a heavy silence, until Sarah finally broke it. "Is that all, guys?"

Stephen and James exchanged a meaningful glance before Stephen gathered his thoughts and broached the subject. "Actually, no. We have a favor to ask," he began, his tone hesitant.

Sarah's mind raced with curiosity. What could two lawyers possibly need from an artist with no ties to the legal world? With a quizzical expression, she turned her attention from one to the other. "Okay. What do you guys need?"

Stephen took a moment to collect himself before he continued. "Anthony was going to give me a flash drive labeled 'confidential'. It's crucial for an upcoming, highly sensitive corporate lawsuit," he explained carefully, treading lightly over the delicate details. "He intended to pass it to me the day after the stakeholders' party."

Sarah winced as memories of her father at the party flooded her mind, a pang of sorrow tightening her chest. He had been so vibrant, so full of life, and now he was gone, leaving behind a void that seemed impossible to fill.

"But, of course, circumstances prevented him from doing so," Stephen continued solemnly, his eyes meeting Sarah's with an empathetic gaze.

"Wouldn't it be at the office?"

"No, I checked. I believe it's likely in his... home office," Stephen replied, his expression betraying a hint of discomfort.

So, there it was. Stephen and James were requesting Sarah to return to the mansion to retrieve the elusive flash drive. Denying it seemed pointless. The prospect of revisiting the empty mansion loomed before her, an unavoidable task she would have to confront eventually. It was time to steel herself against the painful memories and simply get it over with.

With a resigned sigh, she accepted the inevitable request. "Sure," she acquiesced, her voice steady and surprisingly calm. "I'll go search for it in the next couple of days."

Stephen's gratitude was palpable, his relief evident as he effusively thanked her. Oddly, James remained silent, his discomfort almost tangible.

As soon as they left, Sarah felt a wave of exhaustion wash over her, causing her to sink heavily into the couch. She drifted into a light doze, only to snap awake sometime later. The mid-afternoon sunlight filtered through the windows, casting a warm glow that energized her. Though she felt refreshed, the motivation to start on a new canvas eluded her. Her gaze wandered, landing on what was left of the bottle of Opus One Napa Valley Red Wine sitting on the nearby table. A smile crept across her face.

"Been drinking today?" Lucas quipped, a hint of amusement in his tone, as Sarah arrived at his house later that afternoon, the memory of her macabre painting fresh in her mind.

"Yep," she replied flatly, not missing a beat.

"And you drove here?" he inquired further.

"Absolutely not," she retorted, irritation flashing in her eyes at the implication. She had enough sense to recognize the danger of driving under the influence, opting instead to leave her Beemer parked safely in the apartment building's garage and summoning an Uber. Initially, she had considered sleeping off the effects of the alcohol in the solitude of her apartment, but as the sun dipped lower in the sky, the vast emptiness of her surroundings felt suffocating. Plus, there was that eerie crimson painting she had created. Determined to shake off the unease, she had removed it from the easel and leaned it against the wall, facing away. Nonetheless, the sense of isolation weighed heavily on her, prompting her to head over to Lucas's house.

"Let's go to dinner tonight," Sarah suggested, her eyes sparkling with anticipation.

"Sure. Anywhere in particular?" Lucas asked.

"I'm in the mood for Italian."

Lucas's face lit up. "How about that new place in Clayton? Trattoria Italiano, I think it's called. It's got rave reviews."

"Sounds perfect," Sarah agreed.

"Let's see if Emily and Ashley want to join us," he added casually.

Sarah hesitated. "Okay."

"Is there a problem?"

"No, I just thought you wanted it to be just us tonight."

"We've been spending a lot of time together these past few weeks. I figured you'd want to catch up with your friends. But if you'd rather—"

"No, no, that's fine. Give them a call," Sarah interrupted, forcing a smile.

"Great. I'll make reservations for the four of us at 6:30. I'm sure Ashley and Emily would love to see you."

Sarah beamed. "Great." But inside, she was conflicted. There was something in the way Lucas mentioned Emily's name that gnawed at her, a pang of jealousy tugging at her heart. She tried to dismiss it as her imagination running wild, but the feeling lingered.

CHAPTER EIGHT

*T*rattoria Italiano sat in the heart of downtown Clayton, surrounded by grand buildings and lively streets. After the business day wrapped up, the restaurants became the main attraction in the quaint downtown area.

Adjacent to the dining area of Trattoria was its open kitchen, a hive of activity with skilled chefs crafting Italian-inspired dishes. Using fresh, locally sourced ingredients, they turned each plate into a work of art, reflecting their passion and creativity. The menu boasted handmade pastas, wood-fired pizzas, and flavorful braised meats, ensuring a taste of Italy in every bite. Nearby, the gelato station allowed customers to sample flavors before choosing their frozen dessert, rounding out the authentic Italian dining experience.

Sarah sat with Lucas, Emily, and Ashley at a rectangular table in the center of the restaurant. It was roomy, but the tables were closer together than she preferred. Despite having been there countless times before, she couldn't shake the feeling of discomfort. Perhaps she was just more sensitive than usual, especially since her life had taken a turn for the worse recently. And the painting she had done earlier, almost unconsciously, filled with crimson hues and emergency vehicles parked in front of the mansion, certainly didn't help improve her mood.

"More wine, anyone?" Ashley asked, pouring herself a glass from the Chianti Classico Lucas had ordered. They were onto their second bottle already. The first had disappeared quickly among the four of them. Lucas had debated whether to order wine, considering Sarah spent the afternoon polishing off a bottle of wine on her own, but he didn't want to raise any eyebrows with Ashley and Emily. He eased his concerns after Sarah's short nap and two cups of coffee, but he still hoped she'd hold off, feeling a pang of disappointment when she didn't.

"Sure thing," Sarah said, extending her glass to Ashley.

"Me too," Emily chimed in.

The trio giggled as Ashley poured wine into their glasses, spilling a bit on the table. Lucas remained quiet, his smile fixed in place like plastic.

Two wait staff members glided over to their table with practiced ease. One efficiently cleared away the remnants of their mostly devoured salads, while the other expertly placed plates of steaming food before each of them. Ashley opted for the Capellini Pomodoro and Emily chose the Penne Arrabbiata. Lucas, not in the mood for pasta, opted for the delicate flavors of Striped Bass. However, it was Sarah's choice that caught his attention—Pappardelle Bolognese, a dish rich with a hearty meat sauce made from a blend of ground beef, pork, and veal. Lucas couldn't help but flinch slightly at her selection, as it seemed out of character for her. Sarah often leaned towards vegetarian cuisine, though she never officially declared herself a vegetarian. Lucas knew she had a knack for keeping her options open in most aspects of life, but it wasn't until now that he realized it extended to her food choices as well. Nonetheless, he knew the hearty meal would probably help absorb the lingering alcohol in her system, and he felt relieved about that.

"Great to see you," Ashley said to Sarah warmly.

"Likewise. Good to see you both. Sorry for the absence," Sarah replied, acknowledging her friends' understanding.

"No apologies needed, Sarah. We know you've been going through a tough time," Emily chimed in, her empathy palpable. Sarah nodded, touched by their compassion.

Their conversation was interrupted by a young waitress topping up their water glasses. Catching sight of Sarah, she paused, then spoke tentatively, "Ms. Kellerman?"

"Yes?" Sarah responded, curious.

"I attended your last art exhibit. Your work is amazing. I'm a big fan, and I'm studying art at Wash U," the waitress revealed with excitement.

"Thank you so much. Washington University? Nice. Do you know Professor David Lobban?" Sarah inquired.

The waitress's face lit up. "Yes, I'm in one of his classes now. He's fantastic, so patient."

"He's a friend of mine. I received my degree from Williams College, but I attended a few of his workshops when I returned to St. Louis. Then, ended up taking a few of his courses. Great guy. You'll learn a lot from him."

"Are you teaching anywhere?" the waitress asked.

"Not at the moment," Sarah chuckled. "Maybe someday."

"When's your next exhibit?" the waitress inquired eagerly.

"September 12th at Clayton Art Gallery."

"I'll be there for sure. I'm sorry to interrupt your conversation."

"No worries," Sarah reassured her, and the waitress hurried off to attend to another table.

"Whoa," Lucas exclaimed, his eyes wide. "Feels like we're rubbing elbows with a star."

Sarah blushed, while Ashley and Emily exchanged knowing grins.

"Aw, come on, Sarah, you're totally a big deal," Ashley insisted.

"Yeah, you're a rock star with a paintbrush," Emily chimed in, her enthusiasm almost too loud for the cozy restaurant. But that was Emily—bold and bubbly, unapologetically herself. Some might call her a drama queen, but Sarah didn't mind; they'd been friends for ages.

Sarah grinned, feeling a bit overwhelmed by the praise, so she tried to shift the focus. "Hey, Ashley, your eye for interior design is pretty artistic too, you know."

Ashley grinned back, playing along. "Thanks, but it's not quite the same as painting masterpieces."

"What about me?" Emily piped up, mock hurt in her voice. "Navigating the real estate market takes its own kind of artistry."

Sarah didn't feel that way about money, but she smiled at Emily and nodded in agreement, nonetheless. Emily had always seemed a tad envious of her and Ashley's close bond since high school. Despite her occasional overbearing behavior, they made sure to include her.

Lucas chuckled and took a sip of his wine. "Some say making money is the highest form of art."

Emily raised her glass towards Lucas eagerly. "Exactly!" He took the hint and clinked his glass against hers, and Sarah and Ashley applauded, joining in on the comradery.

After the laughter faded, an uneasy silence settled among them. It was evident that Sarah was preoccupied with something.

Lucas was the first to acknowledge it. "You doing alright?" he asked gently. Considering what Sarah had been through lately, it was a reasonable concern. Anyone would feel unsettled after such experiences.

"Yeah, I'm fine," Sarah replied, but her tone betrayed her true feelings.

"What's going on?" Ashley inquired.

Taking a moment to gather her thoughts, Sarah explained, "Two lawyers from my dad's firm need a flash drive he promised them. But he was not able to get it to them for...well...obvious reasons. They think it's at the mansion."

Ashley's shock was evident. "And they're expecting you to retrieve it, like, right now?"

"Yeah, pretty much," Sarah confirmed.

"That's so rude!" Emily burst out, a bit too loudly, earning them a few curious glances from nearby tables.

"They were polite about it," Sarah defended.

"It doesn't matter! Can't they wait a few more weeks until you're ready?" Emily insisted.

Sarah shrugged, uncertain.

Ashley reached out, gently touching Sarah's arm. "Could they search for it themselves?"

Sarah seemed to consider it, then shook her head slowly. "I suppose, but...no, I don't want them poking around the mansion."

"But you let that detective stay and lock up before, didn't you?" Lucas chimed in.

"That was different. I was... out of sorts... and they had a legitimate reason, a real job to do," Sarah explained, shaking her head. "I'm sorry for bringing it up. It's not a big deal. I'll just go and get it. Won't take long."

Lucas leaned in, earnest. "I can do it."

"You wouldn't know where to start."

"Then I'll go with you," he retorted.

Sarah sighed, feeling the frustration building. "No, really. I've got this. I'll go tomorrow and get it over with," she declared, meeting everyone's gaze. "I have to face it eventually. Might as well be now."

They saw that she meant it and decided not to press the matter any further. Emily took a long sip of her drink and leaned back, staring into her wine. "Yes, but you should do it on your own terms, not because you're pressured into it," she murmured, finishing her drink in one go.

Bathed in the gentle moonlight streaming through the curtains, Lucas and Sarah lay side by side in the quiet of his bedroom. The dim light highlighted the contours of their faces, casting shadows that danced across the walls.

Sarah had enjoyed the evening at the restaurant, relishing the chance to escape the confines of both Lucas's house and her own apartment. Yet, beneath the veneer of enjoyment lurked a disquieting realization: she was slipping into a reclusive routine. The thought unsettled her. While she cherished the solitude of her artistic endeavors, she had always thrived on the vibrancy of her social life. The creeping shift in her personality since her father's passing gnawed at her, stirring a fear that she was losing touch with her true self. Was this withdrawal merely a symptom of grief, or was she finally awakening to a new understanding of her identity?

Lucas cleared his throat, breaking the weighty silence between them, "Sarah, there's something I've been meaning to talk to you about."

Sarah turned to look at him, her eyes reflecting the uncertainty that had settled in her mind. "What is it, Lucas?"

He hesitated, searching for the right words. "I've been thinking... about your art."

Her brow furrowed in confusion. "My art? What about it?"

Lucas took a deep breath, steeling himself for her reaction. "I think it might be adding unnecessary pressure to your life."

Sarah's heart skipped a beat, a wave of disbelief washing over her. "What do you mean?"

"I mean, artists tend to be more...moody...and...prone to depression," Lucas explained carefully, his words measured and cautious.

Sarah felt a knot form in her stomach, the weight of his words sinking in. "You think I'm depressed because I'm an artist?"

Lucas shook his head quickly, reaching out to gently take her hand in his. "No, no, that's not what I meant at all. I just...I worry about you, Sarah. I worry that the stress of trying to make it in the art world is taking its toll on you."

"*Trying* to make it? I *am* making it. I'm coming into my own as an artist."

"I know, I know," he said gently, attempting to ease the tension he had ignited. "But the art world, it's notoriously tough to navigate, even for those who've tasted success, like you have. You've suffered the loss of both parents within two years, and now you're shouldering the weight of your dad's estate and business. I'm just worried it might be overwhelming."

Her heart ached at his concern, but she couldn't shake the feeling of hurt that lingered in her chest. "So, what are you saying? That I should just give up on my dreams?"

"No, of course not. But maybe...maybe you could consider focusing more on managing your father's estate."

Sarah's eyes widened in shock, her mind struggling to process his suggestion. "Managing my father's estate? But...I'm an artist, Lucas. That's who I am."

He nodded, his expression earnest. "I know, and I love you for it. But think about it, Sarah. You could brush up on business and law classes, take over his law firm. It could be a way for you to honor his memory, to make something of yourself."

Tears welled up in Sarah's eyes, a mixture of hurt and frustration swirling inside her. "I can't believe you're saying this, Lucas. You're asking me to give up everything I've ever wanted."

"I'm not asking you to give up anything, Sarah," Lucas insisted, his voice soft but determined. "I just want what's best for you. And right now, I think that means focusing on something more stable, more… secure."

What he truly meant was ' more practical,' a truth that lingered unspoken between them, evident in his hesitant demeanor, a fact not lost on Sarah. Though his words stirred frustration within her, they didn't provoke anger. She understood his intentions, his desire for her well-being, yet they only served to deepen the chasm already stretching between them.

"I'll consider it," she murmured.

Sarah turned away from him, her heart heavy with uncertainty. She didn't know what to say, how to make him understand the depth of her passion, the burning desire that drove her to create. All she knew was that she couldn't let go of her dreams, not now, not ever.

CHAPTER NINE

*W*ith the heaviness of Lucas's words hanging over her heart, Sarah tried to find solace in her art studio. The canvas before her beckoned, yet no amount of fervent strokes could lift the dark shroud that enveloped her mood. Each brushstroke seemed to mirror the turmoil within her soul, capturing the essence of her somber state. It was the essence of true artistry: the ability to convey one's innermost feelings and thoughts through the strokes of a brush or the sweep of a pen. Yet, Sarah found herself uneasy with the direction her creativity was leading her, prompting her to lay down her brush and step back.

She stared at the blank canvas, waiting for inspiration to strike. Just as frustration began to creep in, her phone vibrated. It was a video call from Nick Pernod, the young, magnetic businessman she had met at her father's social gathering at the country club. There had been a palpable spark between them.

She answered the call, and Nick's handsome face filled her screen. It looked like he was standing in a well-organized warehouse.

"Hi, Sarah. It's Nick Pernod. We met at Westfield Country Club."

"I remember you," she replied, a smile tugging at her lips.

"I hope you don't mind me calling out of the blue," he said, his tone slightly hesitant.

"No, that's alright," she assured him. "Though I am curious how you got my number."

"I got it from Stephen Millstadt," he admitted, looking a bit sheepish, clearly trying not to come off as creepy.

"That's fine. What can I do for you?"

"I wanted to give you my condolences. I'm sorry I didn't approach you at your father's service. You had a lot of people around you."

"Oh, thank you. I appreciate it."

He gave her a solemn look. "I knew your dad well. He will be missed."

"Yes, he will be," she agreed, the weight of her loss pressing down on her once more. An awkward silence hung between them, then Sarah's eyes shifted to the warehouse behind him. "Is that one of your businesses?" she asked, more to fill the silence than out of genuine interest.

He beamed. "It is now." He turned the phone to show the enormous space filled with boxes and forklifts. He reappeared in the frame. "It's a shipping company in North St. Louis County that I acquired this morning."

"Nice. What part of North County?" she asked, feigning interest.

"Riverview," he said, his enthusiasm evident. "I've been working on this deal for some time. The owner didn't want to sell. It took some convincing."

"Really?" Sarah murmured, barely masking her disinterest.

"Yeah. I buddied up to him. It took time and persuasion. You know, business deals can often happen subversively, like hostile takeovers. But sometimes, you just need to hide in plain sight. Then no one is suspicious of you," he said with a big smile, clearly trying to impress her. But she found such talk a real turnoff.

"Well, congratulations," she said politely. "I'm sorry, but I need to go now, Mr. Pernod."

"Call me Nick."

"Okay, Nick. Thank you for your condolences. I really appreciate it."

His demeanor softened, and he looked genuinely sincere. "Please let me know if you need anything. Anything at all."

"I will," she said, ending the call with a polite smile.

As the screen went dark, she sighed, feeling the weight of the conversation. Nick's attempt at charm had fallen flat, and the business talk had only served to highlight their differences. She turned back to her canvas, hoping to find solace in her art. But no inspiration came.

Feeling stifled in her apartment, Sarah donned a hat, scarf, and sunglasses, and slipped out into the lively streets below. The Central West End beckoned with its array of enticing eateries, bars, and cafes, but she wanted solitude right now. Amidst the bustling crowds, Sarah embarked on a quiet stroll, allowing her mind to meander as she focused solely on the rhythmic cadence of her footsteps, finding solace in the simplicity of the act. With each block traversed, she felt the weight of her worries begin to lift, replaced by a sense of calm.

After meandering through the bustling streets for what felt like an eternity, Sarah found herself standing before a quaint drinking establishment she had never noticed before: Ben's Place. Intrigued by the allure of the unknown, she hesitated for a moment before mustering the courage to step inside.

The bar was small but fancy, oozing charm. A shiny mahogany counter sat on one side, lit up softly by vintage-style lights. Plush leather stools lined the bar neatly, and behind it, crystal decanters held a variety of drinks, sparkling in the light. Everything seemed carefully chosen to make one feel like it was a classy place. Tables with four chairs each were spaced out just right, making the room cozy yet private.

Sarah glanced around and noticed she was the only customer. The bartender, a man, was busy polishing glasses with his back to her. She couldn't see his whole body, but he seemed fit and well-groomed. Hearing her come in, he turned around. He looked about her age, and Sarah was struck by his rugged good looks. His smile was friendly, making her feel welcome. It prompted her to take a seat at the bar.

"What can I get you?" he asked.

Sarah countered with a question of her own, "What red wines do you offer?"

"Cabernet Franc and Merlot."

"Nice," Sarah said, genuinely impressed. She hadn't expected such quality wines at this small bar. He noticed her surprise, having seen this reaction before from other customers, and flashed her a flirtatious grin. Though she found him attractive, she wasn't in the mood for flirting. Her mind was preoccupied with the recent turmoil that filled her life. "I'll have a glass of Merlot, please."

"Coming right up," he said with a smile, his eyes lingering on her as he poured the crimson liquid into a glass.

Sarah scanned the place once more. "How long have you been open? I live nearby but never noticed this place before."

"About three months," he replied as he placed the glass of wine in front of her.

"Thanks," Sarah replied, offering a tight-lipped smile in return. She took a sip of her wine, then gazed into the glass, captivated by the shimmering red liquid reflecting her own image back at her. Her eyes welled with tears as memories flooded her mind—the morning she discovered her father's lifeless body in the pool. Overwhelmed by the sight, she heard her own screams echoing in her mind. She squeezed her eyes shut, hoping to drown out the memories with the sting of her tears.

Amidst the chaos in her mind, another voice, masculine this time, broke through with evident concern. "Hey, are you okay?"

She blinked away the memories and redirected her attention to the person who had just spoken to her. It was the bartender. He kept a respectful distance, careful not to intrude on her personal space, but his gaze remained fixed on her, filled with alarm.

Sarah felt the tears streaming down her cheeks. She didn't bother to hide them; it was clear she was crying. "Just one of those days, you know?" she said, managing a brief smile.

He nodded understandingly, though a flicker of worry remained on his features. "Well, if you ever need someone to talk to, I'm all ears."

She nodded appreciatively.

"I'm Ben, by the way," he introduced himself. He didn't extend his hand, but rather nodded slightly.

A smile tugged at the corner of her lips. "Ben of Ben's Place?"

"Yep, that's me," he confirmed, sweeping a glance around the bar. "This place better work out for me, or I guess I'm living on the street," he added with a wry chuckle.

As Sarah followed Ben's gaze around his establishment, her attention was suddenly captured by a painting hanging on one of the bar's walls. It portrayed a vivid scene: an equestrian competition in St. Charles, Missouri, rendered with striking realism. To her surprise, she recognized it as a print of her own work. Memories flooded back as she recalled the origins of the painting. She had attended the competition with her parents when she was 12 years old. Years later, inspired by old photographs, she had meticulously recreated one of them on canvas.

Her reaction didn't go unnoticed by Ben. "That's a print of a Sarah Kellerman painting," he said with pride evident in his voice. As he admired the painting, Sarah discreetly slipped her sunglasses back on.

"You're a fan of Sarah Kellerman?" she asked, unable to mask her curiosity.

Ben nodded enthusiastically. "Absolutely! Her work is incredible. I'd love to meet her someday."

Flattered yet wary, Sarah concealed her emotions behind her façade. She subtly lowered the brim of her hat, unwilling to reveal the depth of her appreciation. Ben didn't realize it, but he'd inadvertently cheered her up.

Sarah produced a single bill from her purse and laid it on the bar counter. "Thanks for the drink and the conversation."

He reverted to his usual cheerful demeanor. "Sure. Drop by anytime. I'm here most days. Actually, every day."

Sarah chuckled at his wry wit as she turned and made her way out. Before disappearing from view, she stole a brief glance back through the window at him.

Ben retrieved the lone bill from the counter. It turned out to be a hundred-dollar note for a ten-dollar drink. Hurriedly, he dashed out of the bar to offer her change, but she had already vanished into the bustling streets. Returning to his establishment, it struck him that she never mentioned her name. When he first opened the bar, he had sworn not to get entangled with employees or customers, yet he couldn't deny his attraction to her. As he continued preparing for the arrival of his evening shift and anticipating the usual influx of customers starting around 6 p.m., his mind kept returning back to the enigmatic woman, hoping she would grace him with another visit.

After three days, Sarah mustered the courage to return to the mansion to retrieve the flash drive labeled 'confidential' that Stephen requested. Everything about it felt empty and cold – parking in the deserted driveway, unlocking the front door, shutting off the alarm. Nothing seemed natural anymore. The eerie silence enveloping the vast halls gave her an unsettling sensation, as if the very essence of life had been drained from the once-grand estate. Determined to sever ties with the painful memories haunting its walls, she resolved to sell the mansion eventually, longing to escape the weight of sorrow that hung over her.

Despite her best efforts to shake off the feeling of being watched, a lingering sense of unease persisted as she ascended the staircase leading to her father's office on the second floor. Pausing momentarily, she found herself drawn to the painting that hung on the wall—the poignant depiction she created of her father seated at his desk. The simplicity of the scene, with only a laptop and the obscured frame of a photograph, evoked a bittersweet smile as she reflected on the now bittersweet memories it held.

Pushing aside her emotions, Sarah proceeded to her father's home office. Taking a moment to compare the real-life view with the painting that depicted it, she noted the absence of her father's presence in the image and tried to push the pain from her mind. She hastened to his desk and rummaged through the drawers in search of the flash drive, but it was nowhere to be found.

She found it odd that the flash drive wasn't there. Either Stephen was mistaken about it being at the home, or her father kept it in his wall safe, which didn't make any sense to her. If the flash drive contained files related to his law work, there was no reason for it to be in the safe. That was where her father stored the most sensitive and irreplaceable family documents and small heirlooms.

However, with nowhere else to look—barring the thought of combing through the entire mansion, which she refused to entertain—Sarah entered the office's closet, where the safe was secured in a wall and hidden behind a rack of expensive suits.

After her mother passed away, her father had given her the combination to the safe, stating it was a precaution in case something happened to him. Despite her reluctance, she accepted it, feeling uneasy at the thought that merely possessing it might invite trouble. Reluctantly, she entered the combination into her phone's notes, opting not to label what it was for fear of potential security breaches, such as her phone being hacked, or just carelessly losing it.

Retrieving the note, she swiftly opened the safe. Inside, she found it packed with yellowed documents dating back decades, most of which predated her birth. Ignoring their contents for now, she rummaged through until she finally found it—the flash drive, precisely as Stephen had described.

Clutching the flash drive tightly, Sarah hurried out of the room, consumed by the single desire to escape the suffocating atmosphere of the mansion.

As she descended the stairs, she cast a quick glance at the painting adorning the staircase and froze in place. An unsettling feeling crept over her. Despite the overwhelming urge to flee, she turned on her heels and ascended the stairs back to the second floor.

Standing motionless at the threshold of her father's office, Sarah surveyed the room from the exact viewpoint depicted in the painting.

The realization hit Sarah with such force that she felt lightheaded. The laptop was in the wrong position—it had been moved. Detective Nelson had assured her that the police would conduct a walkthrough, merely skimming for any obvious signs of disturbance without touching anything.

Sarah mulled over the possibility that her father might have absentmindedly left the laptop out of place before his swim that morning. But she knew better. His meticulous nature bordered on obsessive-compulsive; he wouldn't have even entertained the idea of taking a swim if the laptop wasn't precisely where it belonged—the exact position depicted in the painting.

However, that morning, Sarah had heard him in his office as she woke up. Then, as she made herself a cup of coffee, she heard him walking around before he entered the pool. It struck her as odd when she heard him leave the house through a side door; normally, he would have used one of the back doors leading to the pool.

Sarah gasped as the sudden truth washed over her with the ferocity of a waterfall. The person she heard that morning wasn't her father. Anthony Kellerman wasn't in his office when Sarah woke up that morning, nor was he walking around the house or exiting through a side door while she brewed her coffee. Anthony Kellerman was floating lifeless in the backyard pool during that time.

The individual Sarah heard that morning was the one who had murdered her father and then searched his laptop for something, neglecting to return it to its rightful place.

Sarah struggled to keep from passing out as she fled the mansion.

CHAPTER TEN

*S*arah's footsteps echoed through the empty hallway of her apartment building as she made her way to the elevator. The dim lights barely pierced the pervasive shadows, casting an unsettling atmosphere. With each stride, fear pulsed through her, overpowering rationality with the relentless rhythm of her pounding heart. Impatiently, she jabbed the elevator button and waited, every second feeling like an eternity until the doors finally opened. Stepping inside, she quickly pressed the button for the tenth floor, eager to reach her destination.

As the elevator ascended, a growing unease enveloped her, like fog creeping over a landscape. The hum of the machinery weighed heavily on her senses as unanswered questions raced through her mind. She shuddered at the thought that her father might have been murdered, wondering who could have done it—and why. Breathing heavily, she pressed against the back wall, fighting against rising panic. Every creak and groan of the elevator magnified her dread.

The elevator abruptly stopped with a loud ding, startling her. As the doors slid open, she held her breath, half expecting someone to be waiting on the other side. To her relief, the corridor beyond was empty.

As Sarah fumbled for her keys and unlocked the door to her apartment, a persistent feeling of being watched lingered, like unseen eyes haunting her from the shadows. Every creak of the floorboards sent shivers down her spine. She stepped inside, closing the door behind her with trembling hands.

Alone in the dimly lit apartment, Sarah's thoughts turned to her father. The events of the past few days replayed in her mind like a haunting melody. The suddenness of his death, the unanswered questions surrounding it – it all seemed like a cruel nightmare from which she couldn't wake.

With a heavy sigh, Sarah sank onto the couch, her mind racing with thoughts of conspiracy and betrayal as she pondered who could want her father dead. Could it have been one of his law partners? A client? Who could benefit from his death? The questions swirled around her like a whirlwind, each one more terrifying than the last.

Unable to bear the suffocating weight of her own thoughts any longer, Sarah dug her phone from her purse and accessed Ashley's number. Sarah sighed in relief when Ashley answered, her voice was like a lifeline in the darkness.

"Hey, Sarah! What's up?" Ashley's voice was filled with warmth and concern, instantly putting Sarah at ease.

"Hey, Ash. Is your offer to stay at your place still on the table?" Sarah inquired, masking the tremor of fear in her voice to avoid worrying Ashley. Beneath her words lay a hint of guilt for choosing to stay with Lucas despite Ashley's earlier offer.

Ashley, sensing Sarah's unease from the subtle trembling in her voice, responded, "Of course. Everything okay?"

"Yes, everything's fine," Sarah replied, her attempt at reassurance falling flat. Then, she pressed the palm of her free hand against her forehead, struggling to contain a sob. "Actually, no, I'm not okay. I'm at my apartment, but...I can't stay here," she stammered, her voice faltering to a near-whisper. "I just can't be alone right now."

"I'll come and pick you up," Ashley said, her voice now grave.

"Thank you, but I can drive myself."

"Are you sure? It is no problem at all."

"Yes. In fact, the drive will actually calm my nerves," Sarah murmured, her tone softening as if she could already feel herself relaxing.

"Okay. I'll see you shortly."

Within an hour, Sarah reached Ashley's apartment, relieved to escape her own place. She packed only essentials, determined to collect the rest of her belongings from Lucas's house over the next few days. The emptiness of her apartment seemed ominous, echoes of that fateful morning at the mansion haunting her. Every creak seemed to mimic the sounds she heard before discovering her father in the pool. Leaving her apartment brought a wave of relief.

In Ashley's apartment, the air felt lighter, the atmosphere more welcoming. Ashley initiated some small talk, which Sarah politely engaged in, though Ashley could sense her disinterest. Understanding her friend's need for space, she helped Sarah carry her luggage into the spare bedroom, then gave her privacy, reassuring her that she was available if needed. As Sarah settled into the room, her thoughts returned to the flash drive she had taken from her father's safe.

With trembling hands, she retrieved the drive from her bag and inserted it into her laptop. The screen flickered to life, casting an eerie glow across the room as Sarah's eyes scanned the contents of the drive.

Two files stared back at her from the screen, their names mocking her with their cryptic simplicity: MASTER NAME LIST and NAME FILES ARCHIVE. With a hesitant click, Sarah opened the first file, her heart pounding in anticipation.

The document that appeared before her was a list of names, each one accompanied by a string of numbers and letters that seemed to hold no significance. She guessed they might be file numbers, but for now they were utterly meaningless to her.

The second file remained encrypted and impenetrable. Anthony had provided Sarah with several passwords he used, just like the combination to his closet safe. Sarah attempted each one, but none granted her access.

Sarah let out a defeated sigh and closed her laptop, the weight of guilt settling heavily within her. It twisted her stomach into knots as she grappled with the ethical dilemma of her actions. Was she betraying her father's trust by delving into his secrets? He never mentioned the flash drive to her, yet Stephen was aware of it. Sure, Stephen was a junior partner, but Anthony had confided in his daughter about many cases over the last two years. So why keep her in the dark about this? Or was she simply overthinking things?

Laughter echoing from the living room interrupted Sarah's thoughts, drawing her attention. Ashley's cheerful voice mingled with Emily's, a welcome distraction. Sarah listened for a moment, thankful not to hear Lucas's presence. Guilt pricked at her conscience for feeling relieved, but she knew she needed a break from him. And this time, she meant it. With a resolute nod, she brushed aside her doubts and left the spare bedroom to join her friends, seeking comfort in their company.

Emily and Ashley greeted Sarah with smiles and open arms as she walked into the living room. Sarah did her best to put on a joyous smile. The heavy weight of grief had been pressing down on her shoulders ever since her father's passing, but it was a burden she tried to bear as silently as possible in an effort to not darken the vibrant spirits of her two closest friends, Emily and Ashley.

"Hey, Sarah!" Emily exclaimed, pulling her into a tight hug. "So good to see you again."

"Yeah, it's been a minute," Ashley added, flashing her a bright smile. "Glad you called me today."

Sarah returned their embraces, feeling a flicker of lightness in her heart. These two were her rock, and together, the three of them have been pillars of support since their youth.

"Thanks for having me," she replied, managing a small smile. "I needed this."

Emily and Ashley exchanged knowing glances, silently acknowledging the weight Sarah carried. But they knew just how to lift her spirits.

"Well, then let's make tonight unforgettable," Emily declared, her eyes sparkling with excitement. "What do you say we hit up Andromeda? It's been ages since we've danced the night away."

"Yeah, just like old times," Ashley added.

Sarah's lips twitched upwards at the suggestion. Andromeda was a club they'd been attending since they'd all turned twenty-one, but their presence there had diminished over the years. It held memories of laughter, wild dance moves, and unforgettable moments with her friends. Maybe tonight, she could forget about her troubles, if only for a little while.

"I'm in," she said, nodding eagerly. "Let's do it."

Ashley clapped her hands together, her enthusiasm contagious. "That settles it then. Andromeda it is!"

They gathered in Ashley's bedroom, excitement buzzing in the air. Emily and Ashley vowed that tonight was going to be their much-needed girls' night out, and they were determined to make it a night to remember. Especially for Sarah.

"Okay, ladies, time to get ready," Ashley declared, pulling open her closet doors to reveal a treasure trove of clothing.

Emily and Ashley exchanged knowing smiles, already diving into the racks of clothes with eager anticipation. Choosing the perfect outfit was serious business, after all. Sarah watched them, a faint smile tugging at her lips as she tried to match their enthusiasm. Deep down, she knew there would come a moment when she'd confide in them about her suspicions regarding what truly happened to her father, but for now, she pushed those thoughts aside, unwilling to let them overshadow the joy of the present moment.

"I'm thinking something fun and flirty," Ashley mused, her fingers skimming over a row of colorful dresses. "What do you think?"

Emily nodded in agreement, her eyes scanning the options before landing on a vibrant red dress that practically screamed confidence and sass.

"This could work," she said, holding it up for Ashley's inspection.

Ashley's eyes lit up at the sight. "Yes! That color is perfect on you."

Meanwhile, Sarah became lost in a sea of skirts and blouses, her brow furrowed in concentration as she searched for just the right ensemble.

"I want something that says 'effortlessly chic'," she explained, holding up a flowy blouse and a pair of high-waisted jeans for consideration.

Emily and Ashley both nodded in approval, already envisioning Sarah rocking the look on the dance floor later that night.

With their outfits chosen, they moved on to the next crucial step: shoes. Ashley's collection of heels lined the bottom of her closet, each pair more glamorous than the last.

"I think I'm going to go with these," Ashley said, holding up a pair of strappy sandals that sparkled in the light.

Sarah and Emily both agreed, knowing that comfort, yet sexy, was key for a night of dancing.

As they slipped into their chosen footwear, they turned their attention to the finishing touches: makeup and jewelry. Emily's vanity was littered with an array of eyeshadow palettes, lipsticks, and brushes, each one carefully curated to create the perfect look.

Ashley selected a deep plum shade. Sarah nodded in approval, already envisioning the stunning effect it would have against Ashley's flawless complexion.

Emily, meanwhile, was busy adding the final touches to her makeup, expertly applying a subtle smoky eyeliner that accentuated her sparkling green eyes.

With their makeup complete, they moved on to jewelry, each selecting pieces that complemented their chosen outfits. Sarah opted for a pair of statement earrings that added a touch of glamour to her look, while Ashley and Emily chose delicate necklaces and bracelets that added just the right amount of sparkle.

Finally, it was time for the final touch: perfume. Emily's dresser was lined with an assortment of fragrances, each one more intoxicating than the last.

"I think I'm going to go with this one," Emily said, selecting a bottle of floral perfume that reminded her of springtime.

Sarah and Ashley both agreed, already inhaling the scent with appreciation.

With their preparations complete, they posed in front of the mirror, admiring their reflections with satisfaction. Ashley and Emily were determined to make this a night to remember, a gesture for Sarah to lift her spirits, a night brimming with laughter, dancing, and the promise of unforgettable memories for years to come.

As they made their way in an Uber to the club in downtown St. Louis, Sarah felt a glimmer of anticipation stirring within her. The pounding music, flashing lights, and throngs of people were just what she needed to drown out the noise in her mind.

Inside Andromeda, the trio found themselves swept up in the pulsing energy of the crowd. Emily dragged them to the dance floor, where they lost themselves in the rhythm of the music. Sarah felt the tension in her shoulders begin to ease as she moved to the beat, letting herself be carried away by the moment.

"This is exactly what I needed," Sarah shouted over the music, a wide grin spreading across her face.

Ashley grinned back, her eyes shining with delight. "I told you! Nothing like a night out with your best friends to chase away the blues."

For hours, they danced and laughed, letting the music wash over them like a healing balm. Yet, as the night advanced, Sarah sensed a restlessness creeping in. The dance had rejuvenated her, but beneath the surface, a faint weariness lingered. It had been some time since she had immersed herself in such partying, and the toll was beginning to show.

"How about we take this party somewhere else? Somewhere a bit more laid-back," Sarah proposed, sinking into a nearby chair to give her feet a break. "There's a new bar that just opened up near my place."

Ashley and Emily readily agreed to relocate the evening's festivities elsewhere. Their primary concern was Sarah's enjoyment, and they were relieved to see her immersed in the moment, reluctant to let the night come to an end just yet.

"Lead the way," she said, a renewed sense of adventure coursing through her veins.

They summoned an Uber to take them to the Central West End. Squeezed snug in the back seat together, laughter bubbled up between the women as they exchanged stories and jokes. The Uber driver, a middle-aged man trying to make a few extra bucks driving for the ride-share company, grinned in the rearview mirror a few times, but didn't try to join in on the girls' conversation.

The pulsating beat of the club still echoed in Sarah's ears as she, Emily, and Ashley stepped out of the Uber and strolled down the crowded Central West End sidewalk to Ben's Place, a serene sanctuary amidst the urban chaos. Sarah led the trio with a confident stride, her heels clicking against the pavement with each step. She had been here before, drawn to the quiet ambiance and the comforting presence of Ben behind the bar.

As they entered, a soft murmur enveloped them, a stark contrast to the noisy chaos of the club they had just left. The bar was dimly lit, the glow of the neon signs casting an ethereal aura over the room. A small crowd had gathered, mingling in hushed conversations as they sipped on their drinks. Behind the counter stood Ben, his familiar face illuminated by the warm light of the overhead lamps.

Sarah led her friends to the bar, memories of her previous visit flooding back to her. Ben's eyes lit up with recognition as he caught sight of her, a warm smile spreading across his lips.

"Hey there," he greeted, his voice laced with a hint of flirtation.

"Hi, Ben," Sarah responded, her tone warm and welcoming.

Ashley and Emily exchanged a swift glance. While Ashley found amusement in the harmless banter, Emily couldn't shake the thought that Sarah's warmth might border on the overly friendly for someone in a committed relationship.

Ben slipped into a casual yet professional demeanor. "What can I get you ladies?" he asked.

"A cosmopolitan," Ashley ordered confidently.

"Dirty Martini," Emily chimed in with a smirk.

Turning to Sarah, Ben awaited her decision. "I'm still deciding," Sarah replied, her gaze thoughtful.

With a nod, Ben turned to prepare the other women's drinks.

"This has been such a blast," Sarah remarked to Emily and Ashley, genuine gratitude evident in her tone. "I can't thank you two enough."

"Hey, it's what friends are for," Ashley replied with a warm smile.

Emily's eyes twinkled mischievously. "And the night's far from over," she teased, adding an air of excitement to their already enjoyable evening.

The three of them shared a deep, knowing laughter that only those with a long history together could understand.

Placing two drinks on the bar counter, one in front of Emily and the other in front of Ashley, Ben grinned. "Here you go, ladies. A Cosmopolitan and a Dirty Martini," he announced before turning his attention to Sarah. "Have you decided?"

"Sorry, I've been chatting with my friends," she said with a chuckle.

"No rush at all. You've got until last call," he teased with a playful smirk.

Ashley lifted her drink. "Em, let's grab a table," she suggested, eager to settle in a cozy spot. Emily hesitated, glancing back at Sarah and Ben at the bar.

"Go ahead," Sarah said, "I'll be there in a minute."

Emily nodded. "Okay," she agreed, her reluctance evident.

With their drinks in hand, they made their way to a small table in the heart of the bar, leaving Sarah behind.

The low hum of gentle chatter and clinking glasses from other bar patrons enveloped Sarah as she scanned the array of spirits lining the shelves.

"I'll just have a glass of white wine, please," she requested, her voice a soft murmur barely audible above the ambient noise.

Ben, the bartender, leaned in attentively, his gaze lingering on her with a curious intensity. "Coming right up," he replied with a friendly smile, his hands moving deftly to fulfill her order.

As he poured the wine, Sarah's gaze drifted to the captivating painting adorning one of the bar's walls—an equestrian competition frozen in time, capturing the raw energy and grace of the moment. A painting she created years ago. Leaning in closer to Ben, she lowered her voice to a whisper, her words tinged with a hint of excitement. "You know, Ben, I'm actually Sarah Kellerman," she confessed, her eyes sparkling with anticipation.

Ben's eyebrows shot up in surprise, his eyes widening in disbelief to the point where he momentarily halted pouring the wine for fear of spilling it.

CHAPTER ELEVEN

"**N**o way! You're *the* Sarah Kellerman?" Ben exclaimed, his voice tinged with awe.

Sarah nodded, a playful smile dancing on her lips. "Guilty as charged," she replied, a sense of satisfaction washing over her.

Ben's expression softened, a warm glow of recognition spreading across his features. "I thought you looked familiar, but I couldn't quite place you. I've seen your photo in a few articles about your work, but it's been a while," he murmured, his tone filled with admiration. "I've always admired your work. It's such an honor to meet you in person."

Sarah's heart swelled with gratitude at his words. "Thank you," she said sincerely, touched by his genuine appreciation. "It means a lot to me."

"You and your friends' drinks are on the house tonight," Ben declared with a generous smile.

Sarah's grin widened. "I appreciate that, but it's not necessary," she replied politely.

"I insist! It's not every day I get to serve a celebrity," Ben asserted, his eyes twinkling with amusement.

"Celebrity? I don't know about that," she chuckled modestly.

"May I join you for a drink?" he asked with a charming smile.

"Of course," she replied, returning his grin.

He poured himself a glass of white wine, and they raised their glasses, the crystal chime of the clink resonating through the air.

Across the room, Emily kept a watchful eye on Sarah and Ben, while Ashley attempted to engage her in conversation. Sensing her distraction, Ashley redirected her attention to the object of Emily's scrutiny. "Is something on your mind?" she inquired, her tone gentle yet probing.

"I just can't help but notice how friendly Sarah is with the bartender," Emily replied, her tone tinged with disapproval.

Ashley shrugged nonchalantly. "They're just having a drink together. Besides, I think Sarah and Lucas might be taking a break."

Emily's eyebrows shot up in surprise. "Has Sarah mentioned anything to you about that?"

Ashley shook her head. "No, but you can kind of tell."

"How?" Emily asked, her curiosity piqued.

"She was with Lucas for a while, then suddenly decided to stay with me instead," Ashley explained. "I didn't pry into it because it's not really my business, but it seems pretty obvious to me."

Emily nodded in understanding, taking a sip of her drink before her expression darkened. "Excuse me, I need to use the restroom," she announced abruptly, a sense of urgency in her tone.

Emily rushed to the women's bathroom. Digging into her purse, she retrieved her phone and swiftly composed a text to Lucas, detailing their whereabouts and subtly suggesting that he should join them. Emily felt a twinge of guilt as she pressed send, but she quickly brushed it aside, convincing herself it was for Sarah's own good. She didn't want Sarah to do something she'd regret later. Since Ashley wasn't helping, Emily felt she had to step up as the better friend. Without waiting for Lucas to reply, she returned to the table, noticing Sarah was still talking to Ben.

At the bar counter, Sarah rummaged in her purse and pulled out a flyer showcasing her upcoming art exhibition; she would be displaying a mix of recent pieces and older favorites. With a mischievous glint in her eye, she handed the flyer to Ben, a playful grin tugging at her lips.

"You might find this interesting," she remarked, her tone tinged with playful humor and a hint of bashfulness, wary of sounding too self-promotional.

Ben's eyes sparkled with excitement as he perused the flyer. "Absolutely," he declared, his enthusiasm palpable. "I wouldn't miss it for the world."

"Great!" Sarah took a sip of her wine. "I should get over to my friends now."

"Sure thing. Just let me know if any of you need more drinks," Ben offered.

"Thanks," Sarah replied, then made her way over to join Ashley and Emily at their table.

They talked for over an hour, three girlfriends with a long and common history, reminiscing about past adventures when life felt lighter and the days stretched out lazily in the summer sun. Outside the bar's wide window, the Central West End's nightlife dwindled, leaving behind a near-empty sidewalk washed in the stark shadows of streetlights. Sarah peered at the almost deserted street, struck by its eerie beauty, like a scene frozen in time. She made a mental note to capture it, maybe return another night and snap a photo to paint later. She already had a title in mind: 'View from Ben's Place'.

The door swung open, and Sarah's gaze locked onto a familiar figure sauntering in with the confidence of a regular. It took her a moment to realize it was Lucas, a surprise guest she hadn't anticipated seeing. A warm smile spread across Lucas's face as he approached their table.

"Last call!" Ben's voice rang out, directed mostly at Lucas, the newcomer.

Lucas waved off the offer with a shake of his head, settling in beside the girls. Ben acknowledged with a nod, though his eyes lingered on Lucas, who casually draped an arm around Sarah.

"How did you know we were here?" Sarah's surprise lingered as she addressed Lucas.

"Emily texted me," he replied casually.

"Yeah, I thought it'd be a nice surprise to cap off the night," Emily interjected quickly, a touch of awkwardness in her tone.

Ashley and Sarah exchanged uncertain glances.

"Is it a problem?" Lucas chimed in with a smirk, attempting to diffuse any tension.

Ashley broke into a grin. "No," she said, "but there goes our girls' night out."

Sarah chuckled softly and reassuringly, "It's perfectly fine, though. The night's nearly over anyway."

Lucas strolled up to the bar and asked for a draft beer, even though Ben had already announced last call. But Ben let it slide since Lucas was with Sarah and her friends. Lucas eyed Ben with a hint of arrogance, as if he thought he was better just because Ben was a bartender. He didn't know Ben actually owned the place, not that it would've mattered to him anyway. Lucas's attitude wasn't lost on Ben, but he found it more amusing than anything else. Lucas returned to the table with his beer mug. It wasn't his usual choice, but since it was getting late, he opted for something lighter.

The four of them chatted casually for a while until Emily turned to Sarah with a question. "Did you ever get those lawyers the thing they needed from your dad's house?"

Sarah nodded. "Yeah, the flash drive. My dad kept it in his safe."

Ashley was perplexed. "Was that a usual spot for him to keep stuff like that?"

Sarah shrugged. "Not really, but it wasn't totally out of the ordinary either." She took a sip of her drink, pondering her next words. After a moment, she decided to dive in. "But I noticed something odd when I was at the mansion."

All eyes were on her now. "What?" Lucas asked, concerned.

"The laptop on my dad's desk had been moved."

They stared at her, waiting for clarification. Sarah met their gaze, expecting them to catch on, but no one did, so she continued. "It's like someone either tampered with it or tried to."

Lucas looked skeptical. "How can you be sure?"

Sarah paused, gathering her thoughts. "My dad was super particular about his desk, and basically everything else in his life. He wouldn't have left the laptop like that when he stepped out of his office."

The others exchanged incredulous glances, struggling to process Sarah's revelation.

"Look. I know that sounds weird, but I knew my dad."

Emily spoke cautiously. "We know you knew him, but what you're describing seems kind of... trivial."

"Not when it came to my dad," Sarah retorted, a hint of defensiveness creeping into her tone. She wasn't keen on having her perception of her father, Anthony Kellerman, questioned. He was a brilliant man, albeit a bit eccentric. They all grasped that to some degree, but Sarah, having lived under the same roof, understood it more intimately. His quirks often tested her mother's patience to its limits.

Lucas leaned forward. "Okay. So... what do you think it means?"

Sarah paused, grappling with the words she longed to express but feared would be met with skepticism. She held back the unsettling notion swirling in her mind – the belief that her father's death was no accident. So far, the reception to her revelations hadn't been supportive. She dreaded the possibility of being dismissed as delusional if she disclosed her suspicion that someone other than her father had prowled through their home on the fateful morning of his demise while she prepared herself a cup of coffee. The weight of that person's presence loomed ominously, and Sarah just couldn't shake the thought that they were likely the very hand behind her father's untimely end. She yearned to confide all of these thoughts in her friends, yet the words eluded her, the truth still too daunting to unveil. At least, not just yet.

Nonetheless, Sarah opted to test the waters of disclosure, if only tentatively. "On that morning... I was in the kitchen and heard someone moving through the house. I assumed it was my dad. But now, I believe he was... already gone."

Lucas furrowed his brow, perplexed. "Who do you think it was?"

Sarah met his gaze briefly before averting her eyes to the table, taking a shallow breath. She wasn't certain if she should continue.

"It's okay, Sarah," Ashley said softly, barely above a whisper. "We're your friends; we're on your side."

"I'm thinking it was a burglar," Sarah offered, aware that she was only divulging part of the truth as she believed it. True, whoever had been there was indeed a burglar if they attempted to access her father's laptop. But they were far more sinister if they had carried out what Sarah suspected.

Ashley regarded her with compassion, though to Sarah's dismay, there was a hint of pity in her expression. Lucas and Emily seemed even more skeptical. None of them were willing to entertain Sarah's words as truth, she could sense it in their eyes. If they couldn't entertain the possibility of a burglar in the mansion that morning, Sarah couldn't even fathom broaching the topic of her father's murder.

Lucas scanned each of the women before fixing his gaze on Sarah. "Sweetheart, I think you might be letting your imagination run a bit wild, especially considering everything you've been through. But that's understandable."

"Especially considering you're an artist," Ashley added. "Artists tend to have vivid imaginations by nature."

"Exactly," Emily chimed in, like someone who didn't want to be left out of the conversation. "You're so creative and imaginative. None of us would even think to consider something...like that."

Sarah wasn't quite sure how to interpret Emily's remark. Was it a compliment or a subtle dig at her for thinking something crazy?

"I'm sure you are all right," Sarah said with a forced chuckle, attempting to lighten the mood she had inadvertently created. Deep down, though, she couldn't shake the feeling that she was onto something important.

After an uneasy silence, Ashley skillfully steered the conversation towards her latest interior design venture, a topic she was passionate about. Eager to shift away from the discomfort Sarah inadvertently introduced, everyone enthusiastically joined in, bombarding Ashley with questions as she animatedly divulged the intricacies of her project. Their lively discussion continued unabated until the bar closed for the night.

They gathered outside the bar, where Ben bid Sarah a subtle farewell wave as he locked up. Though Lucas offered to give the girls a ride to Ashley's place, they opted for an Uber instead, so he drove himself home. Emily made arrangements for her own Uber, planning to retrieve her car from Ashley's in the morning, and Ashley and Sarah shared a ride to Ashley's apartment, wasting no time in retiring to their respective bedrooms once they arrived.

However, Sarah found little rest that night, plagued by unsettling nightmares. In her dreams, a faceless figure lurked in the shadows of the mansion, haunting her every move.

Sarah stepped into Kellerman Law Group, her father's law firm on the 29th floor of the Met Square building in downtown St. Louis. The firm was a bastion of efficiency with its sleek design and contemporary aesthetic. Despite the inviting atmosphere, she wasn't in the mood for socializing with the lawyers and staff who would undoubtedly inquire about her well-being. Their concern was appreciated, of course, but today, she simply wanted to deliver the flash drive to Stephen and leave without any fuss. She wasn't up for the usual small talk and heartfelt inquiries; she just needed to get in and out of the building as quickly as possible.

Stephen's office was cozy but smaller than the senior partners. He and Sarah exchanged pleasantries, but when she handed him the flash drive, she noticed a flicker of tension in his usually composed demeanor. She brushed it off, attributing it to the usual stress of work. He thanked her warmly but had to rush to a meeting, for which he apologized for. Sarah didn't mind, as she wasn't feeling comfortable there anyway. She figured her unease in her father's office mirrored her feelings about the mansion.

Sarah thought she'd feel better once she made her way out of the building and into the parking garage, her senses pricked with discomfort. There, nestled among the rows of cars, sat James in his sleek, sporty Mercedes. Sarah's heart skipped a beat when she noticed him staring at her with an unexpected intensity.

Knowing she'd spotted him, he emerged from his vehicle with a practiced nonchalance, and a casual smile playing on his lips. "Hey, Sarah," he called out, his voice echoing in the concrete cavern of the garage.

Sarah forced herself to return his greeting, though her pulse quickened with each step he took towards her. She couldn't shake the feeling that something was off, that there was more to his presence here than a mere coincidence.

As they exchanged pleasantries, and he said he was just returning from lunch, Sarah couldn't help but notice the subtle tension in James's demeanor, the way his eyes darted around as if searching for something—or someone. She tried to push aside her growing apprehension, reminding herself that James was just one of her late father's colleagues, nothing more.

But as he bid her farewell and disappeared into the depths of the garage, Sarah couldn't shake the lingering sense of unease that settled like a stone in the pit of her stomach. She climbed into her car, the engine roaring to life beneath her, but the feeling of disquiet remained, a nagging presence she couldn't ignore.

As she navigated the familiar streets on her way to Ashley's apartment, Sarah found her thoughts returning to James and his peculiar behavior. Did he follow her there? And why did it leave her with such a sense of foreboding?

The unanswered questions lingered as she parked her car on the street outside Ashley's apartment. Only residents were permitted to park in the underground garage, leaving Sarah with no choice but to find a spot on the curb. She glanced back at the empty street, half-expecting to see James's car lurking in the shadows, but there was nothing there except the quiet hum of suburban life.

With a sigh, Sarah shook her head, chiding herself for letting her imagination run wild. James was just another junior partner at her father's law firm, she reminded herself, nothing more. But as she stepped inside Ashley's apartment and closed the door behind her, she couldn't shake the feeling that something was lurking just beyond the edges of her reality, something she couldn't quite grasp but knew instinctively was there.

CHAPTER TWELVE

*I*n the heart of St. Louis County, Missouri, the city of Clayton exudes an air of refined elegance, where historic architecture meets modern vitality. Its streets weave a tapestry of old-world charm, lined with boutiques, cafes, and art galleries in and near the city. The city comes alive with the laughter of families in Shaw Park, the clink of glasses at upscale bistros, and the melodic strains of live music. Clayton is not just a place; it's a sanctuary where the past melds seamlessly with the present, inviting residents and visitors alike to immerse themselves in its rich mosaic of artistic expression and community spirit.

The date of Sarah's art exhibition had finally arrived, casting a veil of anticipation over her as she stood in the Clayton Art Gallery, her heart pounding with nervous excitement. The room buzzed with energy as guests filtered in, eager to immerse themselves in her world of colors and emotions.

Amidst the throng were Ashley and Emily, their eyes sparkling with pride as they took in the sight of their friend's work adorning the walls. Lucas stood by her side, his reassuring presence a comforting anchor amidst the sea of anticipation.

"So, this is it," Ashley murmured, her voice filled with awe as she gestured to the array of paintings. "You've really outdone yourself, Sarah."

Sarah smiled nervously, her fingers twisting together as she surveyed the room. "Thanks, Ashley. I just hope people like it."

Emily stepped up alongside Sarah and offered a reassuring squeeze of her hand. "They will, trust me. Your art is amazing. It speaks to people."

As the evening unfolded, Sarah found herself swept up in a whirlwind of conversations and compliments. She greeted visitors with a mixture of excitement and trepidation, her heart pounding in her chest with each new interaction.

"Wow, Sarah, these pieces are amazing," one guest exclaimed, studying a particularly intricate painting. "The detail is incredible."

"Thank you," Sarah replied, a rush of warmth flooding her cheeks. "I really wanted to capture the beauty of everyday moments."

Lucas stepped forward, his hand finding Sarah's as he spoke. "She's been working so hard on this. I'm just proud to see her talent on display for everyone to see."

The hours flew by in a blur of laughter and admiration, each moment etching itself into Sarah's memory. She found herself immersed in conversations about her art, sharing stories of inspiration and technique with anyone who would listen. It was as if this art show was an oasis from her current woes, and she wished it could last forever.

At one point, Sarah found herself chatting with a group of curious onlookers, her hands gesturing animatedly as she described her creative process.

"So, what inspires you?" one woman asked, her eyes shining with curiosity.

Sarah paused, her gaze shifting to the paintings surrounding them. "Life, mostly. The beauty of nature, the emotions we all experience. I try to capture those moments and emotions in my work."

The canvas she had meticulously crafted just weeks before flashed vividly in her mind's eye—the scene of emergency vehicles parked before the grandeur of the mansion. Its hues of somber crimson veiled the grim reality lurking beneath its surface. She never completed it, but even if she had, she wouldn't dare display it here. It would undoubtedly attract too much attention and invite countless unwanted questions. With a forced smile aimed at the curious onlookers, she fought to push the haunting image from her thoughts. She hoped that few, if any, made the connection between her and her father, lest it cast a morbid pall over the entire exhibition.

As the evening wore on, the soft glow of gallery lights illuminated Sarah's artwork, casting a warm ambiance throughout the room. Her heart swelled with a mixture of nerves and anticipation as she watched the crowd mingle among her paintings, each stroke of her brush a piece of her soul laid bare for the world to see.

About midway through the evening, a familiar figure strolled into the gallery, and caught Sarah's eye. It was Ben, the owner and head bartender of Ben's Place. He navigated through the crowd with a casual grace, his eyes alight with genuine interest as he surveyed her artwork.

With a nervous smile, Sarah approached him, her hands trembling slightly as she gestured towards her paintings. "Hey, Ben. I'm so glad you could make it."

Ben turned to her, his gaze sweeping over the intricate details of her work. "Sarah, this is awesome. You've really outdone yourself. It's no surprise that your star is rising in the art world."

A rush of warmth flooded Sarah's cheeks at his praise. "I appreciate it, Ben. It means a lot coming from you."

To her surprise, Ben began to discuss the history of realism, his words flowing with a surprising depth of knowledge. Sarah listened with rapt attention, impressed by his insights into the art form she had dedicated her life to.

"You really know your stuff," she remarked, a hint of awe in her voice.

Ben chuckled, scratching the back of his neck sheepishly. "Well, I may have done a bit of research before I came. Had to make sure I didn't embarrass myself in front of a talented artist like yourself."

Sarah was impressed. Not only was he a skilled bartender, but he also took the time to educate himself about her passion. It was a rare quality that spoke volumes about his character.

Ben reached into his pocket and withdrew a business card, handing it to Sarah with a grin. "If you ever need a bartender for another public event like this, or a private one, don't hesitate to give me a call. I'd be honored to lend a hand. I know that sounds like a crass self-promotion, but I would genuinely like to be involved in any or your artistic endeavors."

Sarah accepted the card with a grateful smile. "Thanks, Ben. I'll definitely keep that in mind. And no, it isn't a crass suggestion. You and I are both self-employed, so I completely understand the need to network and promote yourself."

Ben was about to respond when a voice sliced through the air from behind, halting their exchange. "Self-promotion's a given when you're self-employed. I do it all the time," the voice declared with a brashness that caused Sarah to cringe. She didn't need to turn around to know it was Lucas. It wasn't just the familiarity of his voice that bothered her; it was the unmistakable undercurrent of disdain that tainted his words. He made no effort to conceal his disapproval of her interaction with Ben. They faced him and he met Ben's gaze with an icy glint.

Turning to Sarah, Lucas's voice cut through the air like chilled steel. "Hey, babe, everything alright?" His tone, though seemingly casual, carried an overbearing undercurrent as he positioned himself between Sarah and Ben, as if to suggest Ben was bothering her.

Sarah's smile faltered at the sudden interruption, her gaze flickering between Lucas and Ben. She could sense the tension radiating off Lucas in waves, his jealousy palpable even in the dim light of the gallery.

"Sure, Lucas," Sarah replied, her voice tinged with concern on not knowing where this conversation was going.

Lucas's eyes briefly flashed towards Ben, his expression hardening with scorn. "Aren't you that bartender at the place in the

Central West End we were at not too long ago?" he asked, his tone laced with thinly veiled hostility.

Ben arched an eyebrow at Lucas's tone, his own expression guarded but composed. "Yeah. It's called Ben's Place. My name's Ben."

Lucas's smile held a hint of subtle mockery as he spoke. "Oh, how nice. You must be the owner," he quipped.

"Yeah," Ben replied without expression. "And you are…?"

"I'm Lucas. Sarah's boyfriend," he said sharply.

Ben extended his hand in greeting. "Nice to meet you," he said with as much warmth as he could muster, considering the confrontational vibe Lucas was projecting. They shook hands, the firmness of Lucas's grip bordering on excessive. Ben smoothly redirected the conversation. "Sarah and I were just discussing her artwork," he interjected, aiming to diffuse the palpable unease that hung in the air. "Really beautiful stuff. She's very talented."

"How nice. But, if you'll excuse us," he said with forced politeness, "Sarah's friends have been eager to catch up with her." He subtly nodded towards Emily and Ashley, who were engrossed in their own discussion across the gallery, oblivious to what was happening with Sarah and Lucas presently.

Sarah glanced between Lucas and Ben, a knot of unease forming in the pit of her stomach. She could feel the tension between them like a live wire, crackling with the potential for conflict.

Sarah reached out to touch Lucas's arm. "I'll just catch up with them later."

Lucas shot her a withering glance. "Fine," he replied, tightly.

He shifted his gaze towards Ben, a faint smirk playing at the corners of his lips. "I happen to be a tennis instructor," he stated, his tone carrying a hint of challenge. "Always keen on a new opponent. Care to test your skills on the court?"

Ben's expression remained impassive, though a flicker of amusement danced in his eyes. "I don't really play tennis," he admitted, his tone casual. "But I'm willing to give it a shot."

Sarah's heart sank at the prospect of Lucas and Ben facing off on the tennis court. Lucas could push a pro to their limits, his skill unmatched by amateurs. The thought of Ben being humiliated by her boyfriend only added to her unease.

"Lucas, maybe this isn't such a good idea," Sarah said, her voice tinged with apprehension. "You know how good you are, and Ben—"

But Lucas waved off her concerns with a dismissive gesture. "Don't worry about it," he said, his tone brimming with confidence. "It'll be fun. Besides, it's just a friendly game."

"Where do you want to play?" Ben asked.

"Westfield Country Club," Lucas said casually.

Ben's initial surprise at the mention of the location quickly gave way to a sobering realization. In truth, he shouldn't have been taken aback at all. Sarah and her friends belonged to a different echelon—a world of country clubs and privileged circles. He felt a pang of inadequacy, recognizing the vast social divide between them. The idea of ever being welcomed into their exclusive realm seemed utterly far-fetched, a notion he had never entertained until now.

"Oh, yeah, it's in Chesterfield," Ben said, not wanting to feel completely out of touch.

"That's right. When would you like to play?" Lucas inquired, but before he could respond, he added, "How about tomorrow at 11 a.m.?"

Ben hesitated for a moment, then said, "Sure."

With a resigned sigh, Sarah turned her attention away from the two men as Ashley and Emily approached. They enveloped her in their conversation, and she welcomed the distraction.

Ben and Lucas stood shoulder to shoulder, their gazes fixed on a selection of Sarah's paintings. The tension between them hung heavy in the air, tangible enough to slice through even the most vibrant strokes of color on the canvas.

~2~

At the stroke of 11 a.m. , Lucas stood at the front entrance of the prestigious Westfield Country Club, his demeanor crisp with punctuality. Ben, his invited guest, was due to arrive imminently. Lucas had made sure of it. Anticipation buzzed in the air as he awaited Ben's arrival, knowing that his presence as the gatekeeper held significance beyond mere hospitality.

He had arrived early, well before the appointed hour, ensuring that he could orchestrate the day's events to his advantage. Sarah, Ashley, and Emily had joined him at the club's main bar, their laughter spreading through the room as they waited. Lucas had agreed to rendezvous with Ben outside, a calculated move that afforded him a semblance of control over the unfolding situation.

Sarah, ever appreciative of Lucas's thoughtful gesture, was unaware of the ulterior motives simmering beneath the surface. To her, it was a simple act of kindness. Little did she know, Lucas harbored a secret agenda; if Ben entered as Lucas's guest, then Lucas symbolically had power over him. He knew it was petty, but he didn't care.

As the clock struck 11, Ben came walking up the driveway after parking on the guest lot. He approached with a genial smile. After he and Lucas exchanged pleasantries, they entered the club.

Ben was surprised upon seeing Sarah and her friends. Spontaneous hugs were exchanged, masking the underlying tension that lurked beneath the surface regarding Lucas.

The plan for the day was simple yet carefully curated: a drink to kickstart proceedings, followed by a few friendly games of tennis, and culminating in a leisurely lunch shared amongst friends. But beneath the facade of camaraderie, Lucas's mind whirred with strategic precision, each move calculated to assert his dominance and influence over Ben's presence in Sarah's life.

The noon sun blazed relentlessly in the cloudless sky, its scorching rays casting an unyielding glow as Ben and Lucas squared off on the tennis court. Ben, his lean frame exuding confidence, bounced lightly on his toes, his racket twirling in anticipation. On the other side of the net stood Lucas, a seasoned tennis professional, his muscular physique a testament to years of training.

"Ready to taste defeat, Ben?" Lucas taunted, a smirk playing on his lips.

Ben chuckled, a mischievous glint in his eyes. "Is this a game, or are you just here to spout cliched questions, Lucas?"

With a cocky smirk, Lucas tossed the ball into the air and served, igniting the tennis match with electrifying intensity.

From the sidelines, sitting at a table with an umbrella to keep the hot sun off of them, Sarah, Emily, and Ashley watched with rapt attention, their eyes flickering between the two players. Sarah leaned forward, her fingers curling around the edge of her seat. There was an air of concern about her, a furrow in her brow that betrayed her unease. Ashley, the quiet one of the trio, observed with a serene expression, as Emily, who enjoyed the role of being the life of the party, cheered on both players with unbridled enthusiasm.

As the game unfolded, it became apparent that Lucas was leagues ahead of Ben. With every graceful swing of his racket, Lucas effortlessly returned Ben's shots, his movements fluid and precise. Meanwhile, Ben fumbled around the court, his attempts at a decent return met with little success.

"I've got you right where I want you, Lucas!" Ben shouted, his words punctuated by a near stumble that threatened to turn him into a human tumbleweed. "Consider this my strategic deployment of clumsy tactics, lulling you into a false sense of security!"

Emily erupted into laughter at Ben's humor, her giggles filling the air with infectious joy. Even Ashley, typically more reserved, couldn't suppress the grin that spread across her face.

"Give him a break, Lucas!" Sarah called out, her tone betraying just how seriously she was taking the tennis match.

"Just a friendly game, Sarah. Nothing to worry about," Lucas replied, a hint of irritation creeping into his voice at her unwarranted concern for Ben.

Despite his lackluster performance, Ben's charm never waned. "After this, we'll have a contest to see who can mix the best Ramos Gin Fizz!"

"What is that?" Emily shouted out.

With clumsy grace, Ben danced back and forth on the court, breathlessly listing off the ingredients. "An egg white, gin, lemon juice, lime juice, simple syrup, heavy cream, orange flower water…" His voice trailed off as he leaped into the air, miraculously managing to return the ball for a point. "…and club soda!"

The women erupted into cheers and laughter, their voices mingling in a cacophony of amusement.

Lucas seethed with frustration. "I was distracted," he muttered dryly, shooting a pointed look at Ben, who couldn't suppress a triumphant grin.

"Well, I suppose I shouldn't start reciting the ingredients for the Corpse Reviver number two then," Ben quipped, his tone dripping with mischief, "unless we want this tennis match to turn into a séance!"

The ladies guffawed, thoroughly entertained, while Lucas wore his chagrin like an awkward hat on a bad hair day—visible to everyone and impossible to hide.

Ben continued to pepper the game with jokes and witty remarks, drawing laughter from the trio of women on the sidelines. Sarah's concern was momentarily forgotten as she watched Ben's charismatic antics. Ashley nodded in agreement, her expression serene, while Emily cheered on with unwavering enthusiasm.

Lucas couldn't help but feel a twinge of jealousy as he watched Ben effortlessly captivate the attention of the women. It irked him, knowing that no matter how skilled he was on the court, he could never quite compete with Ben's natural charm.

As the game drew to a close, Lucas decided it was time to put an end to the charade. With a powerful serve, he sent the ball whizzing past Ben, who made a feeble attempt to return it. The final point was his, and Lucas emerged victorious with a smug grin.

"Looks like I win again," Lucas declared, his voice laced with triumph.

Ben flashed him a sheepish grin, his breath coming in ragged gasps. "Yeah, yeah, true, you won, but why do you sound like someone who just got served a bowl of sour grapes."

The women shared a collective chuckle at the biting remark, opting not to stoke any more flames of rivalry with Lucas, who shot a pointed glare at Ben. With casual grace, Ben ambled over to the net, offering his hand in a gesture that was as much about reconciliation as it was about sportsmanship. Relenting, Lucas allowed his irritation to dissipate and graciously accepted the offer, clasping Ben's hand in a firm shake. As the tension eased, the women erupted into applause, relieved to witness the men metaphorically burying the hatchet.

As they gathered their things and prepared to leave the court, Sarah approached Lucas with a relieved smile, her concern evident in her eyes. "I'm glad that's over and that you won."

Lucas draped an arm around her shoulders, exhaling a dismissive sigh. "Really, Sarah," he said with some surprise. "I had the game won before we even stepped onto the court."

She didn't like his tone, but she didn't want to push the issue. Not here anyway. "I suppose so. But you've got to admit, Ben had you rattled there for a moment."

With a smirk and a shrug, Lucas chose to remain silent, his thoughts swirling as they made their way off the court together. Despite the outward calm, he couldn't shake the feeling that this rivalry with Ben was far from over.

CHAPTER THIRTEEN

*T*he midday sun hung high in the sky, casting a warm glow over the sprawling covered patio of the country club. Surrounded by lush greenery, the patio offered a serene escape from the hustle and bustle of the golf course below. From their vantage point, Sarah and her friends could overlook the manicured fairways and rolling hills dotted with golfers and their colorful carts.

Seated at a polished wooden table, the group savored the tranquility of the surroundings as they perused the menu. Sarah opted for the shrimp Cobb salad, and Emily and Ashley both chose chicken salads. All the salads came with ripe tomatoes and tangy dressing. Their choices mirrored the bright, sun-kissed atmosphere of the patio, a perfect complement to the warm summer day.

Lucas indulged in an elegant lobster ravioli, served in a rich, creamy sauce and garnished with herbs or shaved truffles. The flavors danced on his palate and left him craving more. It was a meal fit for the refined ambiance of the country club, elevating the lunchtime experience to a culinary delight.

Ben was more of a comfort food sort of guy and opted for a hearty cheeseburger and fries. Though he wasn't part of the country club crowd and figured he never would be, he had to admit the juicy patty, topped with melted cheese and crisp lettuce, as one of the best burgers he'd ever had.

As they lingered over their lunches, chatting amiably while observing the golfers playing on the lush green fairways below, Lucas schemed his next move. Whether it meant tarnishing Ben's image in Sarah's eyes or casting doubt on Sarah in Ben's mind, Lucas was determined to create a rift between them, willing to go to any lengths to achieve his goal.

"Sarah," Lucas began, his tone casual yet loaded with intrigue. "Why don't you tell Ben about how you think there was a burglar at your father's place?"

Sarah's gaze snapped to Lucas, a mixture of incredulity and apprehension flickering in her eyes. Ashley mirrored her surprise, while Emily remained absorbed in her salad, seemingly oblivious to the tension building around the table.

Ben's eyes darted between Sarah and Lucas, seeing trouble hanging in the air like a storm cloud. He knew whatever was brewing wasn't going to bode well.

"I don't think this is the appropriate time or setting, Lucas," Ashley interjected, her voice tinged with caution.

"Of course it is. Sarah shared it when we were all enjoying ourselves at Ben's bar. I fail to see why this setting is any different," Lucas countered, his persistence evident in his tone.

Ben's discomfort intensified as he gently intervened, "It's all right, Sarah. You don't owe anyone an explanation, especially not me."

Lucas bristled at Ben's words, a shiver running down his spine at the way Ben spoke to Sarah. He wasn't about to let Sarah off the hook so easily. "We're just exchanging thoughts, Sarah, same as you did. What harm could there be in that?"

Sarah paused, her mind racing as she considered her next words carefully. She hadn't explicitly invited their opinions; she had merely recounted her suspicions from that fateful morning. Yet, she held back the most crucial revelation—that she believed her father had been murdered. That was a truth she wasn't ready to broach with them, not yet, perhaps not ever.

Throughout the exchange, Emily maintained a stoic silence, a faint glimmer of amusement dancing in her eyes. It was almost as if she found a perverse pleasure in the escalating tension among her friends. Sarah couldn't help but notice the subtle shift in Emily's demeanor, and it unsettled her deeply. A seed of doubt took root in Sarah's mind, questioning whether Emily was truly the trusted friend she had always believed her to be.

Sarah took a sip of her iced tea, using the brief moment to collect her thoughts. She had made a silent resolve to disclose to Ben her beliefs surrounding the events of her father's death. In hindsight, she acknowledged that she had always intended to confide in him eventually. After all, such thoughts weighed heavily on one's conscience, demanding to be shared, much like the cathartic release of unburdening oneself to a therapist.

Sarah regarded Lucas with a flicker of irritation before deciding to get straight to the heart of the matter. "I was in the kitchen, brewing coffee, when I heard footsteps in the house. Initially, I assumed it was my father—it seemed logical. The sounds led me to believe the person exited through either the back or side door, I can't be certain. Later, as I stood by the pool, I assumed I heard my father walking around just before..." She paused, grappling for the right words. Then, just chose not to finish the sentence.

Ben's eyes softened with empathy, but before he could offer solace, Sarah halted him with a raised hand. She drew in a steadying breath. "Looking back, I concluded it couldn't have been my father. He was already gone. It was someone else—a burglar, perhaps— moving about the house."

She sipped her drink with the nonchalance of someone who'd just summarized the plot of a TV series or movie.

But Lucas persisted, his voice edged with a hint of disdain. "Explain your reasoning," he insisted, barely restraining a sneer.

"That's enough, Lucas!" Ashley's retort was sharp, surprising even herself with the intensity of her words. The friendship between Ashley and Sarah dated back to their grade school days, and Ashley wasn't about to watch silently as Lucas launched his verbal assault. His status as Sarah's boyfriend didn't exempt him from accountability in Ashley's eyes.

Lucas raised his palms up in surrender. "Okay, okay," he relented, not wanting to push things too far. Just suggesting that Sarah's odd ideas came from questionable places should be enough to derail any real friendship between her and Ben. Lucas figured Ashley's blow-up, though meant to help Sarah, probably just made things worse for her credibility.

"No, it's fine, I'll explain," Sarah murmured, quieting the table. With everyone's attention fixed on her, she went on, "My dad was really picky about how he arranged stuff on his desk, especially his laptop. It wasn't where it should've been when he died. I'm sure he wouldn't have left it like that if he was planning to go for a swim." She looked around at everyone, making eye contact. "That's it. That's what I think, and I stand by it." She took another sip of her tea.

Lucas watched Ben closely, hoping for a flicker of doubt in his expression. But to his dismay, Ben's eyes widened with concern, his gaze unwavering as he absorbed Sarah's words.

"That's...quite a revelation, Sarah," Ben said slowly, as he set down his burger.

Sarah nodded, her throat tight with emotion. "I know it sounds crazy, but I can't shake the feeling that I'm right about this."

Ben slowly shook his head. "I don't think it's crazy."

Lucas exchanged a worried glance with Emily and Ashley, who sat silently, their expressions mirroring his own concern. This wasn't going according to his plan. He had hoped that Ben would dismiss Sarah's suspicions as unfounded paranoia. But instead, Ben was taking her seriously—too seriously.

"I think you should go to the police," Ben said firmly, his voice leaving no room for argument. "If you have any doubts about what happened, it's important to follow through. A good detective looks for anything unusual, no matter how small."

Sarah nodded, feeling a surge of gratitude towards Ben for believing her. She had feared that no one would take her seriously—that they would all dismiss her fears as the ramblings of a grieving daughter. But Ben's support gave her the courage to speak up, to pursue the truth no matter where it led.

"I will go to the police. Thanks, Ben," Sarah declared, reaching across the table to give Ben's arm a grateful squeeze.

Lucas felt a sinking feeling in the pit of his stomach. His plan to distance Ben from Sarah had backfired spectacularly. Instead of losing interest in her, Ben was more determined than ever to help her uncover the truth.

Sitting in her car in the country club parking lot, Sarah wasted no time in dialing the number on the business card Detective Nelson had given her. She wanted to swiftly arrange an appointment to meet him at the St. Louis County Police Precinct where he was stationed. Once she expressed her urgency, Nelson promptly accommodated her request by opening his schedule for their meeting the very next day.

Inside the police station, the air was heavy with the scent of stale coffee and disinfectant. Sarah sat across from Detective Nelson in his cramped office. The fluorescent lights hummed overhead, casting a harsh glow on the worn desk between them. She hesitated, her nerves coiling like snakes in her stomach as she prepared to reveal her suspicions.

With a deep breath, Sarah recounted to Detective Nelson the unsettling detail she had noticed after her father's passing—the items on his desk had been moved, a stark deviation from his meticulously organized workspace.

Detective Nelson listened attentively, his brow furrowed in contemplation as Sarah laid out her theory. Though his expression remained inscrutable, Sarah detected a glimmer of skepticism in his eyes as she described her father's habits and the significance of the disrupted order on his desk.

As Sarah concluded her account, Detective Nelson eased back into his antiquated wooden office chair, its tired springs creaking in protest as it bore his weight. The worn wheels beneath groaned softly as the chair rocked slightly backward. With a thoughtful expression, Nelson interlocked his fingers, forming a steeple before him, as he mulled over the information Sarah had shared.

He looked her straight in the eyes and spoke as if she were being interrogated. "So, why would someone burgle the house while you and your father were there? I mean, the chance of discovery would be very high, the size of the home notwithstanding, right?"

Sarah sat up, squared her shoulders and steadied her breath. This was her moment of truth. She was about to delve into her deepest suspicions, aware that any misstep could paint her as unstable. She cleared her throat, steeling herself for what lay ahead.

"I believe the person was there at that time, because his plan was to murder my father."

Detective Nelson blinked speechlessly, caught off guard by Sarah's unexpected revelation. But Sarah pressed on, her voice steady and controlled despite the gravity of her words. "I believe someone lay in wait in the woods behind our backyard," she continued, her gaze unwavering. "When my father entered the pool, they emerged and struck him, rendering him unconscious. They then allowed him to drown while they rifled through his computer for who knows what, before slipping away unnoticed."

Nelson leaned forward in his chair, which groaned again, and impatiently drummed his fingers on his desk.

"How could they get through the gate? It's solid metal with a lock."

"I don't know," Sarah responded without hesitation. "But it is just a backyard gate after all, it's not a bank vault. I would think it wouldn't take too high of a skill level to get around that lock."

Detective Nelson nodded, satisfied. "Okay, I see you've given that some thought. But why do you think someone would go to such lengths to harm your father?"

Sarah swallowed hard, the memories of that fateful morning flooding back to her. "I...I'm not sure. But my father was a powerful man. He had enemies."

Nelson's brow furrowed in disbelief. "And you think one of these enemies orchestrated this elaborate scheme to kill him?"

Sarah hesitated, battling against the intensity of Detective Nelson's glare, which seemed to take on a life of its own, attempting to sow seeds of doubt and convince her that she's delusional.

"It's possible," she finally admitted, her voice barely above a whisper.

Detective Nelson regarded her with a mixture of pity and suspicion. "Sarah, I understand that you're grieving. But this theory of yours...it's far-fetched, to say the least."

Sarah's heart sank at his words, her hopes of finding justice for her father slipping further away. "But it's the truth, I just know it is," she insisted, her voice cracking with emotion.

Nelson shook his head, a look of exasperation crossing his features. "I'm sorry, but I can't entertain wild accusations based on speculation. There's no evidence to support your theory."

Sarah's eyes welled with tears as she realized the futility of her efforts. "But what about the items on my father's desk? The laptop, the framed photo..."

Nelson waved a dismissive hand, cutting her off. "Meaningless in a court of law. Saying the items should match their position as that in the painting wouldn't be considered evidence of anything. I'm afraid you're letting your grief cloud your judgment."

Despair washed over Sarah like a tidal wave, leaving her feeling helpless and alone. She had hoped that Detective Nelson would be the one to help her unravel the mystery of her father's death, but now it seemed that even he doubted her sanity.

Nelson took pity on her; it was apparent in his eyes, and he didn't want their meeting to end on a sour note. "Thank you for coming in and sharing your info, Sarah. I always appreciate additional information about any case."

Sarah nodded weakly and rose from her seat. As she made her way to leave the office, she paused, turning back to face Detective Nelson. "One more thing, Detective... Brock," she said, her voice firm despite her trepidation. "It might be worth reconsidering why the surveillance camera by the pool was inoperative. I know your tech team ruled it out as nothing more than a typical glitch of sorts, but it seems pretty... coincidental... so, perhaps it's worth another look."

With that, she exited the room, leaving Nelson to silently contemplate her words in her wake.

As Sarah left the police station, a heavy weight settled in her chest. She couldn't face Ashley's probing questions about the meeting with Detective Nelson. To avoid Ashley's potentially judgmental gaze, she made her way back to her own apartment, seeking solace in the familiarity of her personal space.

Alone in her dimly lit living room, Sarah sank onto the couch, wrapping herself in the comforting embrace of a worn blanket. She flicked on the television, more for the comforting hum of background noise to drown out the silence that weighed heavy in the room, as well as to ease the depressing thoughts swirling in her mind. After a time, exhaustion washed over her like a tidal wave, pulling her into the welcoming depths of sleep.

She awoke, disoriented and groggy, long after sunset. A news anchor's voice filled the room, reporting on a tragic accident downtown. Sarah's heart lurched as she watched the screen, her eyes widening in shock at the familiar face that flashed across the screen.

James, the junior partner at her father's law firm, had died in a single-vehicle car crash. The news report detailed how he had been caught on security cameras, racing down Washington Avenue in downtown St. Louis at over 100 miles per hour before losing control and colliding with a building, his life extinguished in an instant.

A police officer at the scene remarked that the accident might have been caused by either a vehicle malfunction or James's reckless driving. However, they ultimately dismissed the fiery crash as a mere accident.

Sarah's thoughts spun in a whirlwind as she absorbed the news, her suspicions resurfacing with a vengeance. Was it merely chance that James and her father, both esteemed lawyers from the same firm, met their ends in such tragic accidents, mere months apart? The nagging feeling that there was more to their deaths, something sinister lurking beneath the surface, gnawed at her relentlessly.

With a growing sense of apprehension settling in her gut, Sarah realized she couldn't rely on others to unravel the mysteries surrounding her father and his colleague. She knew she had to take matters into her own hands, to dig deeper into the truth before it slipped away forever. And she suspected, with a sinking heart, that time was not on her side.

CHAPTER FOURTEEN

*W*hile Sarah was still sound asleep on her couch 10 stories above the streets of the Central West End, several miles east, sirens blared through the cool night air, casting eerie reflections of red and blue across the glass facades of downtown St. Louis.

Detective Nelson arrived at the scene on Washington Avenue, stepping out of his car to the cacophony of voices, radio chatter, and the distant hum of engines. The acrid scent of burnt rubber and metal filled his nostrils as he approached the wreckage.

Nelson was far out of his jurisdiction as a county cop, but when he heard the name of the accident victim on the news, he made a few calls to some buddies on the St. Louis city homicide squad and asked if he could join the investigation.

Nelson couldn't shake Sarah Kellerman's last words about the conveniently failed surveillance camera at the mansion. Hours later, James Harris, an associate of Sarah's father, was dead from a presumed accident—just like her father had been months earlier. The unsettling pattern of these incidents defied the concept of coincidence, a notion Sarah herself had questioned in their final conversation.

Despite believing that investigating James's death might lead nowhere, Nelson couldn't shake the nagging feeling that he needed to do it to find some closure on the Anthony Kellerman case. The city police department granted him the necessary privileges to investigate it.

"Detective," a young officer greeted him, his face illuminated by the flashing lights. "It's a bad one. Car went up in flames after the crash. Victim's inside."

Nelson nodded, his gaze fixated on the smoldering remains of what had once been a sleek, black Mercedes. He could see the crumpled frame, the shattered windshield, and the blackened skeleton of the vehicle, now reduced to a twisted hunk of metal.

"Any witnesses?" Nelson asked, scanning the crowd gathered behind the police tape.

"Couple of passersby called it in. Said the car was speeding before it lost control and hit the building. Explosion happened almost immediately after impact."

Nelson stepped closer to the car, feeling the residual heat emanate from the wreck. The fire department had done their job extinguishing the flames, but the damage was already done. He could make out the charred remains of a body in the driver's seat, a grim silhouette against the backdrop of scorched leather and metal.

He noticed the license plate, warped and charred but still legible, clinging tenuously to the back of the car. "Was the plate the only way to identify the victim?" he asked, a note of disbelief in his voice. It would be astonishing if this were the case, as it wouldn't follow protocol. They needed to wait for forensics to make a positive identification.

"No, sir," the officer said. He then pointed up the street and added, "H e'd just left The Sapphire Room according to two witnesses who left at the same time. They drove in the same direction and witnessed the accident."

Nelson was familiar with The Sapphire Room. It was located 10 blocks west of their current position on Washington Avenue, an upscale bar he had never visited and had no intention of ever doing so. He had investigated crimes involving wealthy individuals, but mingling with them in a swanky drinking establishment was not his idea of a good time.

The police officer continued, "Those two witnesses, along with the license plate, confirmed it. The car belongs to a leasing company, and their records show it's leased to James Harris. They've provided the necessary documentation to ensure we've identified the correct Harris."

Nelson nodded, already anticipating the next step. Forensics would verify the identification through dental records to make it official. But he knew they had enough evidence to confirm it was James Harris. In fact, the media had already reported it based on an interview with a police officer at the scene. Nelson wouldn't be surprised if the officer received a reprimand from his supervisor for jumping the gun. However, any fallout would be forgotten once the identification was officially confirmed.

He remembered interviewing James Harris not long ago about the death of Anthony Kellerman. The memory of their conversation lingered in his mind, making it all the more unsettling. Just weeks ago, James had been vibrant, his eyes bright with determination. Now, that same young man was gone, reduced to a name on a scorched lease document. The eerie coincidence gnawed at Nelson, a chilling reminder of how quickly life could be extinguished.

Nelson observed the SLMPD Crime Lab van maneuvering through the cluster of police cars, inching as close to the accident scene as possible. He understood that many auto accidents necessitate forensic analysis for accident reconstruction, especially to determine fault for insurance claims, particularly when a fatality is involved. However, his relief stemmed from a different concern. Was this truly an accident, or was there something more sinister at play?

As the forensics team moved in, Nelson made his way back to his car, his mind already racing with possibilities. A high-speed crash in the middle of downtown St. Louis wasn't an everyday occurrence, and the subsequent explosion only added to the mystery.

Detective Nelson strode into the bustling St. Louis County precinct, the early morning light casting long shadows through the tall windows. His captain, Barrett, waved him into her office. She was a sharp, no-nonsense woman in her sixties, with decades of experience etched into her stern yet kind eyes.

"Morning, Captain," Nelson greeted, taking a seat across from her cluttered desk.

"Morning, Nelson. The city agreed to a task force with us regarding the car accident on Washinton Avenue last night," she said, pushing a thin file across the desk.

Nelson opened the file and found the confirmation they had all been expecting. Dental records identified the deceased as James Harris, age 36. "Jesus, that's young," he muttered, his voice carrying more than he intended.

"It is," Barrett said. After a moment, she leaned forward, resting her arms on the desk. "Here's the thing, though. Your involvement is kind of on the hush-hush."

Nelson arched an eyebrow, urging her to continue. "The Anthony Kellerman case is officially closed, and we're not reopening it. However, we need to determine if the death of his associate here is just a terrible coincidence or something more. Kellerman's death was all over the national news, and it's recent enough that ignoring a possible connection could bring unwanted scrutiny to both the city and county police departments. And that scrutiny would be at a national level."

"If it's on the hush-hush, won't that alone draw media coverage?"

"Higher-ups have made a few phone calls to key people in the 24-hour news networks and asked them to leave it alone until we know something. If this is more than a coincidence, we'd rather not spook any persons involved."

"Got it," Nelson replied, his tone flat but his mind buzzing with excitement.

"Well, get to it," Barrett said with a knowing smirk and a wink. She knew he was itching for this and was indulging him. Whether she believed in a connection or not was irrelevant to Nelson. He craved this investigation and didn't care what it took to dive in.

His first stop was to return to the scene of the accident. The mangled wreckage of Harris's car was already towed away, but the skid marks, more visible in the daylight, and scattered debris told a harrowing story. Nelson took a deep breath, picturing the moments leading up to the crash. He needed to understand Harris's final hours.

Next, he visited The Sapphire Room, the upscale bar on Washington Avenue that was 10 blocks west of the accident scene. The bar was a sleek, modern establishment catering to the city's elite. Harris had been there the night of the accident based on witness accounts. According to his bank card records, he had only two drinks.

Inside the dimly lit bar, Nelson approached the bartender, a young man with sharp features and an air of practiced charm.

"I'm Detective Nelson, investigating James Harris's accident. Can I ask you a few questions?" Nelson showed his badge.

The bartender nodded, his face unreadable. "Yeah, I remember Harris. He was here last night. I couldn't believe it when I saw the news." He jerked a thumb over his shoulder at the large flatscreen above the bar, where an afternoon baseball game was on. "One of the regulars had to point it out to me. I was swamped."

"I don't suppose you'd know how many drinks he had?"

"Two," the bartender replied without a moment's hesitation.

Nelson blinked, caught off guard. Harris's bank records also showed two drinks, but the bartender's immediate recall piqued his interest.

"How do you know that? You must've served dozens, maybe hundreds of drinks last night, right?"

"He was a regular, always had two drinks."

"Do you remember what drinks he ordered?"

"A vermouth and tonic, followed by a pale ale."

"Would you say he was drunk when he left?"

The bartender chuckled as he polished a glass. "No, that was his usual. Never seemed to impair him."

Nelson nodded, scribbling in his notepad. While the younger detectives relied on tablets, he trusted his pad of paper—it never crashed or ran out of battery power. "Did he mingle with anyone?"

"No, which was kind of odd."

"What do you mean?"

"James was a social butterfly. Always chatting up groups, trying to strike up conversations with women. Sometimes he succeeded, sometimes he didn't. You know how it goes."

Nelson leaned in. "But he didn't do that last night?"

"Nope. Sat alone at the bar, seemed pretty wrapped up in his thoughts. Normally, I could have a conversation with him easily— it's part of the job. But last night, he was a tough nut to crack. So, I gave him his space."

Nelson absorbed this, doodling absently on his notepad, a habit when nearing the end of an interview.

The cocktail waitress, a young woman with bright eyes and a friendly demeanor, leaned on the bar. She had been listening from nearby. "Sorry to interrupt, but I just wanted to add that Mr. Harris was always polite and tipped well. Last night, he was quieter than usual, but he seemed fine. Didn't look drunk when he left."

Nelson asked if there was anything else, but neither had more to add. He thanked them and requested the surveillance footage.

Back at the precinct, Nelson scrutinized the footage of Harris at the bar. The screen showed him nursing his drinks, interacting with a few patrons, his demeanor calm and collected. But then, something the bartender and cocktail waitress hadn't mentioned caught Nelson's eye. Harris received a phone call while the staff were busy with other customers. The call lasted less than a minute—54 seconds, to be exact. When it ended, Harris abruptly downed his pale ale, slapped a hundred-dollar bill on the bar, and left. His gait was steady, showing no signs of inebriation, but Nelson noticed a shift. Harris seemed clearly agitated, a storm brewing behind his composed facade.

Nelson got a court order to request James Harris's phone records, then he headed to Kellerman Law Group at the Metropolitan Square Building. Stephen, a junior partner at the firm and a colleague of Harris, greeted him in the sleek, minimalist office.

"Detective Nelson, how can I help?" Stephen asked, gesturing for Nelson to sit. He bit back the impulse to say it was good to see him again; that would be wildly inappropriate. Their last encounter had been during the grim aftermath of Anthony's death—a brief, uncomfortable exchange that was more about procedural housekeeping on Nelson's part. No conversation about the loss of his boss and friend could ever be easy. Stephen knew exactly why the detective was here now; the pleasantries were merely a facade. Nelson took the offered seat, the tension in Stephen's voice palpable. Both men understood that this meeting was far from casual, and the air between them crackled with electric tension.

"I'm investigating James Harris's accident. My condolences for your loss."

"Thank you," Stephen replied curtly, eager to bypass the obligatory sympathy. He quickly shifted his focus to Nelson's first statement. "That's...interesting that you're on this case," Stephen said, his brow furrowing in confusion. "Aren't you with the county?"

"I am, but I'm part of a task force for the city."

Stephen raised an eyebrow so subtly that most would miss it, but not Nelson. Trained to catch the smallest details, Nelson had been watching for just such a reaction. He hadn't bothered dancing around the issue. Stephen, a lawyer, would be familiar with police procedures. His late boss, Anthony Kellerman, a former state prosecutor, certainly would have been. Though Stephen's law career had been in civil litigation, Nelson assumed he and Anthony had discussed Anthony's past cases—conversations that likely touched on police tactics. Nelson knew Stephen's reaction could reveal more than words ever could.

"A task force? But it was just an accident, yes?"

"We are required to consider every angle."

"On all cases?" Stephen inquired with a furrowed brow.

Nelson chuckled. "Of course not. But James was doing over 100 miles per hour on a city street. He was not a joy-riding teenager. He was an adult and a professional with a reputation to consider. So, at least on the surface, this would appear to be uncharacteristic of him, or anyone like him. You'd agree, right?"

Stephen nodded, a slight smile playing on his lips. He was impressed; the detective had a keen intellect and sharp instincts, qualities that made Stephen think he might have missed his true calling as an attorney.

Nelson asked him directly about James's drinking habits, and Stephen leaned back in his chair, his expression thoughtful. "James did enjoy his drinks, but he had a high tolerance. He could handle his alcohol better than most. I can't imagine he was drunk after just two drinks. He never was when I was with him."

"Any reason that he might be driving so recklessly?" Nelson probed.

Stephen shook his head. "Not that I can think of. James was always careful, especially with his reputation on the line. Something must have happened after he left the bar."

Nelson left the office, more questions swirling in his mind. He revisited the surveillance footage, this time focusing on the time after Harris left the bar. He traced Harris's route through the city's network of cameras, watching as his car weaving around other cars on the street with increasing speed. Nelson found this behavior from a respected lawyer very confounding.

Nelson's phone buzzed, interrupting his thoughts. It was Barrett. "Nelson, any progress?"

"Some, but nothing concrete yet. Harris left the bar sober. His colleagues say he had a high tolerance, so it's unlikely he was drunk.

But something happened to make him speed through downtown," Nelson reported.

"Well, his phone records arrived," Barrett said. "They're on your desk."

"Great, I'm on my way."

Back at the precinct, Nelson pored over Harris's phone records, zeroing in on the single call he received at the bar. On a hunch, he dialed the number. It rang endlessly, never rolling over to voicemail. Intrigued, Nelson dug deeper and discovered that the number's prefix was linked to a block assigned to carriers known for servicing prepaid or disposable phones.

But that call wasn't the last one on James's phone. He'd made another call just after leaving the bar, and that number was easily accessible to Nelson. It belonged to a woman named Jennifer Watkins. With her name in hand, Nelson checked James's social media accounts and found they were friends on several platforms, with a pattern of frequent interactions. Jennifer worked at a tech firm in Ladue, just outside Clayton. Nelson decided to pay her a visit.

Jennifer's office was in a sleek building filled with young professionals, the hum of innovation and technology in the air. She wasn't entirely surprised to see Nelson; she had anticipated a visit from law enforcement, knowing she was likely the last person to speak to James before the horrific accident.

Nelson asked about their relationship. Jennifer explained that they were just friends who had met at a board game meet-up. "We're all a bunch of gaming nerds," she laughed. James had liked her and hoped for something more, but she had no romantic feelings for him. Despite that, they hung out a few times. They were supposed to meet the night of the accident, but he had called to cancel, which surprised her. James never missed an opportunity to spend time with her.

Nelson pressed for more details about the phone call, the last one James would ever make. Jennifer hesitated, her eyes clouding with the memory. "He sounded...agitated. Mentioned something about needing to meet someone but didn't say who."

Nelson's instincts buzzed with suspicion. "Do you know where he was going?"

Jennifer shook her head. "No, he didn't say. I just assumed it was work-related."

Thanking her, Nelson left the office, his mind racing. Harris receiving a call from someone using a burner phone, then following that with a call to Jennifer, a woman he was attracted to, to cancel their get-together, suggested something more complex than a simple accident. As he walked back to his car, he pondered the possibilities. Who was James meeting, and why the secrecy? The burner phone pointed to something illicit, but what?

Nelson's thoughts churned as he drove back to the precinct, replaying Jennifer's words, the tone of her voice, and the look in her eyes. He didn't sense that she was hiding something; it felt more like she suspected James was involved in something dangerous, something way over his head. Bringing it up might uncover a mess that could tarnish his reputation. Perhaps she believed that, with James gone, it was best to let his past indiscretions—whatever they were—remain buried.

But Nelson couldn't afford to leave any stone unturned. He suspected there was more to this story, layers he needed to peel back. He needed to dig deeper into James's life, his connections, and his secrets. There was a thread connecting all of this, and Nelson was determined to unravel it.

CHAPTER FIFTEEN

*N*elson returned to his office and meticulously reviewed the case files and phone records, hunting for patterns. Nothing stood out. Days passed as he interviewed attorneys at Kellerman Law Group and James's gamer friends, but each lead fizzled. Jennifer had been right—all of James's friends were harmless nerds.

Determined to find a breakthrough, Nelson traced the burner phone's activity. It led nowhere. James Harris had received one call from that burner phone, pinging off a downtown cell tower near the bar where James had been. Despite the proximity, the trail went cold.

Nonetheless, Detective Nelson couldn't shake the conviction that James's death was no accident and that his and Anthony Kellerman's deaths were connected.

Sitting at his desk, he felt the weight of the case pressing down on him. The precinct buzzed with its usual noise, but Nelson was lost in thought, the clamor around him a distant hum.

His phone rang, jolting him back to reality. "Detective Nelson," he answered, his voice a mix of fatigue and curiosity.

"Detective, my name is Nick Pernod."

That immediately grabbed Nelson's attention. He knew that Nick Pernod was a well-known entrepreneur that lived locally but owned several businesses across the country.

Nick continued, "I was an associate of Anthony Kellerman. The last time I saw him was at the stakeholders' event he held at Westfield Country Club this past summer. The night before his tragic accident. I haven't been able to stop thinking about him since. And now his associate, James Harris, is gone. I met him at the country club that night."

"What can I do for you, Mr. Pernod?"

"I think I have some information that might be relevant to your investigation into James Harris's death."

Nelson's interest was instantly piqued. "Go on," he urged, leaning forward in his chair, eyes narrowing with curiosity. Normally, he'd be alarmed if an average citizen knew about this hush-hush investigation. But Nick Pernod was far from average. With connections as deep as any high-ranking politician, there were even whispers of a potential political career in his future. How Nick had uncovered this information was a secondary concern—if he could help crack this case, Nelson was all ears.

"One of my companies manufactures car electronics," Nick explained. "During the event, I overheard James Harris discussing some issues with his vehicle's electronics. Given the circumstances of his death, I think it's important you hear what I have to say."

Within the hour, Nick was sitting across from Nelson in a small, dimly lit interrogation room. Nick, a tall man with a commanding presence, exuded confidence and concern. Nelson gestured for him to begin.

"Many modern cars have WiFi capabilities," Nick began. "This connectivity is both a convenience and a vulnerability. It's possible for a skilled hacker to remotely access a car's electronic systems, including the transmission and brakes. They could essentially control the vehicle, making it accelerate uncontrollably or preventing it from stopping."

Nelson's mind raced. "Are you saying someone could have hacked into James's car?"

"It's conceivable," Nick confirmed. "I know it sounds like something out of a movie, but the technology exists. And even given the sophistication required, it's within the realm of feasibility."

Nelson felt a surge of adrenaline. This might be the breakthrough he had been waiting for. "Our electronic forensics department examined what little remained of the vehicle," he said, his voice steady but charged with newfound energy. "They found some anomalies, but there wasn't enough left to draw concrete conclusions. Your information could be the missing piece."

Nick nodded. "I can provide you with detailed reports on how these systems work and the potential vulnerabilities. It might help your team identify any traces of remote interference."

As Nick spoke, delving into technical aspects that were not necessary for the detective, Nelson's mind was already jumping ahead, planning his next steps. He needed to get this information to the forensics team immediately. If what Nick was saying was true, this changed everything. James Harris wasn't just a victim of a tragic accident; he might have been murdered.

"Thank you, Nick. This could be crucial," Nelson said, standing up and shaking his hand firmly.

After Nick left, Nelson immediately contacted the head of the electronic forensics department, relaying Nick's insights. The team, initially skeptical, began to re-examine the data with fresh eyes. They scrutinized the tiny fragments of the car's onboard systems that had survived the crash, looking for signs of tampering.

Days turned into weeks as the forensic team worked tirelessly. Nelson felt a renewed sense of purpose. He reviewed every detail of the case, cross-referencing Nick's reports with the evidence they had. The more he dug, the more he began to see a pattern.

One evening, as Nelson was deep in thought, his phone buzzed. It was the lead forensic analyst. "Detective, we've found something," she said, her voice tinged with excitement.

Nelson rushed to the lab, his heart pounding. The analyst, a meticulous woman named Dr. Carla Ramirez, met him at the door. "We re-examined the car's electronic control units with Nick Pernod's information in mind. There are definite signs of external tampering. The data logs show unusual access patterns consistent with remote control."

Nelson felt a mix of triumph and anger. Someone had hacked into this vehicle, turning it into an instrument of death. "This means James was murdered," he said, the weight of the revelation settling over him.

Dr. Ramirez nodded. "It's a sophisticated hack, but not undetectable. We're working on tracing the source of the signal that accessed the vehicle's systems."

As Nelson processed this new information, his thoughts turned toward potential suspects. The level of sophistication required pointed to someone with extensive technical knowledge and significant resources. His mind flashed back to the stakeholders' event Nick Pernod had mentioned. Could it have been someone who attended that event? Anthony Kellerman had numerous business rivals and associates, any of whom might have had both the motive and the means. But why target James Harris? No disrespect to the young man, but he was merely a junior partner at Anthony's law firm. What could he have possibly known that would make someone want to kill him?

Determined to dig deeper, Nelson decided he needed to discuss this further with Nick, who moved in these influential circles. A quick phone call later, and Nelson was on his way to Nick's mansion.

Detective Nelson's car glided up the winding driveway, the tires rolling smoothly over the pristine surface. As he stepped out and took a moment to absorb the grandeur of Nick Pernod's mansion in Town and Country, Missouri, he couldn't help but be impressed. The stately facade, adorned with intricate stonework and towering columns, exuded an air of timeless elegance. The meticulously landscaped surroundings added to the serene ambiance, creating a stark contrast to the intensity of the investigation that had brought him here.

The massive mahogany double doors swung open before Nelson could knock, revealing Nick Pernod himself. Impeccably dressed and exuding the confidence of a man accustomed to such opulence, Nick seemed perfectly at home—except for his age. In his thirties, he stood out in this setting of dynastic wealth. His achievements weren't just a product of his privileged background; Nick had excelled academically from childhood through university. His remarkable business acumen had propelled him far ahead of his contemporaries and even surpassed the successes of his own accomplished family.

"Detective Nelson," Nick greeted with a warm, yet purposeful smile. "Nice to see you again. Please, come in."

Inside, the grand foyer's marble floors gleamed under the soft glow of crystal chandeliers. Nelson couldn't help but glance up at the sweeping staircase, its wrought iron banister a piece of art in itself. "Quite a place you have here," Nelson remarked, his voice echoing slightly in the vast space. Though he knew it was a cliché, it felt fitting for a mansion of this grandeur.

"Thank you," Nick replied, leading him into a parlor dominated by a magnificent fireplace. Plush furnishings and rich tapestries added a sense of refined luxury. "Can I offer you a drink? Something to help settle in before we get to business?"

Nelson shook his head, declining politely. "I'm on duty. Let's get straight to it."

Nick nodded, his demeanor shifting from host to the concerned associate. "Of course. Please, have a seat." He gestured to a pair of leather armchairs positioned by a large window that overlooked the sprawling gardens. Nelson sat, taking in the view of the lush lawns and the shimmering pool beyond.

"How can I help, Detective?" Nick asked warmly.

"I need to interview attendees from the stakeholders' party who might have the expertise to remotely control James Harris's car. I'm worried Westfield Country Club will demand a court order for the guest list, which could leak to the media. Can you help me get the list without that hassle?"

Nick was intrigued. "You think the perpetrator might have been someone who attended the event at the country club?"

Nelson shrugged. "I don't know, but I have to start somewhere."

"I understand, Detective," Nick said with a smile. "But as far as I know, I'm the only one who was there that night with the expertise to pull this off."

Nelson chuckled. "You want to turn yourself in?"

"I'll pass, but thanks."

Both men laughed.

Nick steepled his fingers, exuding complete confidence. "I'm not a member of that country club, but I can certainly get a list of attendees. Give me a day—two at the most."

"That would be great, thank you," Nelson said, eyeing him curiously. "I didn't realize you weren't a member."

"I know this is going to sound crass and arrogant, but Westfield is a second-tier country club. I'm a member of Gateway Hills Country Club."

Nelson nodded thoughtfully. He knew Gateway Hills was the most prestigious country club in town. Founded in the late 1800s, it was renowned for its exclusive membership and deep historical significance. The club had been a symbol of elite society since its inception, a place where the city's most influential figures gathered.

After some small talk—a skill Nelson had honed to avoid seeming abrupt at the end of official conversations—Nick walked him to the door.

Nick's expression hardened with determination. "I want to find out who did this as much as you do, Detective. I didn't really know James, but he was an associate of Anthony, who was a friend of mine. Whatever you need, I'm here to help."

Nelson offered a firm handshake. "I'll be in touch. And Nick—stay safe. Whoever is behind this is still out there."

Nick Pernod delivered on his promise the very next day, sending an email to Detective Nelson. The list was lengthy, but Nick had gone the extra mile, marking the most likely candidates with asterisks. One name on the list was Stephen Millstadt, a junior partner at the Kellerman Law Group. Nick included a personal note, stating that although Stephen lacked the technical skills to execute such a scheme, he had observed Stephen and James being very close during a brief chat at a stakeholders' event. Nick speculated that while Stephen might not be the perpetrator, he could potentially have insights into who could have committed such a horrible act. Nick also requested that Nelson keep his name out of any discussion he might have with Stephen. Nelson replied via the email thread, assuring Nick that he certainly would.

Nelson knew he had to tread carefully. The stakes were higher now, and the perpetrator was someone capable of extraordinary measures. As he scrutinized the list of potential suspects, he zeroed in on those with both the technical expertise and possible motives, aware that any misstep could have dire consequences, potentially bringing the wrath of some very powerful people down on him and the police department.

In the ensuing weeks, Nelson and his team embarked on an exhaustive series of interviews and re-interviews. Beyond the names on Nick's list, they questioned IT experts, car electronics specialists, and anyone remotely connected to Anthony and James.

Despite his growing certainty that James's car had been tampered with—thanks to Nick's invaluable assistance—Nelson found himself at an impasse regarding a suspect. Without a significant break in the case, he was effectively at a dead end, the elusive perpetrator still out of reach.

Nelson's thoughts wandered to Sarah Kellerman. She had been adamant that her father, Anthony Kellerman, had not died of natural causes as the initial investigation had concluded. At first, Nelson had dismissed her concerns as the grief-stricken ramblings of a daughter unwilling to accept the sudden loss. But now, with the evidence of foul play in James's death, he wondered if Sarah might be right. Could Anthony's death be connected to James's? The notion was barely above a hunch, but it gnawed at him, compelling him to dig deeper.

Knowing he needed to pursue this line of inquiry somewhat off the record, Nelson reached for his phone and dialed Sarah Kellerman's number. She answered on the third ring, her voice a mixture of curiosity and lingering grief.

"Hello, Detective Nelson," she greeted. He was taken aback that she knew it was him, indicating she had saved his number. That small, thoughtful detail filled him with a comforting sense of assurance.

"Hi, Sarah, how have you been?"

"So-so," she replied, her tone tinged with a hint of sadness. He valued her honesty; they were practically strangers, not close enough for her to owe him such openness, yet she chose to share, and he appreciated it deeply.

"Sarah, I've been reviewing some new evidence, and I believe your concerns about your father's death might be valid," Nelson began, choosing his words carefully. "I think it could be connected to the death of James Harris."

There was a pause on the other end of the line before Sarah spoke again, her voice firmer. "I want to see the file on my father's case, Detective. And the photos taken at our house the morning he died."

She was so direct and to the point that Nelson was taken aback, her words slicing through the air with the precision of a detective's interrogation.

Nelson hesitated. "Sarah, I don't think that's a good idea. Some of those images...they're quite graphic."

"I need to see them," she insisted, her tone brooking no argument. "I have to know what happened."

Reluctantly, Nelson continued. "Alright, I'll give you a copy of the file. But I'll only include the photos of the area surrounding the pool, not the pool itself. It's...it's too much."

Sarah agreed, and they arranged to meet later that day. As Nelson prepared the file, he couldn't shake the feeling that he was crossing a line. But if there was even a chance that Sarah's instincts were correct, he had to follow through.

A few hours later, Sarah met Nelson at a charming little coffee shop called Brew Haven, tucked away in a quiet corner of south St. Louis City. The location was inconvenient for both, but that was precisely the point—they wanted to avoid familiar eyes. For Sarah, whose friends dismissed her worries as mere flights of fancy, and Nelson, who was navigating the shadows on this covert case, discretion was key. They needed a sanctuary where they could converse without fear of being recognized, and Brew Haven, with its cozy nooks and unassuming clientele, offered just that.

Nelson spotted her the instant Sarah walked in. She looked determined, yet fragile, as if she was bracing herself for a wave of pain. Nelson handed her a flash drive, watching as she tucked it in her purse with trembling hands.

"Thank you," she murmured, taking a deep breath.

They each had a specialty brew, engaging in light conversation to pass the time and avoid suspicion from other patrons who might notice if they left too quickly. Nelson felt it was probably overly cautious, but they couldn't afford to be sloppy and attract unwanted attention. Before parting ways, Nelson made Sarah promise not to show the photos or the file to anyone else, nor to keep copies on her computer. He stressed that his job was on the line. Sarah assured him the photos and police file were safe with her. Despite his career-induced cynicism, Nelson believed her.

Back in her loft apartment, Sarah sat at her kitchen table, the file opened on her laptop. She steeled herself and began to sift through the documents and photographs. As she flipped through the images, her stomach churned, and she had to rush to the bathroom, vomiting violently.

After composing herself, Sarah returned to the table and resumed her scrutiny of the photos. Her eyes roamed over the images until something on the side of the pool near the house caught her attention. It seemed out of place, yet she couldn't immediately pinpoint why. She stared unblinkingly at the photo, matching it to her vivid memories of countless summer days spent in that pool.

Then, like a bolt of lightning, it struck her. The deck on that side of the pool—the side no one ever used—was unnaturally, and suspiciously wet. It had never been this drenched, not in all the years she could remember. Her gaze snapped to the corner of the house, where a water spigot with a garden hose attached stood. The hose wasn't neatly coiled as her father always left it; it was wrapped haphazardly, as if someone had used it in a hurry.

Her eyes widened as realization struck like a lightning bolt. Someone had used the hose that morning to wash down that side of the deck. It was clear now—crucial evidence had been deliberately erased. Her pulse raced with the sudden, electrifying revelation.

CHAPTER SIXTEEN

*S*arah sat in a booth at The Moorside Diner, her fingers tapping nervously against the side of her coffee cup. The diner, nestled in the charming heart of Webster Groves, Missouri, was surrounded by tree-lined streets where ancient oaks and maples cast dappled shadows on the historic homes that whispered tales of the town's rich past. Despite the cozy, inviting atmosphere, Sarah's mood remained as dark as a storm cloud. The enticing aroma of freshly brewed coffee wafted through the air, but she barely registered it. Her mind was a tempest of thoughts and emotions, spinning out of control.

She glanced up just as Lucas walked in, his tall frame and confident stride cutting through her mental fog like a lighthouse beam through the mist. They hadn't seen each other for weeks, and his presence was a balm to her chaotic soul. He spotted her and made his way over, a concerned look etched deeply into his features.

"Hey," he said softly, sliding into the booth's bench across from her. "You look like you haven't slept in days. What's going on?"

Sarah took a deep breath, trying to steady herself. She had been bottling up her emotions since receiving the police file and photos from Detective Nelson. Now, sitting here with Lucas, she felt the floodgates straining to burst open.

She told him everything—the standard report concluding her father's death was an accident, and the photos that seemed unremarkable to anyone else. Except for one. That photo carried a significance only she and her father would understand if he were still alive. It showed an unusual amount of water pooled on one side of the deck, and a hose carelessly coiled near the spigot. As she recounted the details, she fought to keep her emotions in check, her voice wavering with the weight of her suspicions.

Lucas reached across the table and took her hand, giving it a reassuring squeeze. "I'm sorry, Sarah. That must have been really hard for you."

She appreciated his concern, but her nerves were on edge, and she urgently needed his opinion. "What do you think about what I just told you?" she asked, her voice tense and impatient.

Lucas sat back in the booth and sighed. Sarah's eyes were piercing, demanding an answer. He couldn't meet her gaze, his discomfort palpable. Relief washed over him when a waiter appeared with a steaming pot of coffee.

"Coffee?" the waiter asked Lucas.

"Sure," Lucas responded.

The waiter turned over the upside-down cup on the table and filled it. He then turned his attention to Sarah. "Top yours off?"

"No," Sarah said, her tone clipped. Realizing she sounded rude, she quickly added, "Thank you." But her eyes never left Lucas. The waiter wandered off, sensing the tension.

"What do you expect me to say?" Lucas finally asked, his voice heavy with uncertainty.

"I just want your thoughts," Sarah insisted.

He leaned forward in the booth and took a sip of his coffee. Now it was his turn to look directly into her eyes, his expression serious. "First, let me ask you, what do you think the significance of the water on the deck and the hose means?"

Sarah's voice trembled slightly as she responded, "That someone else was there. Maybe they left footprints and needed to wash them away."

Lucas sighed, leaning back in his chair. "Sarah, you're still grieving. Your mind is trying to make sense of things that don't need to be overanalyzed."

Sarah felt a pang of frustration. She knew Lucas meant well, but he wasn't listening, not really. "I'm not imagining things, Lucas. There was something off with that one photo."

"Have you discussed this with Emily or Ashley?" Lucas asked, his voice measured but probing.

Sarah sighed heavily, frustration bubbling to the surface. "No, I haven't seen them for some time."

Lucas nodded in that infuriatingly calm way, like a therapist with a troubled client. It wasn't lost on Sarah, and it grated on her nerves. "So... you haven't seen them or me for a little while now, then?"

"What are you getting at, Lucas?" she snapped, her voice rising louder than she intended. A few patrons glanced their way, their curiosity momentarily piqued.

Lucas leaned in, his eyes searching hers. "I'm just saying, Sarah, isolating yourself isn't going to help. You need support, people to talk to."

"Support?" Sarah scoffed, her anger flaring. "I need answers, Lucas. Not empty reassurances and pity."

Lucas shook his head, a sympathetic yet skeptical smile on his face. "Sarah, you just need to move on with your life. Dwelling on these details isn't going to bring your father back."

She felt a surge of anger. "I'm not dwelling on details for no reason. If there's a chance that something happened, something we don't know about, shouldn't we at least consider it?"

"And what if you're right?" Lucas shot back. "What then? Are you going to play detective? Let the police do their job. It's what they're trained to do."

Sarah's eyes filled with tears again, but this time they were tears of frustration and helplessness. "But what if they're missing something? What if they don't see what I see?"

Lucas sighed again, more heavily this time. "Sarah, you're not a detective. You're grieving and you're seeing things that might not be there. I'm worried about you."

She wrapped her arms around herself as if trying to hold herself together. "I thought you would understand," she said quietly. "I thought you would believe me."

"It's not that I don't believe you," Lucas said gently. "I just think you're driving yourself crazy over something that might not mean anything."

Sarah opened her mouth to respond, but a sudden, shrill alarm from Lucas's phone cut through the air, startling both of them. Lucas glanced at his phone, a look of realization and frustration crossing his face.

"Damn," he muttered, silencing the alarm. "I completely forgot I have a session with a tennis client at the country club."

Sarah's shoulders slumped. "So, that's it? We just drop this?"

Lucas reached across the table, gently touching her arm. "No, we don't drop it. We just have to pause. I promise we'll continue this conversation later, okay? I just can't be late for this client."

Sarah nodded reluctantly, her eyes betraying a mix of disappointment and understanding. "Fine. But we need to talk soon, Lucas. I need to figure this out."

Lucas stood, throwing a few bills on the table for the coffee. "I promise, we will. Soon."

As Lucas hurried out of the diner, Sarah watched him go, the door swinging shut behind him with a soft chime. She leaned back in the booth, her coffee growing cold and forgotten. Time slipped away as she stared out the expansive restaurant window, watching the sky darken as the sun sank low on the horizon. Eventually, with a heavy sigh, she paid her bill and left.

She stepped out into the chilly evening air, her mind still reeling. She didn't know what she expected from Lucas, but she had hoped for more support, more understanding. She walked aimlessly, her thoughts spinning in a hundred different directions. The image of the water on the deck kept flashing in her mind, a puzzle piece that didn't fit, a mystery she couldn't let go.

As she wandered through the quiet streets, she thought about her father, Anthony, and the cherished moments they had shared throughout her childhood. The emptiness that now filled her days was overwhelming. She missed him so much it hurt.

She took a short drive to clear her mind, letting the familiar streets of Clayton guide her thoughts. Before she knew it, she found herself at Shaw Park, the place where she and her father had spent so many happy hours together. The park, with its sprawling green lawns and towering trees, was a serene escape in the heart of the city. She sat on a bench, staring out at the darkened playground, the swings swaying gently in the breeze. She could almost hear his deep, reassuring laugh, feel his strong hands guiding her as he taught her to ride a bike, and the pain of his loss washed over her anew.

She pulled out her phone and stared at the number for the police station. She knew Lucas was right about one thing: she wasn't a detective. But she couldn't shake the feeling that she had to do something.

With trembling fingers, she dialed the number and waited for the call to connect. When Detective Nelson answered, she took a deep breath.

"Detective, it's Sarah," she said, her voice trembling with urgency. She recounted what she had learned from the photos, just as she had with Lucas. Detective Nelson listened patiently, acknowledging that there might be more to Anthony's death than Lucas believed. However, he remained skeptical, explaining that the water on the deck wasn't substantial evidence—it wouldn't hold up in court.

"I'm sorry, Sarah, but we need concrete evidence—fingerprints, a witness, a suspect with a clear motive. Right now, we have none of that," Nelson said, his tone firm yet laced with frustration. He wanted to find something substantial as much as she wanted to be believed. The weight of their mutual exasperation hung heavy in the air, leaving them both at an impasse.

Seeing that they struggled with similar obstacles, Sarah offered to assist him in the investigation. Detective Nelson flat out refused. He couldn't involve a civilian; it would jeopardize not only his job but his entire career. More importantly, if something happened to her, the city would be liable.

"Sarah, I understand your frustration," Nelson said, his tone firm but sympathetic. "But you have to trust that we're doing everything we can. Leave the investigating to us."

He ended the call, leaving her feeling detached and cut off, her world crumbling around her.

Sarah strolled down one of the quaint downtown streets of Clayton, the evening air crisp and filled with the mingling scents of coffee and blooming flowers. Normally, such an atmosphere would lift her spirits, but tonight, her mood was as dark as the encroaching night.

She passed by a small indie bookstore called Burke's Books. It's a place she'd visited many times in the past but hadn't been there in a while. Its warm, inviting glow spilling out onto the sidewalk through large glass windows. The cheerful ambiance felt like a cruel contrast to her inner turmoil. As she glanced inside, her heart nearly stopped.

There, at a small table near the back, sat Lucas, his head bent close in conversation with her friend Emily. The soft light illuminated their faces, casting a gentle glow that only made the scene more intimate. Sarah's breath caught in her throat as she saw their hands intertwined on the table between them.

She froze, unable to tear her eyes away from the sight. Emily's smile, Lucas's familiar, comforting presence—it all felt like a betrayal. The bookstore, once a place of comfort and escape, now felt suffocating, its walls closing in on her.

Heartbroken, Sarah turned and hurried away, her vision blurring with unshed tears. The vibrant downtown streets, usually full of life and color, seemed muted as she rushed past. Each step felt heavier, her shoulders weighed down by the shock. She didn't know where she was going, only that she needed to get away from the sight that had just shattered her world.

CHAPTER SEVENTEEN

Sarah lay in her apartment for days, the blinds drawn tight against the outside world. The days blurred together, each one an echo of the last, filled with nothing but a hollow ache. She barely ate, barely moved, her mind stuck on a loop of thoughts about Lucas and Emily. The betrayal she had witnessed gnawed at her, a constant reminder of her loneliness and confusion.

On the fourth day, something snapped. Sarah could no longer stand the silence, the stillness, the oppressive weight of her own thoughts. She needed to do something, anything, to break free from the mire of her despair. She decided to go to Ben's Place, the bar owned by Ben Summers. Ben had been kind, attentive, and she hoped seeing him might offer some solace.

She dressed quickly, not caring much about her appearance, and made her way to the bar. It was a warm day, the sun shining brightly, mocking her dark mood. As she pushed open the door to Ben's Place right as it opened at 11 a.m. , she felt a flicker of hope. But when she asked the bartender if Ben was around, she was told he wasn't working that day.

"Even the owner takes the day off now and then," the bartender said with a grin.

Disappointed but not defeated, Sarah fished out the business card Ben had given her at her art show. She stepped outside, took a deep breath, and dialed the number. It rang a few times before Ben answered, his voice a pleasant surprise.

"Hello?"

"Hi, Ben. It's Sarah Kellerman." The silence on the other end stretched uncomfortably, and Sarah's heart raced. Feeling self-conscious, she hurried on, "You gave me your card at my art show and said—"

"I remember, Sarah! No worries!" he said, his laughter warm and sincere. "You just caught me off guard for a second. It's great to hear from you. How have you been?"

She hesitated, unsure how to respond. His cheerful tone made her reluctant to dampen his mood. "I'm...I'm okay. Actually, I'm standing outside your bar, hoping we could talk, but they said you were off today."

"Yep, true. I generally take just one day off a week. Sorry you picked that day to show up. I wish I was there. I haven't seen you in, oh, probably a month or more."

She was genuinely touched that he had noticed her absence. "Yeah, I'm sorry about that. I've been really busy working on some new paintings." The lie tasted bitter, but she couldn't bring herself to reveal the real reason she had disappeared from her own social life. "I'm sorry I missed you. Maybe I can catch you later in the week at your bar."

"I'm free today if you want to meet up."

His offer caught her off guard, leaving her momentarily speechless. Before she could fully process, the words tumbled out of her mouth. "Sure. Where would you like to meet?"

"How about my place? It's not a five-star resort," he laughed, "but it's comfortable."

He surprised her again. She hadn't expected an invitation to his place. "Okay," she said, intrigued. "What's your address?"

He gave her his address, which was on Gravois Avenue, a busy road in south St. Louis City, near the Bevo Mill. The neighborhood was a far cry from the upscale area where Sarah lived. The houses were smaller, older, and the streets had a rougher, more lived-in look.

Ben lived in a grand corner building that had stood for over a century. Once a sprawling single-family home, it had been transformed decades ago by a general practitioner into multiple units, with the doctor's office occupying the ground floor. The building's age and history lent it a unique charm, with original architectural details hinting at its past life.

Sarah parked her BMW on a narrow side street that intersected with Gravois, right at the corner of Ben's building.

As she walked to the front of Ben's apartment building, she felt a mix of curiosity and apprehension. The building was modest but well-kept. She climbed the narrow staircase to the second floor and knocked on his door. Ben opened it almost immediately, a warm smile on his face.

"Sarah, come in."

She stepped inside, taking in her surroundings. The apartment was small but cozy, filled with personal touches that gave it character. Bookshelves lined the walls, crammed with an eclectic mix of novels, travel guides, and cookbooks. Art prints and posters decorated the space, and a guitar rested in one corner. It was a stark contrast to her own apartment's vast open spaces and high ceilings, with its wall of windows overlooking the city. The intimacy and personal touches of Ben's place felt both comforting and a little overwhelming.

"Nice place," she said, trying to sound casual.

"Thanks," Ben replied. "It's not much, but it's home. Can I get you something to drink?"

"Just water, please."

After getting them both bottles of water, they sat down in the living room, side by side on the sofa, and Sarah took a moment to gather her thoughts. Ben watched her with an open, patient expression, waiting for her to speak.

"I don't really know where to start," she began. "Everything's such a mess right now."

After a moment, Sarah leaned forward, resting her elbows on her knees and clasping her hands tightly. She took a deep, steadying breath, her eyes flickering with uncertainty as she searched for the right words to start her story.

Ben adjusted himself on the sofa, his movements careful as he leaned back, ensuring he gave Sarah the space she needed while trying to read the subtleties of her body language. "Does this have to do with what you told me at the country club about your father?" he asked, his voice soft but probing.

She nodded solemnly, the weight of her unspoken words heavy in the air.

"Take your time," Ben said gently. "I'm here to listen."

She turned to face him, her eyes intense as she began to unravel everything—the suspicions gnawing at her, the confrontation with Lucas, and the unsettling photos. She explained her theories, meticulously detailing the minute observations that convinced her something was terribly wrong. Ben listened intently, his gaze fixed on hers, absorbing every word.

Then she dropped a bombshell. "And then there's the death of James Harris."

"Who?" Ben interrupted, clearly taken aback for the first time.

"The junior lawyer at my dad's law firm. The one whose car accelerated out of control."

Ben's eyes widened in shock. "Downtown?"

"Yeah."

"Oh my god! I saw that on the news, but I had no idea he was connected to your father."

Sarah nodded, the weight of her words hanging in the air between them. "It's all speculation, of course," she admitted. "But I can't shake the feeling that there's something more to all of it."

Ben nodded thoughtfully. "You have a keen eye. It makes sense, considering your art. You notice things others might overlook."

"That's exactly it," she said, feeling a small surge of validation. "It's how I capture images in my paintings. I see the little things, the details that tell the bigger story."

They spent the day together, their conversation moving fluidly between Sarah's current situation and their pasts. She learned that Ben had moved out of his home at 19 , eager to carve his own path. He wasn't estranged from his parents, or anything like that, but they weren't particularly close either. He had a brother he occasionally saw, but his family ties were loose.

"My parents are good people," he said, "but we just don't have much in common. I always felt like I needed to find my own way."

Sarah shared bits of her own history, how she had always been close to her parents. They had nurtured her artistic talents, encouraging her to pursue her passions. How their passing had left a gaping hole in her life, one that she was struggling to fill.

As the afternoon turned into evening, they grew more comfortable with each other. The initial awkwardness faded, replaced by a sense of camaraderie. Ben's easygoing nature was a balm to Sarah's frayed nerves, and she found herself relaxing in his presence.

He took her to a hole-in-the-wall pizza place he loved, Arch City Pizzeria, tucked away off Lindell Boulevard in Midtown. She'd heard of it but had never tried it. They ordered a veggie pizza, and she sensed he chose it knowing it was her favorite. If he were alone, she guessed he'd have indulged in a sausage and pepperoni combo, maybe with mushrooms. When she offered to pay, he insisted on picking up the tab, flashing her a warm smile.

"I'm really glad you called," Ben said as they sat on his small balcony, watching the sunset. "I know things are tough right now, but you're not alone in this."

Sarah smiled, a genuine smile that felt foreign after so many days of sadness. "Thank you, Ben. I needed this more than I realized."

They sat in a comfortable silence for a while, the city sounds drifting up from the street below.

CHAPTER EIGHTEEN

*D*ays passed quietly, each blending into the next with a somber stillness that seemed to pervade Sarah's life. She felt like she was moving through a thick fog, unable to see what lay ahead and barely aware of what she left behind.

One evening, as Sarah sat by her window staring blankly at the darkening sky, her phone rang. The sound was jarring in the silence, and she jumped slightly before reaching for it. Seeing Ben's name on the screen brought a small, fleeting smile to her lips. She took a deep breath and answered.

"Hey, Ben," she said, trying to sound more upbeat than she felt.

"Hi, Sarah. How are you holding up?" Ben's voice was gentle, filled with kindness and concern.

She hesitated, not wanting to burden him with her sadness but also not having the energy to pretend everything was okay. "I'm... managing," she finally replied.

"I've been thinking about you a lot. I wanted to give you some space, but I also wanted you to know that I'm here if you need anything."

Sarah felt a lump in her throat and swallowed hard. "Thank you, Ben." After a long pause, she added softly, "I've been thinking a lot about you too."

Gratitude washed over him, and they slipped into a comfortable rhythm of small talk, discussing mundane topics like upcoming events and the new coffee shop that had just opened in town. It was a relief to focus on something so ordinary, even if only for a few minutes. But Sarah knew that Ben had called for a reason, and she could sense that he was leading up to something more serious.

"Sarah," Ben began, his tone shifting slightly, "I've been thinking about something you said the last time we talked. About your father's laptop. Do you think you should retrieve it? Or at least see the files on it?"

Sarah's heart tightened. She had been avoiding thinking about it, pushing it to the back of her mind where all the painful things seemed to end up. "I know it's probably something I should do," she said quietly. "I just...I haven't been able to bring myself to go back to the mansion."

Ben was silent for a moment, and she could almost hear him choosing his words carefully. "I understand. It must be incredibly difficult to even think about going there. But if, as the detective said, you need real evidence, then..."

Sarah knew he was right, but the thought of going back to the mansion filled her with dread. "I just...I don't know if I can do it, Ben."

"You don't have to do it alone," Ben said firmly. "I'll go with you. We can do this together."

The sincerity in his voice made Sarah's resolve waver. She didn't want to face the mansion or what she might find there, but she also didn't want to let her father down. She took a deep breath, trying to muster the strength she needed. "Okay," she said finally. "Let's do it."

"We don't have to rush. We can go whenever you're ready."

"The sooner, the better," Sarah said, her voice steadier than she felt. "The longer I wait, the harder it will be."

"Alright," Ben said. "How about tomorrow morning?"

The silence stretched on, so long that Ben began to wonder if the call had dropped. He could almost hear his own heartbeat in the quiet. "Sarah?"

"I'm here. Sorry, just thinking. How about we go this evening, after it gets dark? That way we won't draw any attention from the neighbors. My neighbors are great, but I don't want to deal with their condolences and questions right now."

"That sounds like a good idea."

After they hung up, Sarah sat in the darkness for a long time, trying to prepare herself for what lay ahead.

As night fell, Sarah's anxiety grew with the encroaching darkness. She dressed slowly, opting for jeans and a cozy sweater, prioritizing comfort over style. Ben texted her when he arrived and parked discreetly in front of her building. They had agreed to meet there, near his bar, knowing they'd likely need a drink afterward. Sarah suggested taking her BMW to the mansion; the neighbors would recognize it as hers and not raise suspicions. Ben's car, on the other hand, might draw unwanted attention and a call to the police.

Ben greeted her with a warm smile in the lobby when she stepped off the elevator, but she could see the concern in his eyes. "Ready?" he asked gently.

"As ready as I'll ever be," she replied.

The drive to the mansion was quiet, each of them lost in their own thoughts. As they pulled up to the large, imposing gates, Sarah felt a wave of nausea. She clenched her fists, trying to steady herself.

"We can do this," Ben said, as if reading her mind. "Together."

The mansion loomed ahead, its windows dark and foreboding. Sarah parked her BMW in the shadow of a moonlit tree, its branches casting eerie patterns on the ground. She and Ben approached the front door, the concrete driveway echoing their footsteps in the still night. Sarah's hand trembled as she inserted the key, hesitating for a moment before finally turning the lock. As the door creaked open, a wave of memories crashed over her. The familiar scent of the house filled her nostrils, making her almost see her father—or even her mother—coming down the stairs to welcome her.

Ben glanced around for the light switches, but Sarah quickly stopped him. "I'd rather not have the neighbors see the place lit up."

He nodded, understanding her caution. The mansion's numerous large windows allowed the moonlight to filter in, casting an eerie yet sufficient glow throughout the entire interior. For now, the silvery illumination was enough to navigate by.

Ben placed a firm, reassuring hand on her shoulder. "You said the laptop was in his office?"

"Yes," she said, and took a deep breath, steeling herself for what lay ahead.

They ascended the wide staircase side by side, the air thick with tension. As they passed the painting that had set Sarah on this path of discovery, she couldn't help but steal a glance. As before, the colors seemed more reddish than she remembered, even more so than the last time she looked at it. She dismissed it as a trick of her anxious mind.

Ben's gaze lingered on the painting as well, recognizing her signature style. He was tempted to tell her how beautiful it was, a testament to her talent and brilliance, but he knew this wasn't the time for compliments. They had a mission to focus on, and distractions could come later.

They reached the second floor, walked down the dark hallway, and entered Anthony's office, the air inside heavy with a mix of anticipation and dread. The room, lined with dark wood shelves and leather-bound books, felt like a shrine to Anthony's meticulous nature. Everything was in its place, as if he had just stepped out and would return any moment.

Sarah moved to the large mahogany desk, her fingers trailing over its polished surface before coming to rest on the laptop. The sleek device seemed out of place amidst the room's old-world charm. She took a deep breath, glancing at Ben, who gave her an encouraging nod.

With a determined exhale, Sarah opened the laptop and pressed the power button. The screen flickered to life, illuminating the room with a cold, blue glow. She navigated through the login screen with ease, entering her father's password, a combination she knew by heart.

The desktop appeared, cluttered with files and folders, each one a potential piece of the puzzle they were trying to solve. Sarah clicked through the directories, but the sheer volume of documents made it impossible to pinpoint anything significant. Frustration began to gnaw at her.

"There are so many files," she muttered, her voice tinged with helplessness. "How are we supposed to find anything in this mess?"

Ben leaned over her shoulder, scanning the screen. "We need to look for something unusual. Anything that stands out. Of course, it would have to be you who noticed something. I would have no clue."

Sarah nodded, continuing to sift through the digital clutter. As she did, a small detail caught her eye—a timestamp on the system log. She clicked on it, bringing up a more detailed view.

"Ben, look at this," she said, her voice suddenly sharp with focus. "The last login was at 7:08 a.m. on the morning of my father's death."

Ben frowned, trying to make sense of the information. "And that's significant because...?"

"My father always took a swim at exactly 7 a.m.," Sarah explained. "It was part of his daily routine. He never deviated from it, not once. If he logged in at 7:08, something must have happened right after he got in the pool."

"I don't understand," Ben said. Then realization suddenly dawned on him. "Are you saying he was murdered right after he started his swim, and then the killer accessed his laptop?"

Sarah nodded, her heart pounding in her chest. "It's the only thing that makes sense. My father wouldn't have interrupted his swim for anything. Someone must have known his routine and waited for him."

"We need to find out what they were looking for," Ben said, his voice steady despite the tension. "There must be something on this laptop that was important enough to kill for."

Suddenly, a noise broke the stillness—a faint shuffling sound coming from downstairs. Sarah's heart skipped a beat, her eyes wide with fear. Ben, sensing her panic, quickly stepped in front of her, his face set with determination.

"Stay here," he whispered urgently. "I'll go check it out."

Sarah nodded, her hands trembling. Ben grabbed a poker from the office fireplace, its weight solid and reassuring in his grip. He crept towards the door, moving as silently as possible. The mansion's grand staircase loomed ahead, bathed in shadows and moonlight. As he descended the stairs, each step felt like an eternity, the silence amplifying the pounding of his heart as he inched forward with painstaking stealth.

Reaching the first floor, Ben pressed himself against the wall, peering into the living room. A silhouette moved through the darkness, a flashlight beam cutting through the gloom like a knife. The intruder was methodical, scanning each corner and surface, his movements deliberate and unhurried.

Ben's pulse pounded in his ears as he edged closer, keeping his breathing steady. The man moved to the staircase, and Ben's stomach tightened. He had to act before the intruder made it upstairs. Summoning all his courage, Ben took a step forward, and as his shoe met the marble floor, it betrayed him with a soft, traitorous squeak.

The flashlight beam snapped towards him, blinding in its intensity. Ben froze, his heart racing. The silhouette's grip tightened around something metal—a handgun. The intruder cocked the weapon, the sound sharp and menacing in the still air.

CHAPTER NINETEEN

*S*arah knew she couldn't sit by and let Ben face the intruder alone. As soon as he descended the stairs and vanished from sight, she grabbed the fireplace shovel from her father's office and stepped into the hallway. She crept silently through the darkened corridor, her heart pounding like a drum in her chest. Clutching the cold metal handle gave her a shaky sense of security, but the thought of actually using it sent chills down her spine. Each step made the reality of the situation more tangible. The mansion, once a beacon of grandeur and beauty, now felt like an oppressive labyrinth of shadows, each one seemingly reaching out to ensnare her.

As she edged toward the grand staircase, Sarah moved with the stealth of a cat, every step deliberate and soundless. Despite her careful movements, every footfall seemed to echo unnaturally loud in the oppressive stillness of the night. She paused at the top of the stairs, her breath catching in her throat as her eyes scanned the scene below. The dim light from the windows cast eerie shadows, turning the familiar grandeur of the foyer into a menacing tableau.

At first, the foyer at the bottom of the stairs was as still as one of her paintings. Then, suddenly, a sharp white line of a flashlight beam sliced through the darkness, and a silhouetted figure emerged, clutching the light source. The faint moonlight cast an eerie glow around him, making him appear almost ghostly. The sight made Sarah freeze. Terror gripped her as the person stepped to the base of the stairs, poised to ascend and bring them face-to-face. A noise echoed from behind the figure—a clumsy step, perhaps. The figure whirled around, focusing intently on something—or someone—just out of her line of sight. Sarah knew it was Ben.

Suddenly, she saw the glint of a gun in the man's hand, aimed directly at Ben. Panic surged through her, but she knew she had to act immediately. Summoning every ounce of courage, Sarah gripped the shovel tightly and descended the stairs as swiftly and silently as possible.

"Drop your weapon!" the intruder shouted with what seemed like the kind of authority one can only get from being trained. Ben immediately let go of the fireplace poker, which clanged loudly on the floor. The noise reverberated through the silent house, and Sarah recognized her opportunity. With her heart pounding and adrenaline coursing through her veins, she bolted down the stairs, rapidly closing the distance between herself and the gunman.

In her haste, the sound of her footsteps drew his attention. As he pivoted to face her, Sarah didn't hesitate. She swung the shovel with every bit of strength she had, aiming for a decisive blow that could save both her and Ben's lives.

The impact sent the man sprawling onto the floor, his gun and flashlight clattering away from him. Ben's eyes widened in shock, and he instantly darted forward, snatching up the flashlight and aiming its beam at the prone figure. The man groaned and rolled onto his back, one hand rubbing the sore spot on his head where the shovel had struck. The light revealed his face, and Sarah gasped.

"Detective Nelson?" she exclaimed, lowering the shovel slightly.

Nelson, still grimacing from the pain, looked up at them. "Yeah, it's me," he muttered, his voice thick with annoyance. "Nice to see you too, Sarah."

Sarah felt a rush of guilt and embarrassment flood through her. She had just assaulted a police detective. "You should have called out instead of sneaking around. I thought you were a burglar!"

Nelson's lips curled into a sardonic smile as he pushed himself into a sitting position. "And here I thought I'd stumbled upon a burglary in progress. Looks like we were both mistaken." He climbed to his feet, still grinning as he rubbed the back of his head. "I should arrest you for assaulting a police officer," he said with a playful glint in his eye.

Ben was not amused as he stepped forward, his face set in a determined expression. "Detective, this mansion is now owned by Sarah. You had no right to be here without a warrant. As far as we knew, you were an intruder. Unless you have a warrant, you're trespassing."

"I'm just joking, kid."

"What are you doing here?" Sarah asked.

"I came to get the laptop," the detective said.

Ben threw a curious look at Sarah. "The laptop seems to be pretty popular these days."

Nelson glanced at Sarah, who nodded, signaling it was okay to discuss the matter.

"The case has been reopened," Nelson said as he retrieved his gun from the floor and extended his hand to Ben for the flashlight. Ben handed it over as Sarah switched on the foyer lights, illuminating the room and casting sharp shadows around them.

"Is there new evidence in Sarah's dad's case?" Ben asked.

Nelson sighed, rubbing his head in frustration. "And who are you?" he asked, directing his gaze at Ben.

"A friend," Sarah interjected before Ben could respond, immediately feeling a pang of guilt. She mouthed 'sorry' to him. Ben smiled and waved it off, reassuring her it was fine.

But Ben, thoroughly baffled by the situation, turned his attention back to Detective Nelson. "Aren't there official channels for obtaining evidence? It seems odd for the police to be sneaking around a private residence without permission."

Nelson looked at Sarah, silently pleading for assistance. Sarah turned to Ben. "The case isn't officially reopened."

Realization dawned on Ben. "So, you're doing this off the record?"

"Not that it's any of your business," Nelson interjected, "but Sarah can fill you in if she chooses." He turned to Sarah. "May I get the laptop?"

She nodded, and the detective traipsed up the stairs to retrieve the laptop from Anthony's office. He didn't need directions; he had been there on the day of Anthony's death.

Ben waited until the detective was out of sight before turning to Sarah and asking quietly, "Why would he come sneaking around here at night?"

"Well, we're here at night, sneaking around, and it's my house," she replied with a chuckle.

"You know what I mean," he said, smirking.

"He's doing this on his own time, so like us, he's keeping a low profile."

"Okay, but I'm alarmed by this approach."

"Well, he got whacked on the head for his trouble, so I can cut him some slack."

"Whacked on the head by you, by the way," Ben playfully reminded her.

"True."

"Remind me never to get on your bad side."

They both laughed as Detective Nelson descended the steps, the silver laptop under his arm. "Are you laughing at me?" he asked, grinning.

Sarah smiled. "Not at you specifically. More at the situation."

"It's okay. It's kind of funny, actually," Nelson said, holding up the laptop. "Anyway, thanks for this. I'll make sure it's returned as soon as possible," he said, his tone sincere. "And I'll try to avoid any more late-night visits. I'm sorry for startling you both. I should have handled this differently. Now, if you'll excuse me."

"Have a good night, Detective," Sarah said.

"I said you can call me Brock."

"I know but I never felt comfortable with that."

"Fair enough," Nelson said as he headed for the front door.

"Detective?" Ben called out, causing Nelson to turn back. "How did you get into the house, anyway?"

"I have a key," Nelson replied without missing a beat. "I copied it from the one Sarah loaned me."

Sarah's eyes widened in shock. "Is that standard police procedure?"

"No," Nelson admitted, "but when the surveillance camera at the pool failed, I made a copy just in case this turned into a murder investigation. Don't worry. I'll destroy it once the case is truly closed. Just like you'll destroy the file I gave you. Any other questions?"

Sarah slowly shook her head. With a curt nod, Detective Nelson exited through the front door.

Ben turned to Sarah, his eyebrows raised. "This cop is a seriously weird dude."

She let out a long breath, shaking her head in disbelief. "Let's get out of here."

Ben and Sarah left the mansion in silence, the weight of the evening's events hanging heavily between them. The moon cast a pale glow over the grand estate, its once welcoming facade now seeming cold and uninviting. The drive back to Ben's apartment was quiet, each lost in their own thoughts, the tension gradually giving way to exhaustion.

Ben flicked on the light, and the small apartment sprang to life. The comfy space, with its mismatched furniture and budget decor, felt intimate after the mansion's sprawling luxury. Sarah's lips curved into a smile, finding surprising comfort in the contrast after the evening's whirlwind of high drama.

"And so, we return to my humble abode," Ben said with a wry smile, his eyes twinkling. He caught the glimmer in her eyes, a silent acknowledgment of the difference.

"It's cozy," she replied sincerely as she stepped inside.

Ben laughed, a sound that seemed to release some of the tension between them. "Yeah, cozy. That's one way to put it. Wine?"

"Please," Sarah said, sinking into the worn-out sofa.

Ben opened the fridge and retrieved a half-empty bottle of red wine, then grabbed two glasses from the cabinet. With a practiced twist, he popped off the cork and poured them each a generous amount before handing her a glass. "If I were doing this right, I'd let the bottle reach room temperature first, but given tonight..." He raised his glass. They clinked glasses silently and took their first sips, savoring how the wine's warmth began to soothe their frayed nerves.

"Thank you," Ben said after a moment, his voice soft. "For saving my life back there. If you hadn't..."

Sarah shook her head, cutting him off. "Don't. I did what anyone would have done."

"No," Ben insisted, setting his glass down. "You did more than that. You were brave, and you kept your head when things went sideways. I owe you, Sarah."

Sarah looked into his eyes, seeing the sincerity there. "And I owe you for standing up for me against Detective Nelson. That took guts."

They fell into a comfortable silence, sipping their wine, the adrenaline of the night slowly giving way to a sense of camaraderie. Ben moved closer to Sarah on the sofa, his knee brushing against hers. The touch was electric, sending a jolt through both of them.

Before they knew it, they were leaning into each other, their faces inches apart. Ben hesitated for a moment, his eyes searching hers for any sign of hesitation. When he found none, he closed the distance and kissed her. The kiss was soft at first, tentative, but quickly grew more passionate as weeks of unspoken feelings and tension melted away.

Sarah responded eagerly, her hands tangling in his hair, pulling him closer. Ben's hands roamed her back, holding her tight. The world outside ceased to exist; there was only the two of them, the intensity of their connection burning away any lingering doubts.

But as the kiss deepened, Sarah suddenly pulled back, her breath ragged. "Ben, wait," she said, her voice shaky. "I have… a boyfriend."

Ben froze, his eyes wide. "I'm sorry. I thought you and Lucas were…having problems."

Sarah nodded, the reality crashing down on her. "We are. But still…" She hesitated, her mind racing, then continued with resolve. "He's barely been around. It feels like he's abandoned me. I don't even know where he is half the time. I've been so alone, and tonight… tonight you were there for me."

Ben cupped her face in his hands, his eyes filled with understanding. "Sarah, you deserve someone who's there for you, who cares about you. Not someone who leaves you to face everything on your own."

Tears welled up in Sarah's eyes as the truth of his words sank in. Lucas had been distant, wrapped up in his own world, dismissing her concerns without a second thought, and now possibly entangled with one of her friends. But Ben was here – supportive and present. She leaned in and kissed him again, this time without hesitation.

They stumbled towards the bedroom, the air between them thick with desire, an unspoken urgency driving their movements. They fumbled with buttons and zippers, their fingers shaky with anticipation and the need to feel their skin pressed together, their clothes a trail behind them, each discarded piece marking a step closer to the sanctuary they sought.

Once inside the bedroom, they fell onto the bed, their bodies entwined, the soft sheets cradling them as they embraced each other. Their lips met in a feverish kiss, mouths moving in a desperate dance, tasting and exploring. Sarah's hands roamed over Ben's back as his hands mapped out the curves of her body with a reverence that belied the urgency of their need. His fingers traced the delicate line of her collarbone, moved lower to cup her breasts, thumbs brushing over her hardened nipples. Sarah's breath hitched at his touch, her body arching into him, seeking more. Ben obliged, his lips leaving hers to travel down her neck, planting hot, open-mouthed kisses along the way.

The depth of their intimacy was sparked by a night of potent feelings, each touch a plea for connection, each kiss a promise of solace. They moved with a rhythm born of desperation and need, their bodies responding to each other with an instinctive understanding. Sarah's hands threaded through Ben's hair, pulling him closer, her hips lifting to meet his in a raw expression of passion.

As Ben's kisses moved lower, his hands followed, caressing the soft skin of her stomach, her hips, her thighs. Sarah's body trembled beneath his touch, each caress sending shivers of pleasure coursing through her. When his lips finally reached the apex of her thighs, she gasped, her fingers tightening in his hair. Ben paused for a moment, his breath hot against her skin, before his tongue flicked out, tasting her.

Sarah's back arched off the bed, a moan escaping her lips as Ben worshipped her with his mouth. His hands held her hips steady, his tongue working magic that left her breathless and wanting. The sensations built within her, a pressure that grew and grew until she thought she might explode. Just when she thought she couldn't take it anymore, Ben pulled back, his eyes dark with desire as he moved up her body to kiss her deeply, letting her taste herself on his lips.

Their bodies moved together with an intensity that bordered on frantic, the need to be close, to feel, overriding everything else. Sarah wrapped her legs around Ben, pulling him closer, needing to feel him inside her. Ben responded, positioning himself at her entrance and pushing into her slowly, inch by inch, until he was fully seated within her. They both stilled for a moment, savoring the feeling of being joined, hearts beating in unison.

Then they began to move, a slow, sensual rhythm at first that quickly built into something more urgent. Each thrust, each movement, was a testament to the depth of their connection, a physical manifestation of the emotions that had been building between them all night. Their bodies slick with sweat, they moved together as one with a desire that consumed them both.

Sarah held Ben tightly, her breath coming in short, ragged gasps. Ben's hands gripped her hips, his thrusts becoming more forceful, more demanding. The pleasure built between them, a crescendo that grew and grew until it finally crashed over them both in a wave of ecstasy. Sarah cried out, her body shaking with the force of her release, Ben following her over the edge moments later.

Exhausted, they lay together, their arms and legs entwined, the room filled with the sound of their heavy breathing as they came down from their high. As they drifted off to sleep, the world outside faded away, leaving only the two of them, bound together by the intensity of their emotions and the aftermath of their lovemaking.

Outside the apartment, a man dressed in dark, casual clothes lurked in the shadows, his presence barely more than a wisp of darkness against the night. He stood perfectly still, his gaze unwavering, locked onto the window of Ben's apartment. He had been tailing them since they left the mansion, his movements silent and deliberate, always maintaining a careful distance. He was ordered to simply watch and follow, and he was finished for the night. A sinister smile crept across his face, and with one last glance, he melted into the darkness, leaving no trace of his presence, like a ghost slipping back into the void.

CHAPTER TWENTY

*T*he morning sunlight streamed through the windows of the Metro Diner on Grand Avenue in south St. Louis city, casting a warm glow over the checkered floors. The aroma of fresh coffee mingled with the scent of sizzling bacon, creating an inviting atmosphere. Sarah and Ben sat in a corner booth, the events of the previous night lingering between them like an unspoken secret.

They busied themselves with the menus, though neither seemed particularly interested in the food. A waitress appeared, filling their coffee cups with a friendly smile and taking their orders. Once she retreated to the kitchen, they were left in an awkward silence.

As the clatter of dishes and murmur of conversations surrounded them, Ben drummed his fingers on the table, the silence between them becoming almost palpable.

"So," Ben began, his voice carefully casual, "where does last night leave us?"

Sarah glanced up, her stomach tightening at his words. "I...don't know, Ben."

He hesitated, then met her eyes. "What do you think it means for us?"

She sighed, tracing the edge of her coffee cup with her finger. "I'm not sure. There's a lot happening right now. Too much, really. I don't know if I can handle adding more to the mix."

Ben leaned back in his seat, studying her. "Is it Lucas?"

Sarah's eyes flickered with uncertainty. "Partly. I'm trying to figure things out with him. And Emily. Seeing them together could be nothing, but...I don't think it is."

Ben's jaw tightened, and he reached across the table, taking her hand gently. "I get it, Sarah. But we can't pretend last night didn't happen. We can't just sweep it under the rug."

Sarah squeezed his hand, her eyes pleading with him to understand. "I need some time to sort things out with Lucas."

Ben's expression softened, and he gently withdrew his hand. "Is it really about Lucas, or is there something else on your mind?"

Sarah frowned. "What do you mean?"

Ben looked down for a moment, choosing his words carefully. "Is it about who I am? Because... I know I don't quite fit into your world."

Sarah's eyes widened in surprise. "No, Ben. That's not true. It's just...my life is a mess right now. I can't handle another relationship on top of everything else."

Ben looked at her for a long moment, his expression a blend of sadness and understanding. "Alright," he said softly. "I respect your wishes."

Sarah nodded, her heart heavy. "Thank you. It's just for now, I promise. Things are just... complicated."

Ben smiled as he ran a hand through his hair. "Yeah, complicated seems to be the theme lately."

"For sure," Sarah agreed, her smile fading as the reality of their situation settled back in. "I just...I don't want to hurt anyone."

Ben nodded, his expression serious again. "I know. But sometimes, trying not to hurt anyone ends up hurting everyone."

Sarah sighed, knowing he was right but still feeling trapped. "I just need more time."

He leaned in closer, his voice gentle and comforting. "Take all the time you need, Sarah. I'll be here."

Their food arrived, providing a welcome distraction. They ate in silence for a while, the tension slowly easing as they focused on their breakfast.

"Would you want to talk about your father's case?" Ben asked gingerly, concerned that he might be venturing into forbidden territory.

Sarah gave him an appreciative nod. Her father's murder was never far from her mind, and since her other friends had made their dismissive views clear, she was more than happy to discuss it with Ben. He was the only one who seemed to understand.

The waitress returned, refilling their coffee. They waited until after she left before continuing their conversation.

"If it wasn't for the oddity of James Harris's death, my father's death would have remained closed," Sarah said as she shook her head and pushed her scrambled eggs around on her plate. "I feel terrible even thinking about it that way."

Ben looked at her intently, his fork paused halfway to his mouth. "I don't know what you mean."

"Well... I'm glad that Detective Nelson is investigating what happened to my father, but it's awful that it took the death of James for it to happen."

Ben solemnly nodded, setting his fork down and leaning in closer. "Don't feel bad. You wanted your father's death investigated, but it's not like you wanted someone else to die for it to happen. And James dying brings another element to it, assuming they are related."

"What 'element'?" Sarah asked, her brow furrowing.

"It means whoever is responsible is getting desperate."

Sarah's eyes widened with sudden realization. "Yes! This person must've murdered James to cover their tracks, and all they've done is expose themselves to being discovered."

Ben's heart skipped a beat. "Exactly. It also means the killer might not be finished. Maybe all of the lawyers at your dad's firm are in danger."

Sarah's jaw dropped. She hadn't thought of that. "You really think they might go after more people?"

"It's possible," Ben said thoughtfully, his eyes scanning the bustling diner as if he might spot the culprit among the patrons. "If they're desperate enough to kill James to cover their tracks, who knows what else they might do?"

Sarah looked down, her mind racing with the implications.

"Did you tell Detective Nelson about the flash drive Stephen asked you to retrieve from your father's safe?"

Sarah shook her head. "No, I didn't think it was important. But now, I'm starting to wonder if it might be."

"Did your father normally keep flash drives in his safe?"

"Not really. But I didn't really question it. I just figured whatever he kept in his safe was more important than what he kept in his file cabinet. Or it could simply mean he wanted to make sure he didn't lose it."

Ben shrugged and sipped his coffee. He set his cup down and looked her in the eyes. "Could it be that the flash drive really contained info worth killing for?"

Sarah looked down and closed her eyes, the weight of the moment pressing heavily on her. She had been avoiding this realization, the grim possibility that someone might kill for the contents of the drive. The thought had flickered through her mind before, but she had always pushed it aside, unwilling to confront the dark reality.

Then she spoke so softly that Ben had to lean in to catch her words. "Should we warn Stephen? He's the lawyer who requested it." Her expression darkened as she stirred her coffee absently. "But he'd probably think I'm crazy, just like everyone else."

Ben reached across the table and squeezed her hand, his touch warm and reassuring. "Not everyone."

She smiled at him, a flicker of relief in her eyes. "It's good to know I'm not completely alone in this."

"But we should definitely tell Detective Nelson," Ben said, his mind racing. "He needs to know everything."

Sarah nodded slowly, absorbing the weight of the revelation. "Agreed. I should go see him today. Right now, in fact."

"I'll go with you," he said, then hesitated. "That is if you don't mind."

"Of course not. We went on the adventure to the mansion together. No reason you shouldn't go on this one too."

Ben laughed softly, then grew quiet as the gravity of the situation settled on him. "What do you think was on this flash drive?"

"Stephen said it was important for some pending cases and that my father was going to give it to him that day after…" She caught herself, unable to finish the thought.

"It's okay," Ben said softly, with compassion in his eyes. "You don't have to say it."

The conversation shifted to memories of Sarah's father, her voice soft and reflective. She shared more stories of her childhood, her father's laughter echoing in her mind, and though the gravity of the situation was ever-present, her memories brought a fleeting sense of normalcy. Ben listened, offering comfort and a few stories of his own childhood, creating a momentary oasis in their storm of uncertainty.

The diner buzzed with life around them. A child's laughter echoed from a nearby booth, and the clatter of dishes filled the air. The waitress checked on them again, her cheerful demeanor a stark contrast to the heavy conversation. They picked at their meals, neither truly tasting the food in front of them. The vibrant chatter and clinking silverware seemed almost distant, like a soundtrack to a scene they weren't fully part of.

As they finished their meal, the diner had filled up with the lunch crowd, but Sarah barely noticed. She was lost in her thoughts, trying to piece together the puzzle of her father's death. As they walked out, Ben put his arm around her, offering silent support. She leaned into him, grateful for his presence.

Sarah called Detective Nelson, telling him she had something important to discuss in person. She and Ben drove separately to the police station since Ben needed to head to his bar afterward. They arrived and parked, meeting at the entrance before walking in together, their steps in unspoken synchronization. Detective Nelson greeted them with a nod, his expression serious and filled with expectation.

Before Sarah could tell him anything, he interrupted her. "I need to interview you both separately," he said, surprising them both.

"Why?" Sarah asked, stunned.

"You're both suspects," Nelson said.

Ben's mouth dropped open. "Suspects?!?"

Nelson's expression remained impassive. "It's standard procedure to consider everyone who knew the victim to be a potential suspect, especially in cases like this, given the circumstances."

Sarah felt dizzy. "Circumstances? What circumstances?"

Nelson's gaze was steady. "The fact that you benefited significantly from your father's death, Sarah. And Ben, your relationship with Sarah could be seen as a motive since you're not part of her social circle and seemed to have conveniently appeared in her life."

Ben gaped in disbelief and disgust at the detective's insinuation.

"Yeah," Nelson said. "I asked around. I'm a detective, that's what I do."

Sarah's mind raced, her thoughts a jumble of disbelief and fear. "This is insane. I loved my father. I would never—"

Sarah's head swam, and she had to steady herself. Ben's reassuring touch on her shoulder grounded her, reminding her she wasn't alone.

"We're leaving now," she declared defiantly to Nelson.

Nelson's response was immediate and stern. "I have the right to detain you for questioning without arresting you."

Ben, undeterred, asked, "What if we refuse?"

Nelson's eyes hardened. "Then I can arrest you both. But that would be much messier for everyone involved."

Sarah and Ben exchanged tense glances, a silent acknowledgment passing between them. They were losing this high-stakes game of poker, and Nelson held all the aces.

He decided to start with Ben. The young man sat nervously, his hands clasped tightly together on the table, eyes darting around the room. The harsh fluorescent lights overhead cast stark shadows across his face. Nelson's presence was intimidating, and he used it to his advantage, leaning forward to loom over Ben.

Nelson inquired about how Ben and Sarah first met. Ben described the unexpected moment: she had wandered into his bar one afternoon and was immediately struck by the sight of one of her own paintings adorning the wall. Despite being an admirer of her work, Ben insisted he didn't recognize her at first. Skeptical, Nelson pressed harder, finding it improbable that a fan like Ben wouldn't recognize Sarah immediately. The detective then zeroed in on the crux of his interrogation: had Ben stalked Sarah? Did he intentionally rent the bar's location to be near her?

Ben was taken aback, his shock turning into a vehement denial. He shouted at Nelson, calling the accusations absurd. He claimed he had no idea where Sarah lived and had chosen the bar's location based purely on demographics—a fact he could prove. Ben argued that not recognizing her was plausible, given how inconceivable it seemed that she'd randomly wander into his establishment. Besides, she had subtly disguised herself that day.

Yes, he admitted, he was attracted to her, especially after discovering her true identity, but as far as he knew, that wasn't a crime. After hours of relentless badgering, Ben slumped in the uncomfortable chair, utterly exhausted. Satisfied for now, Nelson told him to stay put while he moved on to question Sarah.

He moved to the adjacent room where Sarah waited. She looked calmer than Ben, but her eyes betrayed a lingering sadness. The sterile environment of the interrogation room seemed to amplify the emotional burden she carried. Nelson sat across from her, his gaze steady, dissecting every nuance of her demeanor.

"You came to discuss something with me, right?" he asked, his eyes probing hers.

"Yes," Sarah replied, her irritation palpable. She regretted coming here now, more than ever.

"What would that be?" he inquired, leaning forward slightly.

"I retrieved a flash drive labeled 'confidential' from my father's home safe," she began, her voice steady but tense. "One of the attorneys at his firm requested it. He said it contained crucial information about some legal cases my dad was handling and that my dad intended to give it to him."

"And the attorney's name?"

"Stephen Millstadt."

Detective Nelson paused, jotting the name on a pad of paper before looking back at her. "And why would you think I'd consider that important?" he asked, his tone indifferent, almost dismissive.

Sarah's anger flared. "I assumed the police consider every detail important. You have Ben and me stuck in these interview rooms over what I consider irrelevant information, so I would think you'd be interested in this flash drive."

Nelson leaned back in his hard, uncomfortable chair, eyeing her with a mix of curiosity and skepticism. "How did you get into your dad's safe?" he asked.

"What do you mean?" Sarah retorted, her voice sharp.

"Key or combination?"

"Combination."

"Did he know you had the combination?"

Sarah jumped to her feet, her eyes blazing. "Of course, he knew. He gave it to me."

"Okay," Nelson said calmly, gesturing for her to sit down. "Please, sit."

She sat back down with a heavy sigh. "Are you going to talk to Stephen about this flash drive?" she pressed.

"Yes," he replied, but his voice lacked conviction. Nelson shifted in his seat, a thoughtful look crossing his face. After a moment, he asked, "How did you meet Ben?"

Sarah recounted the same basic story that Ben had told, though with slight variations that could be chalked up to differing memories. She described how she had worn a scarf and sunglasses to subtly disguise herself, wandered into the bar, noticed her own painting, and found it surprisingly easy and pleasant to talk to Ben.

Then, Nelson's questioning took a darker turn. Why had she moved from her apartment back into the mansion? Sarah explained that her mother had died, and she didn't want her father to be alone. Nelson then asked if she had been at the mansion the morning her father, Anthony, died. Exasperation flared in her eyes as she reminded Nelson that he already knew she was there—she had told him that on the day her father died. She didn't like where this line of questioning was leading.

Then came the pivotal question: "Did you have access to the surveillance camera controls?" Sarah's temper exploded. She stood up, declaring that she was done with this interrogation. "Arrest me if you want, but you'll be talking to my attorney next," she snapped, her voice ringing with defiance.

Before Sarah could storm out of the interview room, Detective Nelson calmly said, "I have something you need to see that might change your perspective."

That comment stopped her dead in her tracks. Though she managed to calm her exterior, fury still simmered within. Nelson instructed her to stay put while he fetched Ben, bringing him into the same room. "I'll be back in a moment," he said before leaving.

As soon as the door closed, Sarah and Ben exchanged glances, voicing their frustration over the unfair treatment they had received. Their conversation quickly dwindled into a tense silence as they awaited the detective's return.

After several agonizingly long minutes, the door swung open, and Nelson strode in, holding a large 9x12 envelope. He positioned himself before them, his expression unreadable. With deliberate slowness, he pulled a photograph from the envelope and flicked it onto the table, the image sliding across the surface with a whisper.

"Explain this," he said.

Ben and Sarah leaned forward, examining the grainy image. It showed men unloading crates of alcohol from a truck outside the Westfield Country Club.

"This was taken from a surveillance camera on the day of the stakeholders' social gathering," Nelson said, settling into his seat. He tapped on the image of a figure in the background. "That's Ben," he added, his voice heavy with implication.

Sarah shot Ben a surprised look, but he didn't meet her gaze; his focus was solely on the detective. "So? What does that prove?"

"I don't know. You tell me."

Ben shifted uncomfortably, glancing from the detective to Sarah and back again. "I worked bartending jobs regularly while getting my own bar up and running. I still do occasionally, though less now since I'm busy with my own place." He pointed to the photo. "I didn't know what that event was at the time. I just showed up, did the job, and got paid."

Sarah's voice shook as she turned to him. "Why didn't you tell me?"

"I didn't think it mattered," Ben replied defensively. "It was just another job."

Nelson's eyes flicked between them, gauging their reactions. "Ben, you were at the country club the night before Anthony died, at an event he hosted. Then, in the coming weeks, you befriend Sarah. What would you think if you were me?"

"I would think nothing. I'm a bartender, and bartending gigs are plentiful. And at that event I was a barback; I primarily just kept the bar stocked. I didn't interact with any guests."

"Nonetheless, you wouldn't think it's an unusual coincidence?"

"No," Ben said firmly.

"Of course, you'd say that in your position," Nelson countered. "But what if you were me?"

"I don't know. Only you can answer that."

Detective Nelson pondered for a moment before saying, "Alright, Ben. I don't have enough to hold you, but don't leave town. I may need to speak with you again." He then turned to Sarah. "You can go too, but I might have more questions for you as well."

They both stood. Ben turned to the detective, his face a mix of frustration and sorrow. "I swear, I had nothing to do with Anthony's death," he said, desperation creeping into his voice. "I didn't even know him."

Sarah walked out, and Ben followed, but she kept her distance, a wall of silence between them.

When they left the police station, the sky had darkened, and a chill wind had picked up, carrying with it the scent of rain. Sarah marched towards her car with determined steps, while Ben trailed behind, his movements heavy with the weight of the world on his shoulders. The harsh glow of the mercury vapor lights from the station cast an eerie glow over the scene.

"Sarah, please," Ben pleaded, his voice cracking with raw emotion. "I didn't do anything wrong. The event was just a freelance gig. You have to believe me."

Sarah turned to face him, her eyes icy and her voice barely more than a whisper. "Ben, I don't know what to believe anymore."

Ben watched her walk away, his heart shattered. He wanted to chase after her, to make her understand, but his legs felt like lead. The sense of loss was overwhelming, a physical ache that threatened to consume him.

As they went their separate ways, they were unaware of the figure lurking in the shadows. The man's eyes tracked Sarah and Ben with a chilling intensity, relishing their turmoil.

CHAPTER TWENTY-ONE

*M*atthew crouched in the shadows, his eyes locked on Sarah and Ben as they exited the police station. The dim light of the streetlamps cast long shadows across the pavement, and the air was thick with tension. He watched as they exchanged terse words, their faces masks of frustration and hurt. He'd seen this scene play out countless times before with other targets, and he knew it wouldn't be long before they went their separate ways.

His phone buzzed softly in his pocket, a reminder of his next task. He ignored it for now, his attention fully on the couple. They finally turned away from each other, Sarah heading towards her car with stiff, angry strides, while Ben slumped towards his own vehicle, looking defeated. Matthew waited until they were both out of sight before slipping back into the darkness, leaving behind an aura of unease and unanswered questions.

Matthew's life was one of shadows and secrets. He'd been ordered by his employer to follow Sarah, but he never asked why. Questions were dangerous in his line of work. He didn't even know his employer's name; they communicated solely through burner phones and modulated voices. It was safer that way. Safer for both of them.

He remembered the morning he was sent to kill Anthony Kellerman. The memory was vivid, clear as day, etched into his mind. Before making his move, he infiltrated the surveillance camera system of Anthony's mansion through its Wi-Fi network. His fingers flew over the keyboard, disabling half the cameras, including the one overlooking the pool. It was the only one he needed to disable, but he took out others to avoid drawing undue attention to that specific camera.

He also tampered with the system's internal date, making it appear as though the cameras had failed one by one over the past year. He knew a thorough examination by IT experts would uncover the deception, but he counted on that not happening—Anthony's death would be written off as an accident anyway.

At 6:30 a.m., Matthew parked his vehicle about half a mile down Clayton Road, away from the gated entrance to Greenwood Estates, where Anthony's mansion was located. Moving stealthily through the dense woods separating two subdivisions, he approached Anthony's mansion from the backyard, evading the watchful eyes of the neighbors. The cover of trees and underbrush provided ample concealment as he navigated the uneven terrain, ensuring he remained unseen.

At 6:45 a.m., Matthew picked the lock to the gate leading to the pool area. He then hid in the woods, waiting for the right moment. As the clock struck 7 a.m., Anthony entered the pool for his morning swim. Disguised as a pool cleaning guy, Matthew emerged from his hiding spot, blending with the early morning shadows. The tranquility of the morning was punctuated only by the gentle splashes of Anthony swimming his laps.

Approaching the edge of the pool, Matthew kept his demeanor calm and professional, his rubber mallet hidden behind his back. Anthony swam over, likely ready to inform him that he was there on the wrong day, unaware of the danger lurking just behind the pool cleaner's facade.

The hit was quick and efficient. The large surface of the mallet was perfect for hiding the true cause of Anthony's death, making it look like he had knocked himself out by swimming into the side of the pool. Anthony made quite a splash when he fell back into the water. As Matthew turned to leave, he noticed his wet footprints all over the deck. They would likely evaporate before anyone discovered the body, but he wasn't one to take unnecessary risks. He turned on the spigot and soaked the deck, erasing any evidence of his presence.

Inside the house, Matthew had hurried up the stairs to the office. He needed to copy a file titled 'confidential' from Anthony's laptop and then delete it. Unfortunately, despite his extensive IT background, he couldn't find the file. His frustration mounted as he searched through folders, but the file eluded him. Just as he was about to give up, he heard a noise. Someone was moving around the house.

Peering out of the office door, he saw a beautiful young woman in bed clothes coming out of a room and heading downstairs. He immediately knew it was Sarah Kellerman, Anthony's daughter. Her face was unmistakable; he had studied her profile extensively during the briefings. Knowing he had to leave quickly, he waited until she was out of sight before making his way down the stairs and out a side door of the mansion. He retraced his path through the woods, making his way back to the van he had parked on Clayton Road. Moving quickly but cautiously, he reached the vehicle, climbed in, and drove off without a moment's hesitation.

The aftermath was a blur of burner phones and modulated voices. His employer was furious when Matthew reported he couldn't find the file, but eventually calmed down, saying he'd deal with it.

The next few weeks were a whirlwind of tasks and assignments. One of them involved hacking into the expensive electric car owned by James Harris, an associate of Anthony. The instructions were clear: remotely drive the car at top speed into the corner of an office building, plowing through any pedestrians in the way. It needed to hit the building so hard that the vehicle would be completely destroyed, making it impossible for electronic forensics to reveal it was remotely controlled.

Matthew parked his van on Washington Avenue, eyes trained on the bar's entrance. His pulse quickened as he waited, knowing James would step out soon. His employer had assured him that a well-timed phone call would lure James outside at the precise moment. Matthew's mission was clear, and he was ready with the remote-control hardware in hand.

The job went off without a hitch, or so he thought. The police suspected foul play, and despite the fiery crash, there were always variables that could reveal the truth. His employer wasn't happy but didn't blame Matthew. It was the nature of the business.

Matthew's next task was clear: follow Sarah. Report her every move. She had visited the police too many times, and his employer feared she might know something. He shadowed her from a distance, blending into the background, his presence unnoticed.

The first few days were routine surveillance, but Matthew's instincts told him to stay vigilant. Sarah's life followed a predictable pattern—staying with her boyfriend, then with close friends, returning to her apartment, and occasional outings. However, the bartender introduced an unpredictable element. They grew closer and clearly had sex. Matthew knew from past surveillances that this would definitely complicate their relationship.

Then came the covert meeting at a coffee house with the persistent detective investigating Anthony Kellerman's death. Matthew positioned himself at a nearby table, but their hushed voices thwarted his efforts to eavesdrop. After they left, Matthew lingered, savoring his honey cinnamon latte and almond croissant.

Once he finished, he effortlessly caught up to Sarah. Her predictable routine made tracking her easy, but she seemed more cautious now, frequently glancing over her shoulder and double-checking locked doors. It was as if she knew someone was watching.

This wasn't entirely new for Matthew. He'd encountered subjects in the past who had sensed his presence and slipped into paranoid behavior. In those cases, he always strengthened his resolve and stayed one step ahead. He applied the same strategy with Sarah, ensuring he remained undetected while keeping a close eye on her every move.

Matthew stood in the shadow of his van, watching as Sarah and Ben emerged from the police station. Their weary expressions suggested the hours spent inside had not gone well. They argued, their faces reflecting a mix of frustration and hurt. Though they didn't shout, their words carried easily across the empty parking lot.

"Sarah, please. I didn't do anything wrong. The event was just a freelance gig. You have to believe me," Ben pleaded.

Even from a distance, Matthew could see the coldness in Sarah's eyes. "Ben, I don't know what to believe anymore," she replied icily.

Matthew watched with a detached curiosity. Human emotions were messy and unpredictable. They clouded judgment and made people vulnerable. It was fascinating to observe, but he couldn't let it distract him from his mission.

Finally, Sarah turned on her heels and walked away, her movements stiff with anger. Ben watched her go, a look of despair on his face, before heading to his own car. Matthew noted the time, the details, every nuance of their interaction. You never knew what information might turn out to be valuable.

He waited until they were both out of sight before slipping back into his van. The night was quiet, the only sounds were the distant hum of traffic and the occasional bark of a dog. Matthew's mind was a whirl of calculations and strategies. His employer's orders were clear – he was just to monitor Sarah's movements—but he was also told the situation was fluid. He needed to be adaptable, ready for anything.

Removing his burner phone from his pocket, Matthew texted his employer and apprised him of the situation. He used alternative names for Sarah and Ben – names that his employer understood. The response came quickly: "Stay close to her."

Matthew nodded to himself, slipping the phone back into his pocket. He had a feeling that things were about to get even more complicated. Sarah was clearly on edge, and if she sensed danger, she might do something unpredictable. Far more unpredictable than what she had currently done. He needed to be prepared for every possibility.

The next day, Matthew followed Sarah from a distance, keeping to the shadows. She spent most of the day in her high-rise apartment, only venturing out to a coffee shop and a restaurant for lunch. She walked through the Central West End, perhaps to exercise or clear her head, but there was a noticeable nervous energy about her. She glanced over her shoulder more frequently, her steps quick and purposeful. She was scared, and rightly so.

Matthew sat on a bench, watching her through the restaurant window during lunch, and his mind flashed back to the day he murdered her father. It was supposed to end there. He was paid handsomely and flown out of town that same day. Months passed, filled with other jobs, and he had pretty much forgotten about killing Anthony Kellerman. Then a burner phone was delivered to his PO Box. It was from his employer for the Kellerman job, informing him that the situation had become complicated, and he had another job for Matthew in St. Louis: James Harris, another lawyer at the firm.

Unfortunately, killing Harris reignited scrutiny over Anthony Kellerman's death due to the suspicious timing. This coincidence drove Sarah Kellerman to demand a thorough investigation, stirring up trouble. The prospect of that relentless detective digging deep and unearthing buried secrets sent waves of alarm through Matthew's employer.

So, he paid Matthew very well to remain in town and follow Sarah Kellerman. Matthew had done this type of work long enough to know where it would eventually lead—to Sarah's death. But offing Sarah now would be catastrophic, tipping off even the most oblivious law enforcement to a pattern. It would blow open a major investigation. So, it would have to wait.

For now.

CHAPTER TWENTY-TWO

*T*he morning sun filtered through the gauzy curtains of Sarah's kitchen, casting a warm, honeyed light across the room. The scent of freshly brewed coffee mingled with the faint fragrance of lilacs from the vase on the windowsill. Sarah sat at the kitchen table, her fingers lightly tracing the rim of her porcelain coffee cup, lost in thought. The tranquility of the scene contrasted sharply with the turmoil inside her. She had always trusted her instincts, but recent events had left her questioning everything.

Her phone buzzed on the table with a text message, interrupting her reverie. It was Lucas, again. She debated whether to open it, her heart clashing with her better judgment.

"Hey, can we talk?" the message read, simple and to the point, yet loaded with layers of unspoken emotions. Sarah sighed, her mind swirling with memories and doubts. She typed back a quick reply, agreeing to meet him at a nearby café. She needed closure, if nothing else.

The café was nearly empty when Sarah arrived. She spotted Lucas sitting in a corner booth, his head buried in his hands. He looked up as she approached, his eyes filled with a mix of hope and desperation.

"Sarah," Lucas began, rising awkwardly as she slid into the seat across from him. "Thanks for coming. It's been a while. If I didn't know better, I'd think you were avoiding me," he said with a forced, yet playful smirk.

Sarah's expression was steely, her arms crossed tightly over her chest. "I have been avoiding you."

Lucas's smirk faltered, and for a moment, genuine surprise flickered across his face. Or was it an act?

"Why?" he asked, sounding hurt.

"Because I saw you and Emily holding hands at Burke's Books," Sarah replied, her voice unwavering.

Lucas blinked, his mind clearly racing. An understanding smile formed on his face. "That's it? That's why you're upset? Sarah, that was nothing. Emily lost a big real estate account, and her father was furious with her. I was just giving her a shoulder to cry on."

"Cry? She seemed very happy, not a trace of sadness in that moment," Sarah shot back.

He furrowed his brow, his demeanor shifting. "Where were you at the time?"

"Outside on the sidewalk. I saw you two through the window."

"And you think in that... one moment, you caught what was going on?"

"Well, it seemed—"

"Sure," Lucas interrupted, his tone growing more insistent. "She might've been happy in that second, but had you seen the entire exchange, you would've understood. Emily and I are just friends. Nothing more."

Sarah's eyes narrowed. "You can't tell me that what I saw was nothing."

Lucas leaned forward, his eyes pleading. "Really, Sarah. You didn't see what you think you saw. We were talking, that's all. Emily has been going through a tough time, and I was just being there for her."

Sarah studied his face, searching for any sign of deceit. His expression was earnest, but the nagging doubt in her mind refused to be silenced. "I don't know, Lucas. It didn't look that way to me. It looked more... intimate."

He sighed, his shoulders sagging. "Sarah, that's not what happened. You've, you've just been so stressed and overwhelmed lately. Please, let me help you through this. Let me be there for you."

Sarah looked away, but Lucas's words had already started to chip away at her resolve. She felt a familiar sense of doubt creeping in, wondering if maybe, just maybe, she had misunderstood the situation. "Lucas, I don't know...I'm so tired of all of this. Tired of feeling like I can't trust anyone."

"Then trust me," Lucas insisted. "I love you, Sarah. I never stopped loving you. Let's start over. Let's put all this behind us and move forward together. You and me, like it used to be."

Sarah looked into his eyes, searching for any hint of deceit, but all she saw was the man she had fallen in love with many years ago. The man who had once made her feel like the most important person in the world.

Tears welled up in her eyes as she whispered, "Lucas, I want to believe you. I really do. But I just don't know."

Lucas reached out again, his touch gentle and reassuring. "I know, Sarah. I know you've been through hell. But I'm here now, and I want to make things right. I want to be the person you can lean on. Please, give us another chance."

Her defenses crumbled and she nodded. "Okay, Lucas. Let's try again."

Lucas pulled her into a tight embrace, and as they sat there, holding each other, the past few weeks' pain and turmoil seemed to fade into the background. For the first time in a long while, Sarah felt a glimmer of hope. Maybe, just maybe, they could rebuild what had been lost.

But as she rested her head on Lucas's shoulder, a small voice in the back of her mind warned her to be careful, to guard her heart.

∿

The wine bar was alive with the gentle hum of conversation and the soft clinking of glasses. Sarah and Ashley sat in a cozy corner booth, the flickering candlelight casting a warm glow on their faces. The familiar surroundings and Ashley's comforting presence were exactly what Sarah needed after the whirlwind of the past few weeks.

"To us," Ashley toasted, raising her glass of Pinot Noir.

"To us," Sarah echoed, clinking her glass against Ashley's. She took a sip, savoring the rich, velvety taste of the wine, letting it calm her nerves.

"Thanks for dragging me out tonight," Sarah said, her voice sincere. "I've been a bit of a ghost lately."

Ashley's eyes softened as she reached across the table to squeeze Sarah's hand. "No need to explain. Everyone has their moments. I just want to see you smile again."

Sarah felt a wave of gratitude wash over her. "I'm trying. I got back together with Lucas, but honestly, tonight I just want to focus on us."

Ashley smiled, a flicker of something unreadable in her eyes. "As long as you're happy, that's what matters."

They sat in companionable silence for a moment, the weight of their recent experiences hanging in the air. Then, Ashley spoke again, her tone thoughtful.

"You know, it's funny how life twists and turns. Remember where we started? My folks barely made ends meet, yet somehow, they kept us grounded. Even after my father became successful and everything changed."

Sarah felt a deep connection to her friend's words. "It's easy to lose sight of what's real when everything around you glitters. That's partly why I dove into art—something that felt genuine."

Ashley smiled warmly. "And look at you now, painting your heart out, making a name for yourself. It's impressive."

"Thank you," Sarah said, her voice filled with gratitude. "It hasn't always been easy, but it's been worth it."

"You're stronger than you think, Sarah. Don't let anyone tell you otherwise."

Sarah nodded, feeling a sense of peace settle over her. She knew that no matter what happened, she had friends like Ashley who would stand by her. She had chosen her path as an artist not because it was easy, but because it was true to who she was. And though she would never be a starving artist, thanks to her family's wealth, she knew she would have pursued her art under any circumstance.

They ordered another bottle of wine and a platter of appetizers, the conversation shifting to lighter topics. They talked about their favorite high school memories, the teachers who had inspired them, and the adventures they had dreamed of embarking on. The hours slipped by, filled with laughter and the easy camaraderie that only old friends share.

"Remember when we ditched school to go to that concert downtown?" Ashley asked, her eyes sparkling with mischief.

Sarah laughed, a genuine, carefree sound. "How could I forget? We thought we were so rebellious. And then we had to come up with excuses for our parents."

Ashley grinned. "Simpler times, huh?"

"They were," Sarah agreed, a wistful note in her voice. "But we've come a long way since then. We've grown up."

Ashley nodded. "We have. And we've got the stories to prove it."

"We do, and I'm grateful for the journey we've had."

"Have you seen Emily lately?" Ashley asked.

Sarah tensed, the memory of what she witnessed at the bookstore was still vivid. She longed to confide in Ashley, to unpack the whole scene and seek her insight, but gossip repelled her. "No, I haven't seen Emily in a while."

"Neither have I. I sent her a text to join us, but she didn't respond."

Sarah shrugged. "She's probably just busy."

"Yeah," Ashley replied, her tone distracted. She sensed there was more beneath the surface but chose not to push further.

As they finished their meal and the last of the wine, they promised to stay in touch and meet up more often. Sarah knew how easily people drifted apart. High school friends, inseparable then, often imagined their bond would last a lifetime, but reality had other plans. Yet, Sarah felt a unique connection to Ashley. Ashley's family was first-generation wealthy, yet they never forgot their roots. Despite Sarah's privileged upbringing, her heart set her apart from many of her peers. Perhaps it was her artist's soul, valuing creativity over material wealth. This perspective forged a deep sense of kinship with people like Ashley. And Ben.

Stepping out of the wine bar, the cool night air enveloped them like a comforting embrace. The downtown lights twinkled around them as Sarah and Ashley walked side by side to their cars. For the first time in a long while, Sarah felt a profound contentment. She savored this respite from the chaos of her life, grateful for the simple, soothing moment of friendship.

Sarah stood in the middle of her studio, the familiar scent of paint and turpentine filling the air. The large windows let in the soft afternoon light, casting a gentle glow on her latest canvas. She dipped her brush into a vibrant shade of red, her thoughts wandering as the strokes came to life. The act of painting was a solace, a way to escape the complexities of her world. But lately, even this sanctuary couldn't quiet the nagging doubts in her mind.

Lucas had been a constant presence in her life for years, their relationship a series of passionate reunions and bitter partings. He was charming and confident, with a smile that could light up a room, a quality that made him a respected and successful tennis instructor. They had rekindled their romance yet again a few months ago, and for a while, it had felt like old times. But something had shifted.

Sarah paused, staring at the brush in her hand. The crimson color on the canvas blurred as her mind replayed the countless little moments that had begun to unsettle her. The subtle hints were there if she allowed herself to see them—the casual questions about her family's estate, the way his eyes lingered a little too long on the box of antique jewelry from her long-deceased grandmother that she had but never wore, the seemingly offhand comments about investments and inheritance.

She shook her head, trying to dispel the thoughts. It was unfair, she told herself, to reduce their history to mere transactions. They had shared so much more than that. But doubt, once seeded, had a way of growing, and lately, it seemed to shadow every interaction.

The sound of the apartment door opening broke her reverie. Lucas strolled into the studio, his presence filling the space with effortless grace. He glanced at the canvas and then at her, his smile broadening. "Hey, Picasso," he teased, "how's the masterpiece coming along?"

Sarah forced a smile and set the brush down. "Picasso was known mostly for Cubism and Surrealism—definitely not my style. But it's coming along, slowly but surely," she said, wiping her hands on a cloth.

He moved closer, looking at the painting with an appreciative nod. "I'll never understand how you do it. This looks amazing."

"Thanks," she said softly, her eyes searching his. He seemed genuine, as he always did. But that nagging feeling refused to let go.

"Your work seems to have a bit more red in it than usual."

"Yeah, I've noticed that too," she replied with a grin. "I think it's subconscious. Maybe I'm just going through a red phase."

"I like it, it really stands out," he said, wrapping an arm around her waist and pulling her close. "I've been thinking," he continued casually, "we should take a trip. Just the two of us. Escape from everything for a while."

"That sounds nice," Sarah replied, leaning into him. She wanted to believe in his sincerity, to trust the warmth in his eyes. But the questions gnawed at her. "Where were you thinking?"

"I don't know, somewhere luxurious. Maybe the Caribbean? We could stay at one of those all-inclusive resorts, really pamper ourselves."

She nodded, but her mind was elsewhere. A trip sounded wonderful, a chance to escape and perhaps find clarity. Yet, the mention of luxury, of spending money so freely, felt like another piece of the puzzle falling into place.

As the days passed, Sarah found herself observing Lucas more closely. She noticed how his conversations often steered towards money and status. How he seemed particularly interested in the financial aspects of her art sales, the value of her collections. It wasn't overt, not something she could easily call out. But it was there, a subtle undercurrent she couldn't ignore.

One evening, they attended a charity gala together. The event was grand, filled with the city's elite, and Lucas thrived in the environment, his charm drawing people in effortlessly. Sarah watched him work the room, his interactions smooth and polished. He was in his element, but she felt like an outsider looking in.

During the auction, he leaned in close, whispering, "You should bid on that piece. It would look fantastic in your collection."

Sarah glanced at the item in question, a beautiful sculpture. She smiled politely, but the suggestion felt like another nudge towards spending. "Maybe," she said noncommittally, her gaze roaming around the room.

As the night wore on, she excused herself to get some air. Standing on the balcony, she looked out over the city, her mind racing. The doubts she had tried to push away were becoming impossible to ignore. She thought about their past, the way Lucas had always seemed to reappear when things were going well for her. The times he had vanished when she needed support the most.

"Hey," Lucas's voice pulled her from her thoughts. He joined her on the balcony, wrapping his arms around her from behind. "You good?"

"Yeah," she lied, leaning back against him. "Just needed a moment."

He kissed her temple, his touch warm and familiar. "I get it. These events can be a bit much."

She nodded, but her thoughts were far from the glamour of the gala. Standing there in his embrace, she made a decision. She wouldn't confront him—not yet, anyway. But she would be cautious, guard her heart and her trust.

In the following weeks, Sarah focused on her art, pouring her emotions onto the canvas. She and Lucas continued their relationship, but she kept her distance, emotionally, observing him with a new perspective. He seemed unaware of the change, or perhaps he was simply too confident to notice.

One afternoon, as she worked in her studio, her phone buzzed with a message from her financial advisor—a reminder about a meeting to discuss the investments she had inherited from her father. She glanced at it, then at the painting before her. The contrast between her passion and the constant undercurrent of financial discussions with Lucas felt stark.

Lucas entered the studio, a bright, prideful and arrogant smile on his face. "Hey, I've got us reservations at that new Japanese Kaiseki restaurant downtown. It had a long waiting list, but I dropped your name—you being a famous artist and all—and got us bumped up in line. Thought we could celebrate your latest sale."

Sarah smiled back, but it didn't reach her eyes. "Sounds great," she said, setting her brush down. "Just let me finish up here."

As he left the room, Sarah took a deep breath, the weight of her realizations pressing down on her. She would continue to move forward, but with her eyes wide open. Trust was a fragile thing, easily shattered and difficult to rebuild. She was becoming wary of the man who claimed to love her but seemed more enamored with the life she could provide.

CHAPTER TWENTY-THREE

*I*n the Central West End, Ben was throwing himself into his bar business, trying to numb the pain of his broken heart. The rustic, charming place with exposed brick walls and vintage posters, was his pride and joy. He enjoyed chatting with his regulars and making new customers feel at home, but no matter how busy he kept himself, he couldn't shake the longing for Sarah. Every time he saw a couple sharing a laugh or a tender moment, his thoughts slipped back to her.

One morning, as Ben and another bartender prepared to open the bar, his phone buzzed with a text message. It was from Sarah.

"Can we talk?" the message read.

Ben's heart raced. He hadn't heard from her in weeks. He quickly replied, "Of course. Are you okay?"

A few minutes later, his phone rang. He answered eagerly. "Sarah?"

"Hi, Ben," Sarah's voice was soft, filled with emotion. "I'm sorry for how I treated you. I was so caught up in everything with Lucas, and I didn't realize what I had until it was too late."

Ben's heart ached at the vulnerability in her voice. "It's okay, Sarah. I understand."

"No, it's not okay," Sarah insisted. "You deserve better than that. I've been so foolish, and now I see things clearly. Lucas... he's only interested in my wealth. I should have seen it sooner."

Ben's anger towards Lucas flared up, but he kept his tone gentle. "It's not easy to see things clearly when you're in the middle of it."

"Can you grab lunch?" Sarah asked.

The sun was high in the sky as Ben made his way to Trattoria Italiano, the relatively new eatery nestled in the heart of Clayton, Missouri. The air was filled with the scent of freshly baked bread and rich tomato sauce, mingling with the hustle and bustle of the city. Ben, dressed in his usual casual attire, felt a mix of excitement and trepidation. He hadn't seen Sarah in a while, and the thought of meeting her for lunch brought back a flood of memories.

Sarah was already waiting outside the restaurant, her raven black hair catching the light, making it seem almost like a halo. She wore a simple, yet elegant, dress that flowed with the gentle breeze. As Ben approached, she turned and flashed him a warm smile.

"Ben, it's so good to see you," Sarah said, her eyes reflecting a mix of happiness and uncertainty.

"Sarah," Ben replied, trying to hide his nervousness. "It's been too long."

They embraced briefly, and as they did, the door of the restaurant swung open, revealing Lucas and Emily as they stepped out onto the sidewalk. The atmosphere shifted immediately. Lucas's face twisted into a sneer as he saw Ben and Sarah together. Emily looked away, clearly self-conscious and embarrassed to be seen with Lucas in this moment.

"Well, isn't this a cozy sight?" Lucas's voice dripped with sarcasm.

Sarah tensed beside Ben. "Lucas, this isn't what it looks like."

Lucas's eyes narrowed. "Oh, really? Because it sure looks like you're cheating on me."

Sarah laughed sarcastically. "Oh, how ironic, coming from you, Lucas. What about you and Emily?"

Lucas's face darkened, his jaw tightening.

The restaurant manager, catching a glimpse of the escalating confrontation through the wide front window, hurried out of the restaurant onto the sidewalk. "Excuse me, but I'm going to have to ask you all to take this away from the establishment."

Lucas ignored the manager, his eyes locked on Sarah as his voice cut through the city's noise, drawing the attention of passersby. "Scraping the bottom of the barrel, aren't you, Sarah?" he sneered, his words dripping with disdain.

Ben couldn't just stand by. He stepped between Sarah and Lucas, his eyes filled with steely resolve. "Back off, Lucas, or I'll have the cops here before you can blink."

Lucas laughed right in Ben's face. "Really? You think the police will side with me, a respectable citizen, or a loser bar owner catering to drunks and riffraff?"

"Yeah, well, you should know, I served *you* after all."

Sarah burst into laughter, the sound cutting through Lucas like a knife. His face contorted with rage, his glare sharp enough to shatter glass. "Your new boyfriend's quite the comedian for a miserable loser. Guess that's the charm—misery loves company, right, Sarah?"

Ben smirked. "Better to be a loser on stage than a sad sack in the cheap seats, Lucas."

Sarah laughed again, the sound like a dagger to Lucas's heart.

Lucas stepped up, his face inches from Ben's. "You think you're funny? Maybe I should show you what happens when you mess with me." He shoved Ben hard, nearly knocking him off balance.

Sarah gasped as Ben steadied himself, resisting the urge to punch Lucas for her sake. "Lucas, don't do this," she pleaded.

Lucas laughed harshly. "What? Afraid I'll kick your boyfriend's ass?"

Emily, her face flushed with embarrassment, grabbed Lucas's arm. "Lucas, stop. This isn't worth it."

But Lucas wasn't listening. He shoved Ben again, more forcefully this time. "Come on, Ben. Show me what you got."

Sarah, her eyes wide with worry, stepped between them. "Lucas, enough! This is insane!"

Lucas tried to push past her, almost knocking her over. That was the last straw. Ben, fueled by a protective instinct, delivered a quick, decisive punch to Lucas's face, sending him stumbling backward and onto the pavement.

The crowd that had gathered around gasped in shock, their eyes darting between Ben and the fallen Lucas. Emily rushed to Lucas's side, while Sarah turned to Ben, her expression a mix of relief and concern.

Lucas, clutching his jaw, glared up at Ben. "I'm going to have you arrested for assault!"

Sarah had reached her limit. "Seriously, Lucas? You shoved him twice. He was just defending himself."

"This isn't over," Lucas spat, struggling to get to his feet. "I'm going to sue you."

Sarah stepped closer to Ben, her hand on his arm. "Let's go," she whispered, guiding him away from the scene. As they walked down the sidewalk, the adrenaline began to fade, replaced by a sense of unexpected calm.

"That was intense," Ben said, glancing at Sarah. "Are you all right?"

"I am now," she replied, a small smile forming on her lips. "Thank you for standing up for me. For the second time."

Ben nodded, his own smile growing. "Always."

"And don't worry about him," Sarah said, a hint of a smile playing on her lips, as she jabbed her thumb over her shoulder toward Lucas and Emily. "I own one of the most powerful law firms in the city now."

For a moment, the absurdity of the situation hit them both, and they burst out laughing. The tension that had hung in the air dissipated, replaced by a shared sense of relief as they strolled through the streets of downtown Clayton.

Matthew watched from a distance, his eyes sharp and focused on Sarah and Ben as they walked away from the restaurant. He moved with the crowd, blending in seamlessly, always maintaining a safe but close distance. He couldn't hear every word they said, but he caught enough to piece together the gist of their conversation.

As they paused near the edge of the sidewalk, Matthew managed to get close enough to hear Sarah tell Ben she'd like to show him her apartment and art studio. There was a hint of pride in her tone.

He watched as Sarah and Ben strolled over to her sleek BMW parked nearby. They got in, and as the car pulled out, Matthew swiftly moved to his own vehicle, discreetly parked in the same lot. He had strategically positioned it there earlier, having tailed her meticulously.

He started his engine, keeping a careful distance as he followed them through the city streets. The modern high-rises of Clayton soon gave way to the historic, tree-lined streets of the Central West End. Matthew was meticulous, ensuring he remained undetected as he trailed them. He knew the importance of subtlety in his line of work.

Sarah's BMW turned into an underground parking garage attached to a high-rise building. Matthew parked his car on the street, finding a spot with a clear view of the entrance. He watched as they disappeared into the garage, noting the security measures in place. He knew this building well, having scouted it before. He was aware of the tight security, the layout, the exits, and the vantage points.

He waited patiently, blending into the surroundings. Sarah lived on the tenth floor, which meant he wouldn't be able to see or hear them from outside. Matthew's job was to watch and report back; knowing their location and habits was often enough for Matthew's employer. He could almost picture them now, Sarah showing Ben her art studio, the personal space where she felt most herself.

Ben stood in awe as he stepped into Sarah's high-rise apartment. The expansive view of the cityscape was breathtaking, the floor-to-ceiling windows allowing sunlight to flood the spacious living area. The sleek modern design, coupled with tasteful decor, spoke volumes of Sarah's refined taste. He had always known Sarah was unique, but seeing her home firsthand brought a new level of understanding and respect.

"This place is incredible, Sarah," Ben said, still taking in the surroundings.

Sarah smiled, though it was tinged with a hint of wistfulness. "Let me show you my studio."

She led him down a hallway adorned with elegant light fixtures and vibrant artwork. The walls were lined with frames, some of which held family photos, others abstract pieces that hinted at her artistic journey. They stopped in front of a double door, and with a gentle push, Sarah revealed a room filled with canvases, brushes, and the unmistakable scent of oil paint. This was her sanctuary, a space where her creativity flowed freely.

Ben walked slowly, taking in each painting. There were landscapes, abstract pieces, and portraits. What caught his attention most were the paintings of her parents. Some depicted them together, others individually, but a few stood out because of the profound sadness they conveyed.

"These are amazing," Ben said, pointing to a painting of her parents standing together, their faces somber and distant. "But why do they look so sad in some of these?"

Sarah's expression grew thoughtful as she joined him in front of the painting. "My father's work as a prosecutor exposed him to serious crimes that burdened him deeply. He saw things most people can't even imagine. That's why he eventually left the criminal side of law and moved into corporate legal practice. It was less taxing on him emotionally."

She paused, her gaze shifting to another painting of her mother, her eyes filled with a quiet sorrow. "And my mother...she was often alone. My father disappeared into his work, leaving her to deal with the loneliness. It was just the three of us living in that massive mansion. People can find themselves lost in huge, cavernous spaces, no matter how beautiful they are."

Ben nodded, understanding the complexity of her family dynamics. "That must have been tough."

"It was," Sarah admitted. "But I had a great childhood overall. I had everything I could ever want, but sometimes the mansion felt cold and lonely. The size of it could be overwhelming."

Ben moved to another painting, this one of Sarah as a child, playing in a garden. The vibrancy of the colors contrasted sharply with the melancholic portraits of her parents. "You look happy here," he said, pointing to the painting.

Sarah's face lit up with a genuine smile. "I was. That was my favorite spot in the garden. It was my little sanctuary."

They continued to explore her studio, Ben marveling at the depth and emotion in each piece. He could see how much her art meant to her, how it was an outlet for all the feelings and experiences she had bottled up over the years.

"Your talent is incredible, Sarah," he said, stopping in front of a large canvas depicting a stormy sea. "You put so much of yourself into these."

"Thank you, Ben," she replied softly. "Painting has always been my way of processing everything. The good and the bad."

As they moved further into the studio, they entered a section filled with paintings that were predominantly reddish in color, some almost entirely crimson. Ben paused, taking in the intense hues and the palpable emotion each piece conveyed.

"These are striking," Ben said, gesturing to a particularly vivid crimson canvas. "What inspired these?"

Sarah's expression grew somber. "I painted all of these after my father was murdered. I couldn't help myself. These paintings reflected my mood, my grief."

Ben looked closely at the paintings, captivated by their diversity. Some depicted her parents, others were self-portraits, while a few captured the empty, echoing interiors of the mansion, the sprawling grounds, or autumnal landscapes. Each piece was rendered in a strikingly realistic style, yet a macabre undertone threaded through them all. Though death was never explicitly portrayed, a haunting quality pervaded each scene. It was as if the pain and darkness of her experiences had seeped into the canvas, infusing the mundane with an eerie, poignant depth.

"They're incredibly powerful," Ben said, his voice filled with empathy. "You've captured something profound here."

Sarah nodded, her eyes distant as she recalled the pain of those days. "It was my way of coping, of trying to make sense of something senseless."

Ben moved slowly from one painting to the next, absorbing the depth of emotion in each piece. They spent hours in the studio, Sarah sharing stories behind each painting, Ben listening intently. He felt a deeper connection to her, understanding more about the person she had become through her art and her past.

As the afternoon light began to wane, they moved to the living room, settling on the plush sofa. The conversation turned lighter, filled with laughter and shared memories. But Ben couldn't shake the profound impact her paintings had on him.

"You know, seeing all this, it makes me admire you even more," he said, his voice sincere. "You've turned your... traumatic experiences... into something beautiful."

Sarah's eyes glistened with emotion. "Thank you, Ben. Your support means the world to me."

They sat in comfortable silence for a moment, the city buzzing around them, but in their bubble, everything felt calm and peaceful.

"So, what about you?" Sarah asked, turning the conversation towards Ben. "How did you end up running a bar?"

Ben chuckled, leaning back on the sofa. "It's a long story. After college, I bounced around a bit, trying to figure out what I wanted to do. I always loved the atmosphere of bars—the sense of community, the stories people shared. When the opportunity came to open one, I jumped at it. It felt right."

"And do you enjoy it now that you actually own one?" Sarah asked, genuinely curious.

"I do," Ben replied. "It's not always easy, but it's rewarding. I get to meet all kinds of people, and it keeps me on my toes."

Sarah nodded, understanding the appeal. "Sounds like you found your calling."

"Maybe I did," Ben said with a smile. "Everything else I tried, or whatever job I had, I've gotten bored with. But not my bar."

As the evening turned to night, they continued to talk, their connection growing stronger with each passing moment. Sarah felt a sense of peace she hadn't experienced in a long time. Ben's presence was comforting, his understanding and support unwavering.

They shared a meal, cooked together in her sleek, modern kitchen, the conversation flowing easily. The sadness of her past seemed to fade away as the evening went on.

Later, as they stood on her balcony, overlooking the twinkling city lights, Sarah felt a sense of hope. She turned to Ben, his face illuminated by the soft glow of the city.

"Thank you for being here," she said, her voice filled with emotion.

"You don't have to thank me," Ben replied, taking her hand. "I'm really glad you called."

After a while, they went back into her apartment and Ben spent the night.

Matthew sat in his car, parked inconspicuously outside the high-rise building, his eyes fixed on the entrance. The hours ticked by, and the city around him transitioned from the bustling evening rush to the quiet stillness of midnight. His vigil was methodical, unwavering, but as the night deepened, he finally decided to call it quits. He started the engine and drove off, heading back to the current hotel his employer had arranged for him. The transient nature of his accommodations—hotel to hotel, alias to alias—ensured there would be no trail for the authorities to follow if they ever got wind of his activities.

Settling into the dimly lit hotel room, Matthew's mind wandered back to the day's observations. He found it amusing that Ben, the bartender, was back in Sarah's life. The once-constant figure of Lucas, her on-and-off boyfriend for years, had been unceremoniously kicked to the curb. The fact that Ben appeared to be staying the night suggested that things between him and Sarah were heating up quickly.

This new development sparked an idea. Matthew smiled to himself, a plan forming in his mind. He would float it past his employer tomorrow, certain it would be well-received.

Matthew considered the situation: with the bartender back in Sarah's life, eliminating both of them might be the most effective course of action. The plan would involve staging a suicide pact, leveraging the turmoil in Sarah's life—the relatively recent death of her father and the unresolved questions surrounding James Harris's demise. It was the perfect way to ensure Sarah's removal without suspicion.

As he lay on the hard hotel bed, Matthew's thoughts crystallized. This method would be clean and efficient. The emotional strain Sarah had been under would make it all the more believable. He could already envision the police dismissing it as a tragic story of two troubled souls finding solace in each other's arms for the last time.

The irony of the plan was that it hinged on Ben's presence. Sarah's privileged circle would undoubtedly disapprove of her relationship with someone like him, a bartender. They would be quick to label Ben as a ne'er-do-well who had led Sarah into a dangerous world. This scenario made a staged drug overdose the perfect method. Ben was the ideal scapegoat, making it possible to eliminate Sarah without drawing undue attention. Without him, killing Sarah discreetly would be nearly impossible.

Matthew felt a grim satisfaction as he finalized the plan in his mind. The pieces were aligning perfectly. All he needed now was to execute the plan with his usual precision. Soon, Sarah and Ben would be just another tragic headline, and Matthew would vanish, leaving no trace of his involvement.

Matthew was confident his employer would love the idea. It was ruthless, efficient, and perfect. As he drifted off to sleep, the image of Sarah and Ben together in death— their love story twisted into a final, dark chapter— solidified in his mind, lulling him into a deep, satisfying slumber filled with dreams of murder.

CHAPTER TWENTY-FOUR

*D*etective Nelson sat in his office, the early morning light casting long shadows across the cluttered desk. He rolled the case of Anthony Kellerman's death around in his mind, searching for angles he might have missed. Officially, Anthony Kellerman had drowned in his pool, a tragic accident. It was the story the media and the public believed. But Nelson and his captain knew it was murder. They were the only ones, apart from Anthony's daughter, Sarah, and her boyfriend, Ben.

Nelson leaned back in his chair, rubbing his temples. Although he grilled Sarah and Ben as suspects, he never truly believed they were guilty. Especially Sarah. She reminded him too much of his own daughter, Lisa. Both young women shared a tenacity and vulnerability that struck a chord deep within him. Lisa had been about Sarah's age when she broke off all communication with Nelson.

Sixteen years ago, Nelson had gone through a bitter divorce. His ex-wife had turned Lisa, then a young teen, against him, painting him as a distant, gruff man more married to his job than his family. It wasn't entirely untrue. The job had consumed him, and he had seen too much darkness to remain unaffected, but he tried. Nonetheless, his wife couldn't take it anymore.

The divorce had driven a wedge between him and Lisa, one they had only briefly managed to bridge years later. But his cynical nature, hardened by years of dealing with humanity's worst, had been too much for her. Their reconciliation had been short-lived, and he hadn't spoken to her in years.

Sarah brought all those memories rushing back. It was as if fate had given him another chance, another young woman in need of guidance and protection. But he couldn't afford to let his personal feelings cloud his judgment. His priority was solving Anthony Kellerman's murder.

The man Nelson needed to talk to was Stephen Millstadt. Stephen had asked Sarah to retrieve a flash drive labeled 'confidential' from her father's mansion. That drive could hold the key to unraveling the mystery.

Nelson glanced at the clock. It was almost 9 a.m. He picked up the phone and dialed the Kellerman Law Group. After a few rings, a receptionist answered, and he was soon put through to Stephen.

"Kellerman Law Group, Stephen Millstadt speaking."

"Mr. Millstadt, this is Detective Nelson with the St. Louis County Police Department. I need to ask you some questions about Anthony Kellerman."

Nelson leaned into the heavy silence that stretched between them, then broke it with a firm, "Mr. Millstadt?"

"I'm sorry, Detective, I was just in the middle of something. How can I assist you?"

Nelson wasn't fooled for a second. His cop instincts screamed that Stephen Millstadt's alarm at receiving his call meant he was hiding something. Naturally suspicious of everyone, Nelson had learned to temper his knee-jerk reactions with a careful assessment of his gut feelings.

"I understand you asked Sarah to retrieve a flash drive from her father's mansion. I need to see that drive," Nelson said, his tone casual and nonthreatening. Years on the force had honed his ability to sound disarmingly benign, a skill he now employed with precision.

There was a brief silence before Stephen replied, his tone more guarded. "I'll need to consult with the other attorneys at the firm before I can do that."

Nelson's lips curled into a slight smile. He had rattled Stephen. "I understand, but I need you to be at the station by 1 p.m. today, with or without the drive."

Stephen hesitated. "I'll do my best to be there, Detective."

Nelson hung up, satisfied. If Stephen had something to hide, he now knew Nelson was on to him. Making Stephen sweat was a small victory, but in a case as complex as this, every little edge mattered.

Nelson stared out of his office window, his mind wandering back to Lisa. He wondered where she was, what she was doing. Did she ever think about him? He missed her more than he cared to admit. But now wasn't the time for personal reflections. He had a job to do, and Anthony Kellerman's murder wasn't going to solve itself.

The detective's mind returned to the case. He thought about the dynamics between Sarah, Ben, and Lucas. Lucas had been Sarah's boyfriend, but now he was out of the picture. Was Lucas involved in Anthony's death? And what was on that flash drive? These questions gnawed at Nelson, but he knew he would get his answers soon enough.

He sighed, the weight of the years and the miles showing on his face. The life of a homicide detective was not an easy one, and it had cost him dearly. But it was who he was. It was what he did. And he would see this case through to the end, no matter what it took.

As Detective Nelson sat in his office a few minutes before calling Stephen Millstadt, the morning sun filtered through the floor-to-ceiling windows of Sarah's high-rise apartment, casting a golden glow on the sleek, modern decor. The remnants of last night lingered in the air—a hint of perfume, the slight disarray of the living room, and the warmth of shared intimacy. Sarah glanced at Ben as he stood by the kitchen counter, clad only in his boxer shorts. His athletic physique was evident, every muscle taut and defined. She admired the way his skin seemed to catch the light, the subtle strength in his movements.

They had made breakfast together, a leisurely affair that felt almost like a dance. Now, they sat across from each other at the small dining table, plates of scrambled eggs and toast between them. Sarah, dressed in a skimpy tank top and shorts, sipped her coffee and watched Ben with a mixture of affection and curiosity.

"How do you stay in such great shape?" she began with a smile, "you've never mentioned a workout routine."

Ben smiled, a hint of shyness in his eyes. "I jog a few miles most mornings," he said casually. "Try to hit the gym a couple of times a week."

Sarah raised an eyebrow, sensing his modesty. "A few miles? And just a couple of times a week?"

He shrugged, taking a bite of his toast. "Keeps me fit enough, I guess."

She knew there was more to it. The dedication, the discipline—it was evident in his form, the way his body moved. But she let it slide, appreciating his humility.

They ate in comfortable silence for a while, the sounds of the city below a distant hum. Sarah's thoughts turned to the future. She placed her fork down and looked at him, her expression thoughtful.

"Ben, have you ever thought about what you want to do next? I mean, beyond the bar."

He looked up, a spark of excitement in his eyes. "I've been thinking about opening a restaurant. Maybe even a chain of them someday. Something with a real community feel, you know?"

Sarah smiled, imagining him in his element, creating something tangible and lasting. "That sounds wonderful. You'd be great at it."

"And you?" he asked, his voice gentle. "What about your plans?"

She hesitated, knowing her answer might change the atmosphere. "I've been thinking about leaving St. Louis. Maybe moving to New York City. The art scene there is incredible. It could be a fresh start."

Ben's face remained calm, but she saw the flicker of disappointment in his eyes. He reached across the table and took her hand. "I'd miss you," he said softly. "But you have to do what's right for you. Your art is amazing. It deserves to be seen by as wide an audience as possible."

His understanding touched her deeply. She squeezed his hand, feeling a swell of emotion. "I haven't decided yet. I love St. Louis, grew up here, but with all that's happened…"

"I know, I know," he said softly.

"We could try a long-distance relationship," she suggested, her voice hopeful.

Ben gave a small, rueful smile. "I've never known those to work, honestly. But I'd still like to be a part of your life, somehow."

They fell silent again, the weight of their conversation settling between them. Sarah's mind buzzed with possibilities and uncertainties. She could see the paths diverging before her, each choice carrying its own set of challenges and rewards.

As they finished their breakfast, the quiet solitude of the moment wrapped around them. Each was lost in their own thoughts, contemplating what lay ahead. Sarah glanced at Ben, a blend of gratitude and sadness in her eyes. He had come into her life when she needed him most, and now, as she considered her next move, guilt gnawed at her. He genuinely liked her, and she genuinely liked him. They felt comfortable together. Yet, here she was, contemplating moving on. Was that selfish? He had told her to do what was best for her. Maybe keeping Ben in her life was the best decision. She needed more time to ponder.

The sun climbed higher in the sky, casting its bright light over the city. The day was just beginning, full of potential and promise. Sarah and Ben cleared the table together, their movements synchronized, a silent testament to their connection. They didn't need words to understand each other in that moment; the future was uncertain, but the present was theirs.

As they stood by the sink, washing dishes side by side, Sarah felt a sense of calm. Whatever happened next, she knew they would face it with the same quiet strength that had carried them through so far. And for now, that was enough.

As Sarah and Ben did the dishes and quietly contemplated what the future held for them, Matthew adjusted the cap on his head, the brim casting a shadow over his eyes as he rode the elevator up to Sarah's apartment. The uniform he wore was a perfect replica of the local utility company's attire, complete with a forged ID badge that could fool even the most discerning doorman. The security doorman in the lobby had barely glanced at him, waving him through with a perfunctory nod. Matthew carried a sturdy tool kit, the kind any utility worker might lug around, but inside it, among the wrenches and screwdrivers, was a lethal dose of fentanyl. Enough to kill both Sarah and Ben.

His plan was meticulous. The deaths would be staged to look like a suicide pact—a tragic ending for a couple overwhelmed by circumstances. It was a clean solution, one that would leave minimal traces back to him or his employer. His employer had loved the idea, appreciating the poetic simplicity of it. The elevator hummed softly as it ascended, the floor numbers lighting up one by one. Matthew's mind was calm, his thoughts methodical. He had done this before, and the routine was familiar, almost comforting.

As the elevator neared Sarah's floor, his burner phone vibrated in his pocket. Frowning, he pulled it out and glanced at the screen. A single word flashed: "Change." He knew his employer would be calling any second with revised plans. And right on time, the phone vibrated with an incoming call.

He pressed the phone to his ear, listening intently to the voice on the other end. His employer's tone was calm, precise. Matthew's face remained impassive as he absorbed the new instructions.

A few seconds passed before he responded with a curt nod, even though no one was there to see it. He pocketed the phone and took a deep breath, recalibrating his thoughts to the new directive. The elevator chimed, announcing his arrival at Sarah's floor, but Matthew stayed put. He let the doors slide open and close again, pressing the button for the first floor.

The descent was as smooth and quiet as the ascent. Matthew's mind worked through the new plan, adjusting his expectations and actions with the same precision he applied to all his tasks. By the time the elevator doors opened onto the lobby, he was fully prepared for whatever came next. He walked out of the building, the tool kit swinging lightly at his side, his demeanor unchanged.

Matthew exited onto the bustling street, blending seamlessly into the flow of pedestrians. He walked with purpose, his eyes scanning the surroundings, but his thoughts were on the phone call. The abrupt change of plans suggested something had shifted in the delicate balance of his employer's world. It didn't matter to Matthew why the change had occurred. His job was to execute orders, not question them.

He turned a corner, heading toward a nearby coffee shop. It was a useful place to pause and gather his thoughts. He ordered a black coffee and took a seat by the window, the tool kit placed unobtrusively by his feet. Sipping the hot, bitter liquid, he allowed himself a moment to consider the implications of the new plan.

His employer's voice had been clear and authoritative, but there had been an underlying tension, a hint of urgency. Matthew was skilled at picking up on such nuances; it was part of what made him effective in his line of work. He mentally reviewed the new instructions, ensuring he missed no detail. The plan now required a different approach, but the end goal remained the same: eliminate the targets without leaving a trace.

Matthew finished his coffee and left the shop, merging back into the city's rhythm. He would have to return to his current hotel room to gather new supplies and perhaps modify his disguise. The tool kit, with its hidden compartment of fentanyl, would be stored away for another day. For now, he had a different task to focus on, and he needed to be prepared.

As he walked, his thoughts briefly turned to Sarah and Ben. They were simply names on a list, variables in an equation that needed solving. He had no personal vendetta against them, no emotional connection. They were just assignments, part of the job. But he knew that to be successful, he had to understand them, anticipate their actions and reactions.

He reached his hotel, a nondescript, rundown place on the edge of town where he rented a room under an assumed name. Inside, he methodically unpacked the tool kit, placing the fentanyl in a secure lockbox. He then opened a drawer filled with various IDs and uniforms, selecting the ones that would be most appropriate for his revised mission. Each piece of equipment was carefully chosen and meticulously maintained, ready for whatever situation he might encounter.

Matthew took a moment to review his new plan, the steps unfolding in his mind with clarity and precision. The phone call had changed the immediate task, but his overall objective remained unchanged. He was a professional, and professionals adapted.

After securing everything he needed, Matthew left the hotel, blending once more into the anonymity of the city. His next steps were clear, his mind focused. The game had changed, but the rules were the same. He would do what he always did: follow the plan, execute flawlessly, and disappear without a trace.

As he walked down the sidewalk, Matthew knew one thing for certain: Sarah and Ben's time was running out. Their end would come soon, and he would be the one to deliver it.

CHAPTER TWENTY-FIVE

*D*etective Nelson drummed his fingers impatiently on his desk as the clock reached 1:30 PM. The time for Stephen Millstadt's interview had come and gone, and the man was a no-show. Nelson had a hunch this wouldn't be a straightforward case, but he didn't expect Millstadt to skip out entirely. He waited another hour, hoping Stephen might be late, but as the minutes dragged on, his patience wore thin.

By 3 PM, Nelson's concern had morphed into suspicion. He grabbed his coat and headed to the Kellerman Law Group. Downtown St. Louis hummed with its usual mid-afternoon energy, but Nelson's mind was focused on Stephen Millstadt. Why would a seemingly respectable lawyer dodge a police interview? As an attorney, he should have understood the significance of this situation. At the very least, Nelson expected him to reach out with some legal pretext or obstacle. Complete silence was entirely unexpected.

Arriving at the law firm, Nelson was met with the usual polished facade of legal professionals. He approached the receptionist, flashing his badge. "Detective Nelson. I need to speak with Stephen Millstadt."

The receptionist, a young woman with sharp features and a practiced smile, looked momentarily flustered. "Mr. Millstadt left the office around 10 a.m., Detective."

Nelson frowned. "Did he say if he was going to the police station?"

She shook her head. "No, Detective. He didn't mention anything to me."

Nelson's eyes scanned the room, spotting a cluster of lawyers gathered near the coffee machine. He strode over, his presence commanding attention. "I'm Detective Nelson with the St. Louis County police. Could any of you tell me the whereabouts of Stephen Millstadt."

The lawyers exchanged glances, their professional masks slipping momentarily. One of them, a tall man with graying hair and a stern expression, stepped forward. "I'm sorry, Detective, but Stephen left this morning, and he never said where he was going."

The other attorneys nodded in unison, agreeing with their colleague.

"But it's not like any of us keep tabs on each other," the tall attorney quipped, attempting levity and drawing a few amused grins from the others.

Nelson was not amused, his frustration bubbling just beneath the surface. "Can you at least tell me how he was when he left."

The tall attorney gave Nelson a perplexed look.

"His state of mind? His demeanor? Was he his usual self?" Nelson rattled off, his impatience seeping through his words.

The lawyers looked at each other, uncertainty and perhaps a touch of fear in their eyes. Were they being deliberately evasive, or did they genuinely not know? Before Nelson could press further, a voice from the back spoke up.

"Stephen seemed...out of sorts," said a younger attorney, his voice hesitant. "Not quite himself. I tried to engage him in some small talk, but he was unresponsive and hurried out."

Nelson's gaze zeroed in on the young lawyer. "Out of sorts how? Nervous? Agitated?"

The lawyer shrugged. "Hard to say. Just...distracted, I guess."

Nelson nodded, processing this new piece of the puzzle. He decided to send a couple of officers to Stephen's home. As he left the firm, he called dispatch, issuing the orders.

About half an hour later, back at the precinct, Nelson's phone buzzed. The officers at Stephen's house reported that no one answered the door and the place appeared deserted. Without a warrant, they hadn't entered. Nelson sighed, rubbing the back of his neck. It was looking more and more like Stephen had fled town, but convincing anyone of that was another matter. Even with the captain on his side, he doubted she'd back such a bold assumption at this point. Nelson pondered obtaining a warrant to enter the premises, but he knew a judge wouldn't grant it just for a missed interview. Stephen wasn't officially a suspect yet, and the murders, after all, were months old with no immediate threat present.

Nelson couldn't afford to sit by and do nothing. This wasn't just a missed interview anymore; it felt like the start of a manhunt. He had to tread carefully, though, and keep his suspicions in check. There was still something he could do. Nelson issued an APB on Stephen Millstadt, listing him as a person of interest rather than a suspect. The call went out, and officers across the city and county were alerted to keep an eye out for him, though they weren't actively searching. It was all Nelson could do for now, but it was a start.

By afternoon, the St. Louis Art Museum was a serene haven, its quiet corridors a stark contrast to the turmoil in Sarah's life. She and Ben wandered through the galleries, their fingers intertwined, each step a small escape from the shadows that had fallen over them. The warm afternoon light filtered through the tall windows, casting gentle beams that highlighted the masterpieces around them.

They paused in front of a large, vibrant painting in the abstract art section. The swirls of color seemed to pulse with life, drawing them into its chaotic beauty. Sarah tilted her head, lost in the enigmatic depths of the artwork. Ben put his arm around her shoulders, his presence a comforting anchor in the midst of her turbulent thoughts.

"This one reminds me of us," Ben said softly, his voice barely above a whisper. "Messy, unpredictable, but somehow...it all comes together."

Sarah smiled, a small but genuine smile that reached her eyes. "You're right," she replied. "It does."

They moved on to the next piece, a delicate sculpture of a dancer frozen in a moment of grace. Sarah marveled at the intricacy of the work, the way the artist had captured such fluidity and movement in stone. Ben, ever attentive, watched her with a mixture of admiration and concern. He knew how much she needed this distraction, even if it was just a brief escape from her troubles.

As they wandered through the museum, they found themselves in a gallery dedicated to ancient artifacts. The air was thick with history, the relics of long-lost civilizations whispering secrets from the past. Sarah's gaze lingered on a display of intricately carved amulets, each one telling a story of its own.

"Do you ever wonder about the people who made these?" she mused. "What their lives were like, what they were thinking?"

"Yes," Ben replied. "It's fascinating to think about how connected we are to the past. Though these folks lived lives very different from our own, I'm sure they were similar in most ways. They wanted to be loved and had dreams of better lives. All the same things we think about."

They continued their journey through time, their conversation weaving between the ancient and the personal. Ben's gentle humor and insightful observations brought a sense of normalcy to the day, a reminder of the life that lay beyond the tragedy that Sarah suffered.

They were admiring a particularly striking abstract painting when Sarah's phone buzzed in her pocket, jolting her from her reverie. She glanced at the screen and saw Detective Nelson's name. Her heart skipped a beat.

"Hello?" she answered, her voice tinged with apprehension.

"Sarah, it's Detective Nelson. I have an update on your father's case. Can you come to the station?"

Sarah's pulse quickened. "Hold on," she said, her voice tinged with nervousness. She quickly covered the phone with her hand. "It's Detective Nelson," she whispered to Ben, her eyes wide with anxiety.

Ben's face hardened like stone. He had never liked Nelson, especially after the way the detective had treated them. "What does he want?" he asked, his voice edged with anger.

Her voice wavered. "He wants me to come to the station."

"You think he plans to arrest you?"

She shrugged, fear evident in her expression. "I don't know."

Ben's jaw clenched. "Okay. You have to go, or he'll just send someone to get you. But I'll go with you."

Sarah uncovered the phone. "I'll come, but Ben will be with me."

"That's fine," she heard Nelson say through the phone before he ended the call.

Ben's eyes searched hers for an explanation, and she gave him a tight-lipped smile. "He said he had an update."

They left the museum, the art and history momentarily forgotten as they made their way to the police station. The drive was filled with a heavy silence, each lost in their thoughts. The city outside the car window was bathed in the warm glow of the late afternoon sun, but Sarah felt a chill deep within her.

At the station, Detective Nelson greeted them with a grave expression. He led them through the bustling precinct to a small, dimly lit room, offering them seats before taking his place across the table.

"Thank you for coming on such short notice," Nelson began, his voice steady but tinged with urgency. "I have some important information to share. I requested an interview with Stephen Millstadt to discuss the flash drive you gave him, and he didn't show up for his interview today. I left his office shortly after our phone call, and his colleagues didn't know where he went, but they confirmed he was acting strangely. We checked his home, but he wasn't there. We've been unable to locate him, and as a result, I now consider him our prime suspect in the murder of your father, Anthony Kellerman, and his associate, James Harris."

Sarah's breath caught in her throat. Ben reached over, giving her hand a reassuring squeeze.

Nelson continued, his voice low and deliberate, "He hasn't been officially labeled a suspect, but unofficially, I've made that call. I wanted you to know as we track him down. Here's my theory: Stephen, or someone working with him, entered your father's mansion and..." He hesitated, choosing his words carefully to spare Sarah, "this person… murdered your father in search of a file marked 'confidential'. When they couldn't locate it on the laptop, they had you check the safe for a flash drive, which you found."

Sarah nodded slowly, trying to process the information. "But why would Stephen do this? What could possibly be on that flash drive?"

Nelson sighed, rubbing his temples. "The motivation behind all this is still unclear. But I believe there's vital information on that flash drive, something that Stephen thought was worth killing for."

"What about James?" Sarah asked. "He worked with Stephen. In fact, they visited me together to ask about the flash drive. But, as I recall, Stephen did most of the talking."

"I've considered James Harris's role in this, and I think they might've been in on this together, but Stephen betrayed James and killed him as well."

The room fell silent as the weight of Nelson's words settled over them. Sarah's mind raced, trying to piece together the puzzle. She had never given Stephen much thought, but to think he was capable of murder was a different reality altogether.

Ben leaned forward, his brow furrowed. "Do you have any idea where Stephen might be now?"

Nelson shook his head. "We've issued an APB and are searching for him, but so far, no leads. We need to find him before he disappears completely."

The detective's words hung in the air, heavy with urgency. A surge of determination washed over Sarah. She couldn't let her father's killer evade justice. Even if Stephen was innocent, he needed to be thoroughly investigated to rule him out. There had to be something she was missing; some clue yet to be uncovered.

The sterile environment of the police station, with its harsh fluorescent lighting and constant buzz of activity, felt oppressive. Sarah glanced around, her gaze landing on a bulletin board cluttered with case files and mugshots. The reality of their situation pressed in on her.

"Detective," she said, her voice steady despite the turmoil inside her, "we'll do whatever it takes to help you find Stephen."

Nelson gave her a small, appreciative nod. "I'll keep you updated on any developments. In the meantime, stay vigilant. If you hear from him, or learn about his whereabouts, let me know immediately."

As they left the station, the sun was setting, casting long shadows across the city. Sarah's mind was a whirlwind of thoughts and emotions. Ben stayed close, and she welcomed his comforting presence.

Sarah and Ben walked across the police station parking lot, their footsteps echoing against the asphalt. The air was crisp, and the late afternoon sun cast long shadows, painting the scene in shades of gold and amber. Sarah's thoughts were tangled, her mind racing with the revelations from Detective Nelson. She glanced at Ben, his brow furrowed in concentration as he walked beside her.

"I'm glad we're not suspects anymore, but I'm really disturbed at what Detective Nelson told us," Sarah said, her voice tinged with a mix of anger and sadness. "I hope this mystery is close to being solved."

Ben nodded, his gaze steady and reassuring. "Yeah, I have a different perspective of Nelson now. I think he will get to the bottom of it, Sarah."

As they approached her sleek black BMW, Sarah noticed a man leaning against the side of his car a few spaces away. He was dressed in faded jeans and a plain t-shirt, his car hood up, and he was talking on a cellphone. He seemed to be in distress, begging the person on the other end of the line for help with his car.

The man noticed Sarah and Ben and turned towards them, a hopeful expression on his face. "Excuse me," he called out politely, lowering his phone. "I'm really sorry to bother you, but could you give me a jump? My battery died, and I'm kind of stuck here."

Sarah felt a flush of embarrassment. "I'm sorry, but I don't have any jumper cables," she admitted, glancing apologetically at Ben.

The man sighed and shook his head. "I don't have any either. Thank you anyway."

Sarah nodded sympathetically. "I hope you can get your car issues resolved soon. Good luck."

The man smiled weakly and returned to his phone, continuing his conversation. Sarah turned her attention back to Ben as they reached her car.

"I really think I'm going to sell the mansion," she said, her voice taking on a firmer tone. "I don't ever want to go there anymore, but I need to get my personal things, some family stuff, and my art supplies. I want to get my art supplies first." She tapped her key fob and unlocked the car. "Can you help me do this in the morning?"

Ben didn't hesitate. "Of course, Sarah."

They both got into the BMW, and as they drove off, Sarah felt a strange mix of relief and apprehension. She glanced in the rearview mirror, watching the man with the broken-down car shrink into the distance.

Matthew lowered the dummy smartphone he carried, a device that could light up and appear functional but was incapable of connecting to WiFi or the cell tower. It was just a prop, a clever tool to help him blend in and be ignored. The irony amused him endlessly: the man the police were hunting—the killer of both Anthony Kellerman and James Harris—was right there in their parking lot, casually chatting with his next two victims. These victims were intricately connected to the very case Detective Nelson was investigating.

Earlier in the day, Matthew had stolen a car to fulfill the assignment his employer had abruptly handed him as he rode the elevator in Sarah's apartment building. After completing that task, he tailed Sarah and Ben from her apartment to the art museum and finally to the police station, parking the car near Sarah's BMW. The thrill of risking capture while conversing with them was intoxicating—an adrenaline rush like no other. But the encounter yielded more than just a rush. They had unwittingly handed him a huge and unexpected gift: he overheard their plan to visit the mansion in the morning.

Matthew discreetly watched Sarah and Ben disappear from the lot, a cold smile curling his lips. He waited a few moments before slipping into the driver's seat of the 'dead' car. He turned the key, and the engine roared to life. As he drove away, his mind raced with plans and possibilities.

The tidbit of information he had overheard was priceless. He knew exactly what he needed to do next. Tomorrow morning, Sarah Kellerman and Ben Summer would die of a fentanyl overdose, and the mansion would burn to the ground. The anticipation made him giddy, like a child on Christmas Eve.

CHAPTER TWENTY-SIX

*B*en and Sarah set out for the mansion in the morning sun as it bathed the streets of the Central West End in a soft golden glow. They were in Ben's van, a sturdy vehicle he primarily used for moving supplies and items associated with his bar. Today, though, the van served a different purpose. Sarah needed to move her personal items and art supplies out of the mansion, marking the beginning of a larger effort to transition out of her old life and into the new. As they drove, Sarah felt a mixture of excitement and apprehension about the tasks ahead.

"Thanks for helping me with this, Ben," Sarah said, her eyes following the familiar route. "It's a lot to handle alone."

Ben understood she wasn't just talking about the physical effort of the move. The emotional weight of simply being at the mansion was almost too much for her to bear.

"Anytime, Sarah," Ben replied, his tone warm and reassuring. "I'm just glad I can be here for you."

As the van rolled along, Sarah glanced out the window, her expression clouding with melancholy.

"You know, Ben," Sarah began hesitantly, "I haven't talked to Emily since I saw her with Lucas."

Ben's eyes flicked towards her before returning to the road. "That must have been hard."

"It was," Sarah admitted softly. Seeing Emily and Lucas at the bookstore felt like a dagger to her heart, a moment seared vividly into her memory.

"But now, I see it more clearly. Lucas and I have been on and off for so long, and honestly, I was the one who kept instigating the breakups. I can understand why he wanted to move on."

Ben nodded, his expression thoughtful. "It takes a lot to come to that realization, but please don't beat yourself up over it. Human relationship dynamics are never easy."

"I know," she said thoughtfully. "I guess I'm not really upset with them anymore," Sarah continued, feeling a weight lift as she spoke. "It's just...messy." She paused for a moment. "And his constant talk of money grated on me, but that's who he is; that's how he was raised. Everyone in my circle was. I can't really hold that against him."

Ben nodded thoughtfully. "I'm here to listen, Sarah. Always."

Their conversation lapsed into a comfortable silence as they neared the mansion. The sprawling estate came into view, its grandeur tempered by the memories it held for Sarah. They parked in front and walked to the door. Sarah got out her keys, but before entering, she immediately noticed something was not right.

"The alarm's been shut off," she said, frowning.

Ben's brow furrowed. "Would a power outage cause that?"

"No, the place has a generator, and the alarm panel has a battery backup," Sarah replied, her mind racing. "Last time we were here, we had that scare with Detective Nelson. I must've forgotten to set it in all the chaos."

Ben nodded, but his eyes were still scanning the surroundings. "Let's just be careful."

They made their way inside, heading upstairs to Sarah's bedroom first. The room was filled with the remnants of her past—a collection of personal items that held memories both sweet and bittersweet. Sarah ran her fingers over a photo frame, lost in thought.

"After I moved out, my mom wanted to leave my bedroom the same, almost as if it were a shrine," Sarah said with a reserved laugh. "It's not like they needed the space." She sighed and glanced around the room. "I just want to take my art supplies today, but let's go ahead and pack this room up to get on our next load."

"Whatever you want to do," Ben said with a nod.

They began carefully wrapping items in bubble wrap and placing them in boxes.

"I spent so much time in this room growing up," she said softly. "It was my sanctuary." She frequently paused her packing, her eyes lingering over the cherished possessions of her youth. Family photos and snapshots of her with Ashley, Emily, and Lucas from high school brought tears to her eyes. Ben remained silent, continuing to box items, allowing her to lose herself in the bittersweet memories.

"You've faced so much," Ben said gently. "But in the fairly short time we've spent together, I've seen that you always find a way through, Sarah."

"Thanks, Ben," she said, smiling briefly before turning back to her packing.

They worked quietly, filling boxes in a silence that stretched on for some time.

Sarah broke the silence as she packed a box of keepsakes. "I'm concerned, Ben."

"About what?"

"We're so different. What if we're not compatible in the long run?"

"I've thought about that too," Ben admitted, carefully wrapping a set of books. "But I think it's worth trying. Even if it means figuring out the long-distance thing. I've got several bartenders up to speed at my place, so I can visit you in New York on a regular basis. I mean, if that's what you want me to do."

Sarah smiled, feeling a bit more reassured. He was willing to give it a try without pressuring her. "Yeah, that would be great."

With Sarah's bedroom packed up, they moved to the second room, which had been converted into an art studio. The room held a special place in her heart; it was where she found solace and a creative outlet during her formative years, encouraged by her parents. It was also where she returned for comfort during her mother's illness and after her passing.

Sarah surveyed the room, feeling a mix of nostalgia and determination. "It's going to be hard to leave this behind." She shook her head. "The memories," she said softly.

"But you're moving forward," Ben said, smiling at her. "And that's a good thing."

As they gathered the art supplies, their conversation continued to flow. Ben spoke about his bar and the challenges of running a small business. Sarah shared her dreams of exhibiting her work in galleries and the anxiety that came with such aspirations.

"I believe in you, Sarah," Ben said firmly. "You have so much talent. New York is going to love you."

Sarah laughed, feeling a blush rise to her cheeks. "I'm not sure what to say about that."

He chuckled. "A thanks will do just fine, but you don't have to say anything if you don't want."

"I'm sorry, Ben," she said with a grin. "Compliments can embarrass me."

"Well, get used to it. I think the people of the New York art scene will be complimenting you a lot."

They shared a good laugh as they packed up the last of the art supplies. Sarah looked around the room one final time. It was filled with memories of late nights spent painting, moments of inspiration, and times of sorrow. It had been her refuge, but it was time to move on.

"Ready?" Ben asked, balancing a box on his hip.

Sarah took a deep breath and nodded. "Ready."

They carefully carried the boxes down the hallway, their steps echoing in the empty mansion. Sarah felt a mix of emotions—sadness at leaving, but also hope for the future. She glanced at Ben, who was carrying a telescoping aluminum tripod easel along with his box and felt a surge of gratitude.

"Thank you, Ben," she said quietly.

He looked at her, his expression tender. "For what?"

"For being here," Sarah replied. "For everything."

Ben smiled. "Always, Sarah. Always."

As they reached the top of the stairs, Sarah paused, looking back at the rooms they had packed up. It was a significant moment, a turning point in her life. She was leaving behind her past, but she was also stepping into a future filled with possibilities.

"One last look?" Ben asked, sensing her hesitation.

Sarah nodded, taking it all in one final time. "One last look."

Just as Sarah turned toward the stairs, she caught a glimpse of a figure darting from the open door of a room across the hallway. It was a man, not particularly large or imposing, but wiry and athletic. She jerked her head and got a good look at him—it was the man from the police station parking lot, the one who had pretended to have car trouble. Recognition flooded her, but before she could react, the man barreled into Ben, sending him tumbling down the marble staircase.

Ben instinctively released the box and tripod easel, twisting his body to avoid smashing his head on the steps. His arms and legs took the brunt of the impact, the sound of his fall echoing through the grand foyer.

The man turned to Sarah with a wicked grin, his eyes gleaming with malicious delight. He lunged for her, and she screamed, the sound piercing the air like a siren.

Matthew's arrival at the mansion was shrouded in the same eerie quiet that had enveloped him the first time he'd been there, the morning he murdered Sarah's father, Anthony. He parked his unassuming white van on the adjacent street just before sunrise and slipped into the dense woods that bordered the back of the opulent estate. His movements were fluid and precise, a testament to his years of experience in the shadows. With his laptop slung over his shoulder, he moved silently through the underbrush, stopping just short of the mansion's backyard.

He took a moment to survey his surroundings, noting with satisfaction that the security had not improved since his last visit. The mansion's WiFi network flickered to life on his screen, and within minutes, he had breached its defenses. A cold smile spread across his face as he observed the network status. Half of the surveillance cameras were still inoperative, just as he had anticipated. He quickly disabled the alarm system, then hid his laptop in some bushes and approached the house.

Matthew broke a window on the side of the mansion, carefully selecting one that could only be viewed by a camera that was, fortunately for him, disabled. The sound of shattering glass was barely audible, swallowed by the surrounding forest. He slipped inside, his presence like a dark specter in the grand but dimly lit interior. The mansion's silence was almost oppressive, the kind that presses on your eardrums and makes your heart beat louder.

He moved to the second floor, where Anthony's office was located, and took up his position in an adjacent room. From here, he had a clear line of sight to the hallway and stairs. His breathing was steady, his mind focused. Hours passed as he lay in wait, the darkness gradually yielding to the light of dawn, and eventually to the brightness of midmorning.

The quiet was finally broken by the soft click of the front door opening. Matthew tensed, his senses sharpening. He could hear their voices—Sarah and Ben, talking in hushed tones. They ascended the stairs, their footsteps slow and hesitant. He could make out snippets of their conversation, a mix of relief and lingering sadness. They were discussing their budding relationship, the emotions raw and unfiltered. The irony wasn't lost on Matthew; they spoke of a future that would never come.

He waited, timing his attack with the precision of a hunter. The moment they left the room Sarah had used as an art studio and approached the stairs, he made his move. Matthew rushed out of his hiding place, his footsteps silent and swift. He shoved Ben down the stairs with a single, brutal motion. The young man's body tumbled down, limbs flailing, until he lay motionless at the bottom.

Sarah's scream echoed through the mansion, a sound of pure terror and desperation. She dropped her supplies and raced down the stairs, with Matthew in close pursuit. They collided on the first-floor landing, and a fierce struggle ensued. Sarah fought with all her strength, but Matthew was too strong, his grip unyielding. He forced her down, pinning her to the floor as he withdrew a syringe from his pocket.

"This won't take long," he muttered, his voice devoid of emotion.

But before he could administer the fatal dose, a sudden, sharp pain exploded in the back of his head. Ben, bloodied and bruised, had managed to retrieve the aluminum tripod easel that had followed him down the stairs, and swung it with all his might. Matthew staggered, more enraged than hurt, and turned his attention to Ben. He knocked the tripod from Ben's grasp and lunged at him, seizing him by the throat.

Matthew's grip tightened, and he prepared to plunge the syringe into Ben's neck. But a searing pain in his back made him freeze. Sarah had extended the metallic pointy legs of the tripod and stabbed him. Matthew whirled around, his vision blurred by pain and fury, just in time to see Sarah lunge at him again. This time, the tripod leg drove into his eye.

Blinded and in agony, Matthew's survival instincts kicked in. He turned to flee, but Ben, fueled by a mix of adrenaline and rage, tackled him from behind. They crashed to the floor, and Ben began pounding the back of Matthew's head with his fists. Each blow was delivered with a ferocity that spoke of desperation and fear.

Sarah, panting and wide-eyed, pulled Ben off, thinking Matthew was finished. But Matthew's body started to convulse violently. The realization hit them both simultaneously—he had accidentally injected himself with a syringe that he clutched during the struggle. They both pondered the contents of the syringe as they watched this man—this intruder—tremble on the floor, realizing from his reaction that it must be something deadly. His body twitched uncontrollably, his breath coming in shallow gasps.

Sarah and Ben stood transfixed, staring at the man whose identity and role in recent tragedies was still unknown to them, now watched as his life ebbed away. The mansion, a silent witness to countless sorrows, now bore witness to the demise of the man that had caused so much heartbreak.

Ben wrapped his arms around Sarah, pulling her close. They were both shaking, the adrenaline beginning to wear off, leaving them exhausted and shell-shocked.

"Who was this guy?" Ben muttered, his voice echoing in the silence.

Sarah stared at Matthew's spasming body for a long moment, still in deep shock. "I have no idea," she whispered, her voice barely audible.

Matthew's body finally lay still on the floor, the convulsions having ceased. The mansion, once a symbol of wealth and power, now stood as a silent testament to the horrors that had unfolded within its walls.

But as Sarah and Ben clung to each other, the reality of their situation began to set in. The mansion had once again become a crime scene, this time with a man dead by their hands. Though it was in self-defense, they couldn't escape the fact that they had caused his death. More importantly, could they prove it?

The future they had talked about, the one they had dreamed of, was now uncertain.

CHAPTER TWENTY-SEVEN

*D*etective Nelson arrived at the mansion with a battalion of police officers, their vehicles forming a barricade around the property. The once-quiet neighborhood buzzed with activity as neighbors stepped out onto their lawns, drawn by the commotion and eager to catch a glimpse of the scene unfolding before them. For the second time in less than a year, the mansion had become the center of a dark spectacle, and the air was thick with curiosity and judgment.

Matthew's lifeless body was carried out on a stretcher, his face covered, leaving only the mystery of his identity. As the paramedics moved him to the waiting ambulance, several IDs were discovered in his possession, each bearing a different name from various states. They also found a burner phone and an inoperative smartphone. The forensics team would have to untangle the web of aliases to uncover who Matthew truly was. The weight of the neighbors' stares bore down on Sarah, who stood on the mansion's driveway, feeling exposed and scrutinized. She could almost hear their whispers, their judgments about the woman whose mansion had become a repeated crime scene.

Beside her, Ben stood tall and resolute, his support for her never wavering. He met the eyes of the onlookers with a defiant gaze, daring anyone to cast aspersions on Sarah. He knew the truth, and he would not let her bear the brunt of the neighborhood's gossip alone. As Detective Nelson approached, his expression serious but not unkind, Ben braced himself for the inevitable questioning.

"Do you have any idea who this man was?" Detective Nelson asked, his tone sharp and probing, as if he already suspected they were hiding something.

Sarah shook her head and described their encounter with the man in the police station parking lot. Nelson's expression tightened as he realized how close this man had been to all of them. The thought that he could be lurking so near sent a shiver down his spine.

Ben stepped forward with a firm tone. "Detective, you need to understand—we were defending ourselves. The man died accidentally, by his own hand. We didn't intend for this to happen."

Detective Nelson nodded, making notes. "We'll need to take statements from both of you. And we'll need to try to figure out this man's identity. This could take some time."

As the scene unfolded, the media arrived, turning the mansion into a circus. Reporters jockeyed for position, cameras rolling live broadcasts that would soon flood the city and, by day's end, likely hit the national news cycle. Sarah watched the chaos with a sinking heart, knowing that her privacy was shattered once again.

The arrival of Ashley, Emily, and Lucas brought a moment of respite. They had seen the news and rushed over, their concern evident in their faces. The trio enveloped Sarah in a tight embrace, their support a balm to her frayed nerves.

"It's going to be okay," Ashley whispered, her voice filled with conviction.

Sarah nodded, grateful for their presence. The recent past, with its complicated emotions and relationships, seemed distant now. The fact that she had lost Lucas to Emily no longer mattered. They had all moved forward, accepting the new dynamics. Sarah was with Ben now, and Emily was with Lucas. Peace had settled over the once turbulent relationships, and it was a comfort to all involved.

Ashley and Emily watched as Lucas hugged Sarah and then shook Ben's hand, a rare moment of unity amidst the chaos. Seeing them together, Ashley leaned closer to Emily and murmured, "Tragedy really puts things into perspective, doesn't it?"

Emily nodded, a tear glistening in her eye. "Yeah, it really does."

Lucas, standing beside Emily, added, "We're in this together. No matter what."

Sarah felt a surge of gratitude and love for her friends. They had come together in her time of need, putting aside their past grievances.

As the day wore on, the police continued their work, gathering evidence and interviewing witnesses. The media circus showed no signs of abating and was brewing into a full-blown media storm. Sarah shook her head as she watched it, knowing that this incident would be dissected and discussed for days to come.

$$\sim$$

The same day that Matthew died, police forensics hit a roadblock. There was nothing in the national fingerprint database to identify him, indicating that he had never been arrested in his entire life. But then, they struck pay dirt with dental records. His name was Matthew Heller.

The breakthrough came from a set of dental records from Saint Paul, Minnesota, five years earlier. Matthew had undergone dental work there after an impact to his jaw. He had claimed the injury was due to slipping and falling on the ice, but when Detective Nelson heard this, he theorized it was more likely from a struggle—a victim fighting back with a punch to the face.

As a new patient, Matthew had full X-rays taken, providing detailed records. These records were entered into the national database after Matthew failed to show up for a follow-up appointment. Coincidentally, this was around the time the body of an unknown man, loosely fitting Matthew's age and body type, was found in Crosby

Lake. The dental records revealed the body wasn't Matthew's, but it led to his dental records being placed into the database.

Further investigation revealed that Matthew used to work in IT in Las Vegas until he left his job about eight years ago. At that time, there had been numerous disappearances and murders in and around Las Vegas. Nelson speculated that Matthew was a serial killer who decided to pursue it full-time. However, without a stable source of income, he had to offer his services to those who needed to "eliminate" problems.

Matthew apparently became proficient in his gruesome trade, using his IT skills to stay off the grid for the most part. Nelson built a strong case, presenting his theory to his captain that Matthew wasn't killing entirely at his own leisure but was working for someone.

The connections between the victims, Anthony and James, and the intended victims, Sarah and Ben, suggested a common link. Nelson floated the idea that Matthew worked for Stephen, given the interconnectedness of the victims. The fact that Stephen had yet to surface added weight to his theory.

The captain agreed there was enough evidence for Nelson to obtain a warrant to enter Stephen's residence. The potential link between Stephen and Matthew, combined with Stephen's suspicious absence, made it a compelling lead.

If Stephen was indeed behind the orchestrated attacks and murders, then bringing him in could unravel the entire web of deceit and violence that had ensnared Sarah and Ben. It was a pivotal moment, a chance to bring justice and stop the cycle of killings.

As he prepared the paperwork for the warrant, Nelson couldn't shake the image of Matthew's lifeless body being carried out of the mansion. The man had been a ghost, operating in the shadows, but now, his identity was known. It was time to shine a light on whoever had been pulling the strings. Nelson was ready to bring this dark chapter to a close and put this case to bed.

With a warrant in hand, Detective Nelson led a police raid on Stephen's house in Richmond Heights, which was a charming St. Louis municipality known for its tree-lined streets, family-friendly parks, and a blend of historic and modern homes. The quiet suburb, usually a picture of tranquility, now buzzed with the flashing lights of police cars and the hum of anxious officers preparing for the unexpected.

The team approached Stephen's two-story brick house, its façade a deceptive veneer of normalcy amidst the chaos unraveling within. Nelson's heart pounded as he signaled his team to breach the door. It swung open with a crash, the sound echoing through the silent neighborhood.

Inside, the air was heavy with an eerie stillness. The officers fanned out, their flashlights cutting through the dimly lit rooms. Nelson's instincts told him something was terribly wrong. His gut feeling was confirmed when he entered the living room and found Stephen hanging from a ceiling beam, a crude noose around his neck. Nearby, on a table, were several empty bottles of prescription strength sedatives, suggesting Stephen had used them to muster the nerve to hang himself. The scene was macabre, a stark contrast to the tidy suburban home.

"Get the coroner," Nelson barked, his voice steady but laced with frustration. He reasoned that Stephen had known the police were closing in and had chosen death over capture.

The team meticulously searched the house, but their efforts yielded nothing incriminating. They were looking for the flash drive Sarah had given Stephen, hoping it contained vital evidence. But there was no sign of it. Every drawer, every hidden compartment, came up empty. The search only deepened Nelson's frustration. They were at a dead end in terms of solid evidence.

Circumstantial evidence, however, painted a damning picture. It strongly suggested that Stephen had been Matthew Heller's accomplice in the killings. But the exact nature of their connection, and their motive, remained elusive. The lack of concrete proof gnawed at Nelson.

Then, just as Nelson was beginning to piece together a coherent theory, forensics called. They confirmed a high dose of sedatives in Stephen's system, and that he died by hanging, but then they dropped a bombshell. Stephen had died twelve hours before Matthew's attempt to murder Sarah and Ben. The revelation made no sense. If Matthew had been working for Stephen, why would he try to kill Sarah after Stephen had already taken his own life? The timeline didn't add up, throwing a wrench into Nelson's already convoluted investigation.

Nelson rubbed his temples, feeling the onset of a severe headache. The case was spiraling into a labyrinth of confusion. Each new piece of information seemed to contradict the last, creating a tangled web of motives and actions that defied logic.

Back at the precinct, Nelson pored over the evidence, his mind racing. Stephen's suicide, Matthew's attack, the missing flash drive— it all felt like pieces of a puzzle that refused to fit together. He knew he was missing something crucial, some key detail that would unlock the truth.

Nelson scrutinized the phone log in Matthew's burner phone. Every entry was either an incoming call or a cryptic, coded text from the same number. Matthew had never made an outgoing call. Nelson dialed the mysterious number from the burner phone, but there was no answer, not even a voicemail setup. Undeterred, he waited and tried again from a phone at the police station. Still, nothing. A quick call to the cellular carrier revealed that the number belonged to another burner phone, leading Nelson to a frustrating dead end. The only useful data he could extract was a record of the phone pinging off various cell towers over the months.

With a heavy sigh, Nelson acknowledged the futility of chasing this lead any further. He needed to pivot. The one person connected to all three victims—Anthony, James, and Stephen—might hold the key. Resolute, he picked up his personal cell and called Sarah Kellerman.

As Sarah stepped inside Detective Nelson's office, she noticed the cluttered desk overflowing with case files, photographs, and the faint aroma of stale coffee.

"Sarah, thanks for coming in," Nelson greeted her, rising from his chair. His eyes were heavy with fatigue, but there was a spark of determination in them. "This case has me befuddled and since you're related to one of the victims, and somewhat knew the other two, I thought I'd see if you had any insight that could assist me."

"Of course, Detective. Anything I can do to help," she replied, taking a seat across from him.

Nelson settled back into his chair and gathered his thoughts. "Stephen Millstadt was dead twelve hours before Matthew Heller attempted to kill you and Ben, making it unlikely that they were associated. That in itself is a puzzling detail."

"Why?"

"Because if Heller was hired by Stephen to kill you, why would he even try to, if his 'employer' was already deceased? I mean, if he was paid in advance, wouldn't he just leave town with the money rather than risk doing the 'job', since the person he would be doing the job for was already dead?"

"Maybe he didn't know Stephen was dead," Sarah said, matter-of-factly.

"That's a good point, but then why would Stephen commit suicide before he knew the outcome of the attempt on your life?"

Sarah sat back in the chair and furrowed her brow. "Yeah, you're right. This doesn't make sense."

"On top of that, Matthew Heller received phone calls and texts on his burner phone from another burner phone. Presumably from whoever had hired him. But we checked Stephen's whereabouts and learned that two of those calls occurred while Stephen was in depositions, and one came while he was in court. So, Stephen essentially had an alibi. That leaves us with knowing nothing about the person that Heller was working for other than their rough location based on cell tower info."

Sarah leaned forward, her interest piqued. "What are those locations?"

"They're scattered all over the city and county," Nelson said, glancing at the phone records on his desk. "Clayton, downtown St. Louis, Ladue, Creve Coeur, Brentwood, Riverview, Ballwin—"

"Wait," Sarah interrupted. "Riverview?"

Nelson nodded. "Yes, why?"

"Other than downtown, most of those places are in West County, and fairly wealthy communities. But Riverview is pretty far north and a lower middle-class area. Based on the other locations, it seems pretty out of place. Why would there be calls coming from there?"

Nelson rubbed his chin thoughtfully. "I honestly have no idea."

"Are there specific dates for the Riverview calls?" Sarah pressed.

Nelson shuffled through the phone records on his desk until he located the necessary one. "They all started in mid-July of last year."

Sarah pulled out her cellphone and scrolled through her call log, her brow furrowed in concentration. Finally, she looked up at Nelson. "Did you receive any calls on July 13th?" she asked.

He glanced at the phone record and his eyes widened in surprise. "Yeah. In fact, the first call came on that date." He scrunched his face in confusion. "How did you know that?"

"That's when I received a video call from Nick Pernod. Nick had just acquired a company in Riverview."

Nelson raised an eyebrow. "That is a compelling coincidence, but unfortunately, it's just circumstantial evidence at best. And it doesn't make much sense. Nick Pernod is a highly respected businessman and was instrumental in determining that James Harris's car was controlled remotely, proving his death was a murder and not an accident."

"How could he possibly know that?"

"Nick owns a company that makes electronic parts for automobiles."

Sarah leaned forward, her eyes narrowing. "So, then Nick actually has a company that could've made the necessary equipment to control James's car?"

Nelson paused, considering her point. "You're right, but why would Nick help us discover that? He would only expose himself as a suspect."

Sarah gets a thoughtful look. "During our call, he mentioned something about hostile business takeovers, saying, 'sometimes, you just need to hide in plain sight. Then no one is suspicious of you.'"

Nelson's eyes widened, impressed. "You have an amazing attention to detail, Sarah."

She blushed, feeling a mixture of embarrassment and pride. "Many people have said that. But there's something else. Before I gave Stephen the flash drive, I briefly viewed it on my laptop. I know I shouldn't have, but I felt I had a right since it belonged to my father. I saw a list of names. I didn't recognize any of them except for one—Nick Pernod. It meant nothing to me at the time, so I just filed it away in my mind, but in light of what you're telling me now…" she didn't finish the sentence as she felt she'd made her point.

Nelson's mind raced with possibilities. "This changes everything. Nick might be more involved than we thought. But we need solid evidence."

Sarah nodded, her heart pounding. "What do we do now?"

Nelson stood up, determination etched on his face. "You don't need to do anything. It's all on me now." He looked her straight in the eyes. "Thank you so much, Sarah. You've been more than helpful."

"Anything to catch the persons responsible for my father's death."

After Sarah left Nelson's office, the detective sank into his chair, the weight of the revelations pressing down on him. He picked up his office phone and dialed his captain. Time was dwindling fast. They needed to move quickly before Nick Pernod realized they were onto him and disappeared without a trace.

CHAPTER TWENTY-EIGHT

*T*he morning sun cast long shadows as police cars surrounded Nicholas Pernod's business headquarters, located in a newer downtown Clayton office building, their lights flashing ominously. Detective Nelson led the team of officers as they moved with practiced precision. The busy street was soon buzzing with the hum of police activity, the tension in the air palpable.

Nelson had orchestrated the raid meticulously, knowing they needed to catch Nicholas off guard. They breached the front door and stormed inside, their movements swift and calculated. Nelson's heart pounded with anticipation as he navigated the corridors of the sleek office building.

Nelson rushed into Nick Pernod's office with determined intensity. He knew Nick would be there; officers had staked out his mansion overnight and tailed him to his office in the morning.

"What the hell is this?" Nick demanded, rising abruptly from his desk chair, his face flushed with anger.

"Mr. Pernod, you are under arrest for conspiracy to commit murder, and we have warrants to search these premises and all of your businesses," Nelson declared, his voice steady and unyielding. Nick Pernod, being who he was, had considerable political clout, glared at him, but Nelson remained unfazed. Despite the nerves gnawing at him over the potential backlash Nick could unleash on him and the police department, Nelson's poker face revealed nothing but confidence.

As Nick was led away in handcuffs, he snarled at Nelson. "I helped you with the James Harris case, and this is the thanks I get? I don't look kindly on betrayal, cop. You're going to regret this."

The uniformed officers hustled him out of the office, and Nelson finally allowed himself a sigh of relief, the tension momentarily easing from his shoulders.

Nelson ordered his team to search every office and room in Nick's wing of the building. The officers, well-briefed on what to look for, quickly located their target. The flash drive labeled 'Confidential' was sitting in Nick Pernod's top desk drawer, as plain as day. Nelson wasn't surprised. Someone like Pernod, who believed himself above the law and untouchable, wouldn't bother hiding such incriminating evidence. It was a stark reminder of Pernod's arrogance, and just fortified Nelson's determination to serve justice.

It didn't take long for the police department's IT experts to access the files on the flash drive and uncover the information that had caused so much death and disruption. One of Anthony Kellerman's final acts before leaving his role as state prosecutor was to compile all the evidence he had on various individuals with criminal ties and hand it off to his successor. That crucial list of names and the accompanying evidence were all on the flash drive. As Sarah had mentioned, Nick Pernod was prominently featured on that list, and his criminal ties ran deep, revealing a virtual empire of corruption and illicit activities.

Unfortunately, that handoff never occurred due to Anthony's untimely death. Not until now, at least.

After Detective Nelson handed the flash drive over to the new state prosecutor, he sat down to interview Nick Pernod while he was in police custody. The room was crowded with Nick's defense attorneys, creating a tense atmosphere. Despite the wealth of information on the flash drive, Nelson focused exclusively on the deaths of Anthony Kellerman, James Harris, and Stephen Millstadt. The crimes detailed on the flash drive were not the detective's concern; the state prosecutor could tackle those. Nelson was only interested in the murders of the three men.

Nick and his attorneys stonewalled the interrogation, repeatedly denying any connection to the murders. Their simple defense—"Nick knows nothing about that"—seemed frustratingly effective. But just as it appeared Nick might wriggle free, a crucial piece of evidence surfaced.

Matthew Heller's laptop was discovered in the woods behind the Kellerman mansion, throwing a wrench into Nick's defense.

Once the police IT team broke through the laptop's security, Nick Pernod learned firsthand the dangers of trusting a serial killer. Matthew Heller had retooled his burner phone to record his conversations with Nick onto his laptop. Additionally, he maintained a video log on his laptop detailing all his activities for Nick Pernod. Although Matthew wasn't supposed to know his employer's identity, his expertise in surveillance allowed him to gather incriminating evidence against Nick, ensuring revenge if he were ever betrayed or killed.

Voice recognition technology, powered by advanced AI, easily defeated the voice modulation, and identified Nick Pernod's voice in the recordings from the burner phone. These files, along with Matthew's comprehensive video logs, outlined his activities for Nick and revealed additional information about Nick's clandestine operations. Matthew's meticulous documentation left no doubt about Nick's involvement, sealing his fate.

The phone recordings and video logs pieced together a damning timeline of events. When Nick learned Anthony might have evidence against him, he tried to cozy up to him to gauge what he knew. That tactic failed, but Nick discovered through other sources that Anthony had crucial information stored in a computer file. Desperate, Nick ordered Matthew to murder Anthony, making it look like an accident, and retrieve the file.

When the file wasn't found, Nick had Matthew disguise himself as a telecommunications technician hired to work on the phone system at Kellerman Law Group. Matthew planted bugs throughout the offices, which revealed that Anthony had confided in Stephen and James about the flash drive at the stakeholders' event, shortly after Nick had spoken with him.

Nick offered Stephen a staggering amount of money to get the drive. Stephen enlisted James to help, but when James got cold feet and decided to hand the drive over to the new prosecutor, Nick acted quickly. He retrieved the drive from Stephen and then had Matthew murder James, making it look like an accident, to prevent him from blabbing to the authorities.

Nick then posed as the hero, revealing that James was murdered, and subtly steered the police towards Stephen as the mastermind. He subsequently had Matthew kill Stephen before the police could arrest him. Finally, to tie up loose ends, Nick ordered Matthew to eliminate Sarah before she could piece everything together.

When that plan failed, Nick Pernod's entire life unraveled. The evidence against him was overwhelming, yet his deep pockets ensured his attorneys would craft a defense designed to drag the trial out indefinitely. Despite their efforts, Nick was deemed a flight risk and remained behind bars throughout the proceedings. Pundits and politicians speculated that, regardless of the trial's outcome, Nick Pernod's life was irreparably shattered. His personal and financial standing lay in ruins, and his businesses teetered on the brink of collapse, forever tarnished by his now infamous name.

EPILOGUE

 *S*arah Kellerman stood on the front steps of the grand mansion she had called home for most of her life. The imposing structure, with its ivy-clad walls and sprawling grounds, looked more like a relic from another era than the place where she had spent her childhood. Today was the final day she would set foot inside its cavernous rooms. She took a deep breath, the weight of the past few months pressing heavily on her chest.

Detective Nelson arrived promptly, his expression a mixture of professional detachment and personal concern. Over the past several months, he had become more than just the officer in charge of her father's murder investigation; he had become a confidant and, in many ways, a friend.

"Morning, Sarah," Nelson greeted her with a nod.

"Morning, Detective," she replied, managing a small smile. "Thanks for meeting me here."

Nelson glanced up at the mansion. "Hard to believe it's all over, isn't it?"

Sarah nodded. "It is. But it's time for closure."

They walked through the grand entrance together, the sound of their footsteps echoing through the empty halls. The house felt like a mausoleum now, devoid of the warmth and life it once held. As they made their way to the second-floor office, where so much of the drama had started, Sarah's thoughts drifted back to her father, Anthony Kellerman. His meticulous nature had been both a blessing and a curse, leading her to the discovery that his death was no accident.

They reached the office, and Sarah paused at the door. The room looked exactly as it had the day she found him, except for one crucial detail: the laptop on the desk. After Detective Nelson had returned the laptop at the conclusion of the investigation, she put it in the exact position depicted in her painting, a painting that had ultimately revealed the truth about her father's demise. She did that in honor of her father.

"Do you remember the first time we met here at the mansion?" Nelson asked, breaking the silence.

Sarah nodded. "I do. You asked me about my father's habits, his routines. It all felt so surreal."

"And now, with Nick Pernod charged with multiple crimes, and the trials underway, it seems justice is finally being served," Nelson said.

"Yes," Sarah agreed. "It's a bittersweet victory though; it can't bring my father back. Or any of the other victims."

They spent a few moments in silence, each lost in their own thoughts. The office, once a sanctuary where her father delved into intellectual pursuits and studied law, had also been a haven for quiet reflection. Now, it stood as a stark symbol of the exposed secrets that had shattered Sarah's world.

"Sarah, I know this has been an incredibly difficult journey for you," Nelson said softly. "But you've shown remarkable strength and resilience. Your father would be proud."

Tears welled up in Sarah's eyes, but she quickly blinked them away. "Thank you, Detective. For everything. This case couldn't have been solved without you."

With their final words exchanged, Nelson offered a reassuring nod and left the room, leaving Sarah to her memories. She took one last look around before heading down the hall to one of the mansion's many rooms, where Ben was busy packing up her family's belongings. She found him carefully wrapping a delicate porcelain figurine in bubble wrap.

Together, they moved through the house, packing up heirlooms, mementos, photos, and other important items. Each object they carefully wrapped and placed in a box carried a piece of her past, a reminder of the family she had lost. It was a melancholic process, but it was also a necessary one.

When they finished packing the boxes, they started collecting her paintings that were displayed throughout the mansion.

As the afternoon wore on, they finally reached the last painting. It hung on the grand staircase—the portrait of her father in his home office, sitting at his desk. This was the painting that had sparked her journey into uncovering and solving the crime. Sarah paused, her hand hovering inches from the canvas. She was conflicted, unsure if she wanted to move it. She looked to Ben for support; he nodded reassuringly.

Together, they lifted the painting off the wall, and carefully carried it down the stairs. "I'll never forget him or my mother. Or what they did for me," Sarah said, solemnly.

With the mansion finally emptied and the last of her father's legacy safely packed away, Sarah and Ben took a moment to stand in the now-empty foyer. The house, once filled with laughter and love, now stood as a testament to the passage of time and the inevitability of change.

"Are you ready to go?" Ben asked, his voice gentle.

Sarah took one last look around. "Yes. It's time."

Ben and Sarah stepped out of the mansion, the grand wooden doors closing behind them with a soft, definitive thud. The warm afternoon sun cast a golden glow over the sprawling estate. The once vibrant gardens were now quiet, a gentle breeze rustling through the leaves. As they walked down the stone steps, hand in hand, Sarah glanced back one last time at the place she had always called home. The mansion, now stripped of its cherished belongings, stood as a silent sentinel to her past, soon to be adorned with a discreet "For Sale" sign. With a mixture of nostalgia and hopeful anticipation, they got into their car, and drove away for the final time.

~

The warm light of the early evening filtered through the windows of Ben's bar, casting a soft, inviting glow over the rustic wooden tables and polished bar top. The atmosphere was relaxed, filled with the low hum of conversation and the occasional clink of glasses. In the corner, Sarah and Ben had claimed a cozy booth, waiting for their friends to arrive.

Ashley was the first to walk in, her vibrant smile lighting up the room. She spotted them and waved, making her way over with her usual grace. Sliding into the booth, she radiated warmth and cheer. Ben poured her a drink, and they exchanged a look of easy familiarity, the comfort of long-standing friendship evident in their eyes.

Moments later, the door swung open again, and Lucas and Emily entered together. Their arrival was marked by a shared sense of calm, their previous animosities now a distant memory. They made their way to the booth, greeting Sarah and Ben with friendly nods and easy smiles. As they settled into their seats, the group felt complete, a circle of friends reunited after a long and tumultuous journey. Despite being a recent addition to the group, Ben felt completely accepted by Sarah's friends, seamlessly blending into their close-knit dynamic.

Drinks were ordered, and the initial awkwardness quickly dissipated. The conversation flowed effortlessly, punctuated by genuine laughter and occasional reflective silences. The weight of past conflicts seemed to lift, replaced by a newfound sense of camaraderie.

As the evening wore on, they reminisced about old times, their shared experiences weaving a tapestry of memories that bound them together. They silently acknowledged the challenges they had faced, the mistakes they had made, and the lessons they had learned. The air was filled with the healing balm of forgiveness, smoothing over old wounds without the need for words.

Sarah looked around the table, her heart swelling with gratitude. Despite everything they had been through, they had managed to find their way back to each other. There was an unspoken understanding that they had all grown and changed, yet their bonds had endured. In the glow of the bar's warm light, they shared a moment of collective peace, a silent toast to new beginnings and lasting friendships.

Sarah and Ben stepped out of Sarah's apartment building; the afternoon sun wrapped them in gentle comfort as they towed their luggage behind. The Uber they had requested was only a couple of minutes away, according to the app.

"I'm glad you postponed moving to NYC," Ben said, his voice full of relief.

Sarah shrugged, a playful glint in her eyes. "I haven't completely decided to go yet, you know that."

He flashed her a sly grin. "I know, but I'm pretty sure New York is calling your name, like a siren song."

Sarah raised an eyebrow, impressed. "Look at you, knowing your Greek mythology and everything."

"Yep. I'm a multitalented bartender. I can mix up a mean ouzo, too," he said with a wink.

She gave him a perplexed look, and he chuckled. "It's a famous Greek drink," he explained. "No one ever orders it, though."

Sarah laughed. "Probably because no one's ever heard of it."

The Uber pulled up, and the driver stepped out to load their luggage into the trunk. Ben turned to Sarah as they watched.

"So, after Greece, where do you want to go?" he asked.

"I don't know. Do you have any ideas?"

"I'm leaving that up to you. You're the program director on this trip," he said with a wide grin.

"You okay just leaving your bar behind for a while?"

"I've got a good manager. He'll keep things running smoothly. I'm just so glad to see you happy."

Sarah gave him an appreciative, loving smile. "Thanks. I'm so happy you're coming with me."

"I wouldn't want to be anywhere else."

They shared a tender kiss before sliding into the Uber. As they rode toward Lambert International Airport, Sarah felt a deep sense of peace settle over her. She had faced her past, uncovered the truth, and found justice for her father. Now, it was time to embrace the future, side by side with Ben.

Together, they would explore the world and each other, discovering new places and new facets of their relationship. The future was uncertain, but they were ready to face it together, with hearts full of hope and a shared sense of adventure.

ABOUT THE AUTHOR

*J*ana Sawyer is a new voice in romantic suspense fiction, based in St. Louis, Missouri. Her debut novel, The Crimson Canvas, intertwines romance, mystery, and danger in a gripping narrative set against the backdrop of the art world. Born and raised in St. Louis, Jana pursued a degree in English Literature at Washington University, where she discovered her passion for writing suspenseful and emotionally rich stories.

When she's not writing, Jana enjoys exploring the vibrant arts scene in her hometown, taking long walks in Forest Park, and experimenting with new recipes in her kitchen. She lives in a charming historic home with her two Chihuahuas, Hemingway and Bronte. The Crimson Canvas marks the beginning of what promises to be a compelling career in romantic suspense.

Made in the USA
Monee, IL
16 September 2024

65884646R00151